PRAISE FOR THE

TALES FROM THE POISONED APPLE
SERIES

"Mooney is magical. With thrilling adventure, swoon-worthy romance, mystery, and humor, you'll want to escape your world for that of Pricked—again and again."

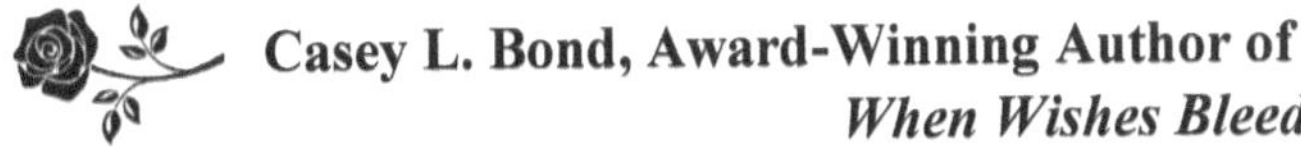 **Casey L. Bond, Award-Winning Author of** *When Wishes Bleed*

"Scott Mooney has truly written a great novel with some great twists and a little bit of heart."

 **The Nerd Daily**

"…an intriguing blend of modern times and fairy tale lore…"

 **InD'tale Magazine**

"…perfect for fans of Neil Gaiman and Victoria Schwab. A smart, funny, exhilarating read."

 **Jaded Book Reviews**

THE END OF THE ROSE

TALES FROM THE
POISONED APPLE
BOOK THREE

SCOTT MOONEY

OWL HOLLOW PRESS

Owl Hollow Press, LLC, Springville, UT 84663

The End of the Rose: Tales from the Poisoned Apple Book Three

Library of Congress Cataloging-in-Publication Data
Pricked / S. Mooney — First edition.

Summary: Briar Pryce thought she was saving the Poisoned Apple, New York City's borough of bootleg curses and graffiti-strewn castles. But when she freed every princess in town from their sleeping spells, she woke a giant deep underground, threatening the very foundation of her world.

ISBN 978-1-958109-53-3 (paperback)
ISBN 978-1-958109-52-6 (e-book)

*Para Hércules, quem me fez ficar muito mais
fácil escrever histórias de amor.*

ONCE UPON THE END TIMES...

I was hiding out in Central Park with my magic mirror set on Do Not Disturb. It was a damp and misty Tuesday in early spring, and as I sat on a bench by the Great Lawn, the surrounding skyscrapers faded in and out of view above the trees, obscured by the massive columns of fog drifting past like sailing ships. For a few moments as the mist enveloped me, it was easy to feel like the world around me had disappeared. Or I'd disappeared from it.

But the city always came back, whether I liked it or not.

It felt like I was alone, or about as alone as you ever get in Manhattan. The humidity had kept most people indoors, with just a steady drip of joggers to keep me company, floating through the haze like health-conscious, spandex-wearing ghosts. A pair of girls in private school uniforms skittered along one of the paths coming from the Met, their teenage cackles muffled by the thick mist.

Ostensibly, I was doing the crossword. Or at least that was my excuse for doing nothing. I'm not particularly good at puzzles for a part-time detective, but the frustrating ritual of filling out the answers, erasing the answers, and swearing excessively at the answers at least gave me something to focus on.

It was better than letting my thoughts wander around unsupervised, at least most days. Assuming *The Witchdale Weekly* crossword didn't decide to personally screw with my head.

Take, for instance, nine across. "A hero at their lowest point." Six letters, ending in D.

I groaned and scrubbed my face, but it didn't stop the answers from coming into my head uninvited.

Stupid.

Ruined.

Coward.

I know I'd called myself all those and more in the last six months since I'd broken a curse and accidentally broken the world. And that's why I wasn't in any rush to call myself a hero either.

Of their own volition, my hands clenched into fists, a familiar, impotent anger coursing through them until the neat grids of the crossword crinkled into a mess of lines and letters. My pulse thudded, and somehow the humid air around me felt hot, too hot—

"Hey—*let go!*"

My vision, already tunneling a bit around the edges, snapped to the edge of the nearest baseball field, where one of the two teens was struggling with an older guy over her purse. His motions were sharp and feral, jerking the chain of the expensive bag out of the hands of the young girl.

I was on my feet before I had a chance to think, the strap of my messenger bag tangled through the crook of my elbow. My fingers felt like they'd swollen into Gray's Papaya hot dogs as I rushed to disentangle myself and—do what? Charge forward? Draw my dagger and stab the guy?

I hadn't carried any roses with me in months. Roses meant magic, and my powers had done enough harm for a lifetime.

Finally freeing myself, I took two stumbling steps forward before the young girl's friend got involved. She was willowy, with auburn hair and a spattering of freckles that reminded me of a fawn, but her movements had no Bambi-like hesitation. Adding her strength to her friend's, she was able to pull their attacker forward and past them, the criminal stumbling in the slick grass.

"Give it here, *bitch*," the older man's voice rasped, his pale skin turning red with fury and exertion. His hand flicked out from his coat pocket, and the glint of a switchblade made my blood run cold. But I was still so far, and terror froze my legs to the ground, useless—

But the freckle-faced girl's eyes were glinting too, and as the man approached her, she nimbly dodged the first ragged swing of the blade, got inside his guard, and delivered an uppercut that sent the purse snatcher flying ten feet into the air. He landed a few dozen feet away on the edge of the baseball diamond in a puff of dust, twitching and groaning.

The two schoolgirls walked forward to retrieve the purse and give him a kick in the ribs for good measure. As they walked back in my direction, they seemed to notice me for the first time, and I noticed they had the familiar sheen of fellow residents of New York City's most magical zip code.

"Are you two okay?" I asked as they passed my bench. The girl who'd delivered the knockout was shaking out her wrist, but otherwise they seemed fine.

"All good," her friend said, clutching her bag a little more tightly than she had been. She shot an appreciative look at her friend.

"Most fun I've had all day," the other girl quipped, her smile moving her freckles into new constellations. "Gotta thank the Rose for that super strength."

So she wasn't just an Upper East Side private-school type.

She was an actual princess.

The Royal looked me up and down, taking in my soggy cardigan and unsettled expression. When she spoke, her flippant attitude was replaced with genuine concern. "Are *you* okay?"

It was a fair question. And one I had no idea how to answer.

I WAITED IN THE PARK for another few hours before the thick mist started to turn to actual rain and the streetlights came on, shrouded in rainbow halos by the humid haze. With a sigh, I gathered my things and started down the prismatically lit path towards Belvedere Castle.

A family of French tourists in raincoats was taking pictures of Turtle Pond from the castle's outlook, but only their youngest daughter saw me as I slipped open the heavy wooden door to the tower's interior. I couldn't help giving her a conspiratorial wink as she tried unsuccessfully to get her parents' attention. Her cries of "*une voleuse grande!*" faded as I slid the door shut.

The patter of rain grew louder as it ran in rivulets along the castle's lead windows, making the green ivy along the window-panes bounce. I made my way down the stone staircase in the last dregs of the day's light, the way so familiar I could find it with my eyes closed. At the end of the staircase, I scanned the stones for a moment before an arched doorway appeared, the dark wood a little more worn and weathered than I remembered.

Then again, who wasn't a bit more beat up than usual?

A rush of dry, subterranean air blew up around me as I opened the door, pushing the frayed ends of my grey cardigan back behind me. The shift in atmosphere was a welcome change as I entered the ruined hallway beyond. Scattered stones littered the floor in front of me, and one of the hall's decorative Doric columns lay on its side, cracks on the mosaic floor marking where it had fallen.

Another victim of the Shudders.

Soon, the cracked hallway surrounding me gave way to a muddy forest path, lined by crumbled masonry and the first buds of spring. Ahead, a stone archway stood at the crest of a small hill, the stool sitting beside it conspicuously vacant. There hadn't been much call for Doormen in recent months, and Horace, who normally manned that post, had left months ago for an extended vacation in the Bahamas, mentioning something about "not wanting to go through another Ragnarok, thank you kindly."

Seeing the sorry state of the Poisoned Apple beyond the hill, I couldn't blame him.

Once the fairy tale reflection of New York City, my hometown had gone from a children's bedtime story to *Children of Men*. The cheerful cottages of Commontown were in shambles where large Shudders had driven up ridges of rock between the wooden buildings. Some buildings clung stubbornly to life but twisted at new angles from the wracked earth beneath. The Gingerbread Tenements had been the hardest hit, as confectionary-based architecture always is. Even Castle Fortnight, the glittering gem of the City that Always Dreams, had been compromised, some of its famous white towers listing dangerously on the now unstable ground of the Apple.

I checked my pocket watch as I made my way into the outskirts of town. Plenty of time to make it to the Woodsman's Log before meeting up with Cade for our usual Tuesday Happy Hour…not-date.

The streets of the Apple were hollow, and not because of the weather. People had stuck it out for the first few weeks of the Shudders, but as the months dragged on, the denizens of the Apple were leaving for less dangerous areas. Those that remained were just as run down as the buildings: a harried troll ushered her two kids along in front of her, all of their dim yellow eyes glued to the cobblestones. They ignored the jingling flagon of an Eisenhans panhandling on the corner, his metallic skin barely covered in the cold. A cardboard sign to his right read SHUDDERS TOOK MY HOME. PLEASE HELP.

I tossed him ten bucks, but I couldn't meet his eyes. It felt like if he looked at me, really saw me, he'd see the truth about who was to blame for his situation. Like the trolls, I kept my eyes on the ground after that.

Blessedly soon, the comforting outline of the Woodsman's Log came into view, still standing tall and proving definitively that we will all be outlived by cockroaches and dive bars. The squat Tudor looked like an English country pub by way of Bushwick, graffiti dotting its stone foundation with the prismatic colors of the Poisoned Apple. Pushing open the familiar doors, I smelled cheap mead and despair. The bar inside was cavernous, by which I mean dark and poorly ventilated; ever since the magic rations, the Log had been getting by on good old candlelight, which gave things a cozy, albeit war-torn sort of vibe.

"Briar, over here," a low voice said from behind me. Cade Arden had staked out an entire booth hidden in a corner, and nobody was likely to give him flack for it. Tall and obnoxiously well muscled, the Red Hood ranger treated me to a crooked grin as he rose to his impressive height and opened his arms. Underneath his soft, grey henley, Cade smelled like the misty pine forests where he hunted monsters. If I moved a little more quickly than usual to give him a bear hug, if I grabbed him a little more desperately, he had the kind heart not to mention it.

"You started Happy Hour without me?" I asked, ending the hug after the appropriate three back-pats and throwing my bag in the booth.

"I was waiting for you, obviously," he said. When I crooked

an eyebrow, he amended, "I did get some lembas-breaded chicken fingers but they…they didn't make it." The smirk he gave me was anything but repentant.

I chuckled at my old friend despite myself and turned to the back of the room. "I'll order some more."

Cade was always hungry when he finished a shift with the Red Hoods, the Poisoned Apple's first line of defense against the creatures who roamed the Afterwoods surrounding the city. Most of the time the Hoods were more park rangers than paladins, only removing the more aggressive monsters who threatened the edges of town. But the Shudders had woken more and more of the forest's darker inhabitants, and Cade and the rest of the Red Hoods were running ragged trying to defend the Apple's borders.

A long oak bar took up the majority of the main room of the Woodsman's Log, its dark surface scored by the carvings of decades-worth of drunks and delinquents, depicting everything from dirty pictures to ancient Sumerian runes. Ensconced behind it like a queen in exile, Josefina Campbell rocked an oversized black hoodie and a gunmetal grey tiara while she made a pair of Midgard Mules. The Woodsman's Log's resident drag queen gave me a wink of recognition as she finished with the two valkyries in power suits across from me. A cyclops in a poncho gave me the eye as I leaned on the bar, but whatever he saw on my face made him turn and go back to his drink.

"How's it going, Bri?" Josefina called, pulling two flagons of my favorite mead. "Does Cade want more chicken fingers?"

"Sure does. I might even get to have a couple if I wrestle him for it."

She cast a heavily eye-shadowed look towards Cade as he lounged in our booth, a muscled arm thrown casually over the back of the wooden divider. "I mean, I've done worse for less…" Her sly smile lit up her face as she patted my hand on the bar. Her next words were softer. "How've you been, honey?"

I looked away, sure I couldn't bullshit the bartender if I tried. "Hanging in there." An accurate if incomplete statement. "How are you, Jo?"

She threw up her hands after sliding over our meads. "Not sure, honestly. The sky didn't fall today, so things could be worse. I'll put off going full Chicken Little for one more day."

I raised my mead to her in a salute as she grabbed my tip off the bar. "Here's to one more day."

She smiled, but I could smell the pain and fear that were just underneath the surface of her bravado. Most people had a whiff of it these days.

Cade straightened up from his slouch as I put the mead in front of him. "Thanks. Next round is on me." In front of him was the crumpled-up crossword I'd had in my bag from earlier.

"Going through my stuff now, Arden?" I scowled as I settled down across from him.

"It fell out when you tossed your bag. What happened? Did this crossword personally offend you?"

"Yes, actually," I grumbled.

"You used to find these relaxing," Cade mused.

Cade had been my roommate until recently, when, in a fit of uncharacteristic maturity, we decided that living together was just giving oxygen to the embers of our squashed high-school romance. While it was weird not having his steady, familiar presence at home as the world became so very unsteady, the longstanding tension we'd lived with had finally dissipated. Our weekly catch-up sessions had honestly been a lifeline of normalcy in the strange new world the Shudders had created.

"Do you want help?" he said, gesturing down at the puzzle he'd smoothed out.

"No," I snapped, but seeing his blond eyebrows rise, I

groaned. "Fine. What is it?"

"Thirteen down, the team mascot for the winners of the 2014 World Broadsword Melee Championship. You have 'Duergar.'"

"Yeah, for the Deira Duergar."

"It's a trick question. The Duergar had their title revoked a year later, since half their team turned out to be homunculi. So the runner-ups became winners by default, the Golden City Griffins."

"You ever think what your brain would be able to do without the freakish amount of sports knowledge taking up ninety percent of it?"

Cade grinned and guzzled some mead. "I hope to never find out."

My sigh was perhaps a little overdramatic as I erased thirteen down. That means all the answers I'd berated myself with for "a hero at their lowest point" needed to end in G, not D.

I jumped as Cade's hand rested on mine, a frown darkening his face. "It's not a big deal, Bri. It's okay to make mistakes."

My hand pulled away of its own accord, and I shook my head, tears welling in my eyes. If I'd had the ability to speak, I'd have said something along the lines of:

Not when my mistakes are destroying the city I love.

CADE LEFT TO MEET UP with some of his old high school jousting buddies, so an hour later I was walking back to Havmercy by myself. The two meads I'd quaffed provided a pleasant disconnect between my head and my boots, but so far, they seemed to be getting me home without issues.

My boots must've decided to take the shortcut under the

Jack B. Nimble Memorial Overpass, which was sketchy at the best of times, and much more so now that the Shudders had shifted the broken cobblestones into a forty-five degree angle. My conscious mind knew that. But whatever half-drunk subroutine was moving my feet didn't know—or didn't care.

A steady, low-volume stream of my favorite curse words was my only companion as I shuffled down the slope towards the overpass, trying to keep myself from slipping on the slick wet stone. My profanities only increased as I saw a new bit of street art decorating the graceful stone arches in front of me. In bright red and white, someone had painted the word HOPE, only the O was a brilliantly detailed rose blossom.

I paused for a second, massaging my suddenly aching temples.

It had only been six months since the resolution of the Apple's previous existential crisis, but it felt like a lifetime. Something had been torturing the town's sleeping princesses, immersing them in nightmares and causing them to scream. Soon they were sleepwalking and attacking people with freakish strength, and the entire town was on edge. With the help of my friends, I was able to figure out what was going on and break the spell, waking every princess in the Apple with my magic.

The official story was that a brilliant wizard at the Academy of the Iron Wand, my friend Professor Tamsin Davies, had undone the curses. But rumors circled of princesses waking up covered in rose petals, feeding into the existing legend of an anonymous magician known as the Rose, who had the unique power to influence people's emotions—a magic thought to be impossible, even in our city of impossibilities. The more optimistic types in the Apple thought the Rose was still out there, working to stop the Shudders and save us all.

Little did they know she was so messed up that she couldn't even stop a Central Park mugging.

The ground evened out as I made my way into the shadows underneath the overpass, the sound of a single carriage rumbling along the road above. I moved cautiously, picking my way through the broken glass of liquor bottles and off-brand mana potions. Whoever normally spent their nights here was nowhere to be found, wisely deciding that the underside of a bridge wasn't the best place to party when the ground kept shifting. Once upon a time all you had to worry about were trolls.

My shoulders relaxed once I was out from underneath the shadow of the bridge, which is just when a hand grabbed them.

Without thinking, I sunk down and spun, my boots gripping the cobblestones for power as I thrust my left elbow back into my attacker's ribcage. My other forearm pushed forward as I twisted around with the rest of my momentum, coming up under the chin of the cloaked figure and pushing him back into the stone column of the overpass, revealing a familiar, if unwanted, face.

"Easy! Easy, Briar, it's me," Isaak Krakelev panted, genuine fear on his handsome, fine-boned face.

"You say that like it's going to stop me from kicking your ass."

The Royal Lothario didn't look great. His black, shoulder-length hair hung lank and unwashed, matching the exhausted half-moons sitting underneath his eyes. The dim silver light of the wisp-lamps on the streets above us caught the sheen of sickly sweat along his forehead.

As much as it felt good to feel the power of pressing his light frame into the wall behind him, I begrudgingly dropped my arm and stepped back.

"You really shouldn't be walking alone in the dark," Isaak gasped out, my blow to his ribs still tightening his voice.

"Says the reason why it's not safe to walk alone in the dark. What do you want, Krakelev?"

"I didn't mean to scare you."

"That's not an apology."

Isaak let out an exasperated huff. "I'm sorry. I needed to talk to you, and a buddy said he spotted you at the Log earlier."

"Are you having me followed?"

"Don't flatter yourself," he said with a smile. "I have eyes everywhere. Or in this case, eye."

The cyclops at the bar. I made a mental note to find him and give him a very personal reenactment of the story of Odysseus.

"And what was so important you couldn't just send me a mirror message like a normal person?"

His lips twitched into a poor facsimile of his trademark lecherous grin. "Is it that painful to spend time with me?"

I groaned with frustration and turned to leave. "Good night, Isaak. If you touch me again, I'll shut you up with my dagger, not my fist."

"Wait," his voice creaked out from behind me, a tinge of desperation edging the prep-school elocution. "You owe me, Briar Pryce. You made a promise. One flower delivery of my choice."

I whirled on him. "Seriously? The world is falling apart and *this* is what you're choosing to do with your time?"

He sized me up, the playboy façade slipping for just a second, showing the vulnerable hurt underneath. "This is the only thing that's important."

I'd met Isaak while working a kidnapping case, trying to find a non-magical Columbia student who'd been magically stolen. He'd been a suspect at first, and later helped provide some information that led to the kidnapper, his ex-girlfriend, Miranda Grimmour. But in exchange, I'd promised him a rose delivery, no questions asked.

And the Poisoned Apple is not the sort of place that lets a promise go unfulfilled.

"What does it matter?" I grumbled, already resigning myself to whatever inane errand he had for me. "The only girl who ever touched your cold, dead heart is locked up in the White Tower. I put her there."

In response, he raised his eyebrows arrogantly, and his meaning suddenly became clear.

"No," I said instantly. "Absolutely not. You want me to smuggle magic into the White Tower? That's impossible."

"Not magic," he countered, digging into the black leather pouch on his hip. "Just a flower."

He pulled out a strange flower, deep black from stem to flower, but some kind of...

"A daffodil? All of this so you can make me deliver an emo daffodil to Miranda Grimmour?"

"It's from my family's special garden, brought over from the old country. They only bloom once a generation. I just—with everything going on, I needed to show Miranda that I still..." He trailed off with an attempt at a macho shrug.

"Then why not deliver it yourself?"

"She kidnapped a Know-Naught and nearly started a civil war within the Multiarchy. Her visitation privileges are...limited. But I'm sure you could find a way."

Isaak's tone made it clear he knew that he had me over a barrel. The magic suffusing the Poisoned Apple has a way of making things go really, really badly for anyone who goes back on a promise or bargain. But that didn't mean I had to like it.

"Fine," I said, snatching the bloom from his hands. "Is there any specific message you want me to deliver with it? Please say it's not a poem—"

"Tell her this: our future blooms out of the stone our parents left us."

I rolled my eyes as I jotted it down on the back of my crossword. "What the Hecate is that? It sounds like a trigger phrase to activate a KGB sleeper agent."

"It's…" His pale features reddened a bit. "It's a line from a song I wrote her."

My knee-jerk response was to mercilessly mock him for this, but given how vulnerable he looked in that moment, and that the world was crumbling around us, I remained uncharacteristically quiet and put the flower in my bag.

Isaak seemed as surprised by my lack of teasing as I was, and merely nodded. "Thank you, Briar. I don't know how things will work out with the Shudders, or the Apple, but…if you can't say 'I love you' when the world is ending, when can you say it?"

I didn't have a response to that, so I just grunted a goodbye, and let the Royal romantic vanish into the syringe-filled shadows underneath the overpass.

"HOW DID HE EVEN MANAGE to sneak up on you like that?" Alice said as she placed a steaming-hot mug of chamomile tea in front of me. I'd made it home in one piece and gratefully accepted my roommates' offer of tea and a debrief. "The streets are practically deserted after dark these days." She pushed a strand of her black hair behind her ears; she'd gotten a short, spiky undercut a few weeks ago, and was constantly toying with it. It looked badass, calling attention to her graceful neck and kind, heart-shaped face.

We'd rearranged our furniture after Cade moved out, and the three of us were sitting in what we'd christened the breakfast nook, which was just a small glass table and some mismatched chairs by the window, but it had become our de facto place to hang out and catch up after a long day. Our glass-slipper-shaped bong was sometimes involved.

"There were always rumors about the Krakelevs," my other roommate, Jacqui recalled. "That their bloodline was mixed with something darker. Lidérc, if I'm remembering correctly. Basically Hungarian incubi. Could explain his light step." Leaning back in her chair, she unbuttoned the sleeves of her graceful cream blouse and pushed them up. While Alice was wearing a Hello Kitty t-shirt and high-waisted jeans, Jacqui had come from a town hall meeting and looked every inch the leader she was, albeit she'd traded her pumps for pink, fluffy slippers.

"Or the mead I'd had with Cade made me a little less cautious than I should've been," I admitted. "Regardless, he would've tracked me down one way or another. And I don't have a choice—I've got to make the delivery for him."

I cradled my She-Ra mug in both hands, blowing on it as my roommates exchanged a look. "Maybe, it's…maybe it's not a bad thing," Alice said as lightly as she could.

"What do you mean?"

"Briar, you've been—look, you've been through so much, things have gotten really hard but…maybe this will be a good thing to focus on. Get you out of your rut," Alice said, trying to infuse cheer into every syllable.

"My *rut*?" I said acidly. "I'm not a Hallmark-movie heroine who has issues with work-life balance. The Apple is literally collapsing around us."

"I think what Alice is trying to say," Jacqui added diplomatically, "is that you've been spending so much time in the Otherworld, sitting around Central Park doing crosswords, and…it feels like you're running away, Bri."

I felt my hands curl into fists around my tea, and it was all I could do to take a deep breath and not jump across the table at them. "I'm doing my best," I spat out. "I tried to play the savior when the princesses were screaming, and look how that ended up. There are plenty of other wannabe heroes out there. Can't it be someone else's turn?" My lungs were gasping, the words tumbling out without any input from my conscious mind. Then, quieter, "Why does it always have to be me?"

Looking up from the steaming surface of my chamomile, I expected to see anger, judgment, disgust—all the things I'd been lobbing at myself for six months. But the only emotion I could see in my friends' eyes, the only feeling I could smell on their breath, was concern.

"Briar, this isn't us saying you need to save the world," Alice said thoughtfully. "We want you to be okay. Not for us, not for the Apple. But for you. And maybe this delivery is just…a first step. Towards getting yourself back."

I thought of Alice, carefree, awestruck Alice, getting home from her long shifts as a maid in Castle Fortnight and making lists of all the necessities the people in Commontown might need during the Shudders. She'd organized a whole network of people, connecting those in need with supplies donated by the Royals (or quietly liberated from under their noses). She hadn't asked to be a hero, either.

"It's a lot," Jacqui added. "Learning about your family, losing Antoine, and now the Shudders? The last year has been an epic shitstorm, for you more than most. But you're someone who's at her best when what she does has meaning. And I don't think escaping to Manhattan is giving you that."

Jacqui, former princess and current community council member, left her privileged family behind and was doing her best to use her voice to help the people of the Apple, those who were vulnerable even before the Shudders started. Because of her advocacy, the city was begrudgingly investing in structural reinforcements in the Gingerbread Tenements, saving homes and saving lives.

Neither of them was perfect. They were my messy, loud,

loving best friends, and this year was wearing on them, too. But they hadn't given up. They weren't moping around the city feeling sorry for themselves.

My voice sounded lost and hollow as I rasped out, "You don't get it. *This is my fault.* I broke the sleeping spell, and that woke the giant underneath the Apple. The Shudders are just him starting to stretch and waken. Sooner or later, he's going to finish waking up, and everything we know will be *gone.*"

My tears made the entire room blur, but I saw both my friends reach out to grab my hands. "We don't know that," Alice said softly. "Think about the last six months. We had no idea things were going to turn out this way. How can we know what life will be like six months from now?"

"But I can't—I can't fix it," I squeaked out.

"No one's asking you to," Jacqui said. "But you can do *something.* Deliver Isaak's emotional message to his long-lost love. It's not going to fix everything, but it's *something.* And if you won't do it for that Royal dirtbag, do it for yourself."

I sniffed, hiding my face behind the mug as I took a deep sip. The calming, floral taste of the warm tea dripping down my throat softened me from the inside out, and I nodded, not trusting my voice in that moment.

Alice squeezed my elbow. "Besides, worse-case scenario is Miranda hates the flower and then Isaak gets a rude awakening that his ex doesn't owe him a Grimmsdamn thing." She looked down at her watch. "I gotta go—I'm helping distribute torchstones in Liars' Square. See ya later, babe." She gave Jacqui a peck on the cheek as she grabbed her peacoat and skipped out the front door.

That was another thing I couldn't have predicted six months ago. Jacqui and Alice had never been on my romantic radar, and then something just *shifted,* and it made total sense. There weren't any big dramatic confessions of love or flower deliveries, they just went from friends to girlfriends. From cuddling while watching *Real Housewraiths* to cuddling even more while watching *Real Housewraiths*. Some couples just click, no grand romantic gestures required.

I watched Jacqui's tender smile as her eyes followed her girlfriend out the door. She turned back to me, and for a moment almost looked guilty. "How's Antoine?" she asked softly.

"He's fine," I said automatically, before I could actually think about the question. "He's worried about me," I amended. "We're supposed to talk later."

The cherry on top of my Terrible, Horrible, No Good, Very Bad Quest was a magical mishap involving Antoine DuCarr, Knight Bachelor and my sometimes detective partner. He had been trying to get to me for the final showdown, went through a very suspicious portal, and ended up...*somewhere else*. Alice called it the Mirror Mainframe; some sort of in-between place that connects all the magic mirrors in the Poisoned Apple. Our efforts to get him back to this reality had so far produced few results, so he was stuck communicating with this world through mirror messages and calls, but not really here.

The irony, of course, is that we'd never been closer. After finally acknowledging our feelings for each other and after one heart-pounding makeout session, we'd figured out what we wanted just in time for him to get trapped in another realm.

It sometimes felt like even my happy endings were losses.

"Tell him I said hi," Jacqui said with a sad smile as she got up to leave.

"Jacqs?" I asked softly. Something about the tone in my voice made her freeze, one hand on the wooden chair across from me. "How are you handling this so well? The Shudders, the uncertainty, the *everything*—"

"Well? I wouldn't say well." She collapsed back into the chair and shook her head. "The pressure, the hurt, everywhere you look—it gets to me sometimes. I had a full-on breakdown with Alice last night."

"Really?" I said.

"Oh yeah. Heaving sobs, ugly crying. I was basically a James Van Der Beek GIF."

"How are you today?" I asked, realizing in my rush to tell my friends about what had happened that I'd barely asked them about themselves.

"Honestly? Better. I think I just needed to get it out. Alice was beyond understanding." She gave my hand another squeeze. "She reminded me of her epic freakout last month when her hours at the castle were cut back…I think we all just have to save each other, whenever we can. And trust that someone will be there when we need it."

A lump in my throat formed, but it seemed like a good lump, so I just nodded. "I should call Antoine," I managed, grabbing her mug so I could wash it. The least I could do. "And thanks, Jacqui."

"I'll be in my room if you need me," my oldest friend said, and I knew she meant it.

THE DEEP BROWN EYES of Antoine DuCarr stared at me from the pillow next to mine and, at the same time, from a world away. I'd propped my mirror up so it could emit the glowing blue sparks forming his face in a way that could almost make me believe he was curled up in bed next to me.

Almost.

"Sounds like a long day," he murmured, his kind voice un-distorted by the strange, magical medium of our communication. I didn't mind his sparkly form, because I knew his face so well;

the curly chestnut hair, the kind brown eyes, the long, graceful limbs with an impressive amount of muscle in them. The slight scratch of the stubble around his lips. Even at the edge of the SparkleCast, around his waist, where he faded to nothing, I could fill in with my memories of his usually khaki-clad legs.

"Long. Draining. Full of those pesky emotion-thingies."

"We can hang up, if you need to rest," he offered, but I shook my head. Some days talking to him was the only thing that calmed me down enough to sleep.

"I'm good," I smiled. "Unless you have somewhere else to be?"

He laughed, and despite everything that had happened, I smiled. With my eyes closed, it was like we were back to our normal snarky, bantering selves. I felt lighter than I had in a long time.

"If there's one complaint I have about this magical nether world, it's the lack of decent nightlife. What's a knight supposed to do at night?" While he was there, Antoine didn't seem to sleep or eat or do any of the other usual human things. It was like he had become a part of the magical ether that surrounded him.

"When you're back, we'll have to burn up all your lingering energy with some epic dance parties." I grinned. As painful as it was, making our list of what we were going to do when we were reunited had become a habit. A reminder that this current arrangement wasn't forever. A defiant declarative that his return was a question of when.

Not if.

"Definitely. I'll take you to my favorite discotheque. The one I told you about, in Paris."

"Paris?"

"Sure, why not? I just…" He got quiet. "I miss it all. I miss the world. I miss *you*."

"I miss you, too."

"But at the same time…it's kind of funny, right? We used all the time we spent together *not* talking about us and our relationship, and now that's all we can do."

"Do we have different definitions of the word funny?"

"What I mean is—despite everything, I'm glad we've gotten to spend time together like this. I'm grateful."

I smiled and reached out my hand. On his side of the bed, a small cluster of sparks mirrored me, forming his strong, long-fingered hand, as if he were pressing it up against mine.

"Who knew we could make inter-dimensional long distance work?" I smiled, not shying away from the look of pure adoration in his eyes.

"And when I'm back…I want to do all of it. Dancing in Paris, soaking in the hot springs of Atlantis, stargazing in the Rocky Mountains…"

"Do you not have stars there?"

"Not really. There's a big swirly…cloud thing. I think it represents the sum of all human knowledge, but there aren't any constellations, so it's kinda boring."

I laughed, curling over on my back as I looked up at the ceiling of my bedroom, where the dim lights of the Poisoned Apple peeked through my curtains, playing across the wooden beams.

Once I wasn't looking directly at him, I felt a little braver. "Do you think Jacqui's right? Have I been running away?"

He paused for a second, but I knew him well enough to know it was the pause he took when he needed to think about something tough, really chewing it between his mental molars until it was soft enough to digest—a contemplative habit I was failing to learn from him.

"I don't think you've been running. I think you've been surviving," he said evenly when he was done considering. The timbre in his tone was pure kindness, without a trace of judgment. "But I do think they're right. You've been stuck in this cycle for months, torturing yourself for something that isn't your fault."

"I broke the sleeping curse—"

"You saved the princesses. It had unexpected consequences, but it was the right thing to do. You saw them suffering, and you did what you could to end it."

My hands twisted the blankets that I'd brought up around my shoulders. "I just—it feels like a punishment."

"Waking the giant underneath the Apple was a side effect, not an outcome. The only punishment here is the one you're giving yourself unnecessarily. Briar, you weren't the one who set everything in motion. You acted out of empathy and kindness, and I never want you to feel bad about doing that."

Somehow these words were painful to hear, a hot knife cauterizing the wounds I'd been walking around with for months—healing, but also hurting like a mothergooser. I resisted the urge to hide under the blankets from Antoine's truth barrage and instead scrubbed my hands over my face and let out a long, low breath.

I looked back at him, and even with the heavy subject matter, he was smiling, looking at me like I was a happily ever after in the flesh. "I'd say forgive yourself, but you've done nothing that needs forgiveness. Just…remember, the world tells a much better story with you in it, Briar Pryce."

I smiled back, in awe of how I could feel so good and so shitty, all at the same Grimmsdamn time.

ANTOINE FINALLY CONVINCED ME I should hang up and get some sleep, and I sadly watched the blue sparkles of his form retreat back into my magic mirror, leaving my room gloomy and dark. As much as I tried to follow his advice and turn off my churning brain, pretty soon I was staring at the ceiling, letting the events of the day whip around me until I was short of breath.

The world tells a much better story with you in it.

Antoine's voice filled my head, causing all the other voices keeping me awake to quiet for a moment. And just like that, another chorus of sensations replaced them, giving his simple words the depth and texture of truth. Cade's familiar bear hug, holding me up when my legs felt tired and weak. The smell of chamomile tea as Alice put it in front of me, her warm hand lingering on mine without expecting anything in return. The image of Jacqui rolling up her sleeves across the table from me, ready to fight anyone who made me feel bad about myself, even when that person was me.

My friends were all heroes in their own ways. And they'd been saving me, every day of these last six months. Finally, *finally*, I felt ready to do my part to save them.

I felt so warm and sad and grateful and hopeless and human that it was just too much. The dam broke within me, leaving me somewhere between laughing and crying, all the emotions cascading down my cheeks. I had gotten so used to the feeling of almost crying, fighting off tears with a rabid desperation, and yet I couldn't remember the last time I'd actually let myself let go, if even for a moment, alone in my bed at night.

By the time my sobs left me, I felt a good sort of exhaustion, the pleasant soreness from laying down a heavy burden. My interior landscape was like the streets of the Apple after a rain, wet but with a refreshing scent of clean stone. Before I let the shitty voices back in, I pulled my covers off and walked to where my bag sat on the side of my desk. Pulling out the cross-word, I scribbled in my answer, smiling even as a tardy tear fell on the newsprint.

Afterwards, I felt better, despite knowing that my response might be wrong. Maybe I'd have to erase it later, but if so, who cares? For once, I relaxed the part of me that needed to be right, needed to know all the answers before putting my own ideas out there.

For now, I knew my answer to describe a hero at her lowest point.

I ran my finger over the word *TRYING*, made a soft sound somewhere between a chuckle and a sob, and went back to bed.

I PAUSED AT THE BOTTOM of the stairs, our house lit only by moonlight. I shook my head, trying fruitlessly to remember why I'd come downstairs. There was something I had to do, something important, but my mind was a hazy blank, as empty as the darkened living room in front of me.

I was supposed to do something, wasn't I?

Confused, I considered going back to bed, pulling the soft covers over my head and forgetting whatever sharp feeling of obligation that lingered in my mind. It was just on the tip of my mental tongue, something big, something important, but I couldn't for the life of me remember what it was.

Hoping to get a breath of fresh air, I opened the French doors in our kitchen, flicking the switch for the lanterns outside so I didn't trip and knock the forgotten task out of my head by force.

But the light that came on didn't illuminate my garden as I'd left it.

Ash, dark and thick, covered the remains of my roses, which still smoldered on the edge of a barren and destroyed Afterwoods. More burning embers floated down from the dark red sky above, so choked with smoke that not a single star shined through. The remains of trellises and trees, blackened with soot, reached into the air like hands reaching out for help from the wreckage of the earth.

My boots hit the edge of the doorjamb as I staggered backwards, landing with a thud on my butt. This wasn't real. This couldn't be real. I scrambled to my feet and rushed to the front door, throwing it open and hoping against hope that the view would be better.

Instead, I saw a flash of the Poisoned Apple in ruins, fires raging and sirens blazing. A thick haze of smoke and screams kept me from seeing any one crisis in detail, as instead the misery around me swirled into a merry-go-round of suffering. A witch's wooden tower crumbled before my eyes, green lighting erupting as the spell circuits blew, lighting a nearby house with arcane flame. A group of commoners, hands empty of anything but a few stray children and pets, tried to run from the chaos into the forest, but a haunting howl and the sound of snarling and gnashing teeth was all that met them.

A resounding crash shook the foundation of the cottage, sending me careening off kilter as I tried to clutch the wall to stay upright, my head swimming. From the chaos in front of me, a dark silhouette, taller than any skyscraper, straightened up to its full height and stepped towards our cottage. I stumbled back, so small in the face of something so overwhelmingly big that it blocked the sky, and I ran. Another crash nearly toppled me to the ground, closer this time, much closer, and I knew the next step would come right down on the roof.

The backdoor was still twenty feet away, and time felt like it slowed down as I braced for impact. Just as I rounded the couch and began my final sprint, I noticed a small figure standing in the middle of my ruined garden. A child in cream-colored linen overalls, with fluffy hair and delicate green skin the shade of a beech leaf, waved at me, bouncing from bare foot to bare foot. While their form looked about ten years old, something about their iridescent amber eyes felt much, much older.

"Run!" I screamed, flailing my arms as if through sheer will I could push the child away from what was coming. Instead, the child stomped their foot impatiently and pointed down to the earth beneath them.

A resounding crack split the house as an impact sundered the roof above me, sending splintered timbers and beams into my path. The door was only a scant few feet away, but as I felt the shudders of my home collapsing under a giant's foot, I knew I wouldn't make it.

The last thing I saw before the walls came tumbling down around me was the patch of earth by the child's feet, where a single beansprout grew, unheedful of the ash and ruin around it.

MY DREAM LEFT ME unsettled, tossing and turning with images of a burnt city behind my eyelids. It was around sunrise when sleep finally evaded me fully, so I figured I might as well start my day. Cool mist blocked the earliest strains of sunlight, giving the Poisoned Apple a welcome blanket of peace; with the world obscured, it was almost possible to think the Shudders had been just another insubstantial nightmare. I went downstairs to the kitchen and was making a cup of tea and a bowl of Goblin Grahams when I noticed the intruder in our backyard.

I went out to meet him after pouring a second mug of tea.

"You really don't have to do this, Pop," I said, handing over a Garfield mug so faded it looked like he'd been eating lasagna with bleach. My father's kind brown eyes wrinkled in gratitude as he raised his mug in a salute. "I promise I'm going to get around to fixing up my garden."

Last year, when I'd woken the sleeping princesses, it had taken every petal of every rose in my garden to break the curse, freeing the princesses but also waking the giant. While the damage was nothing near as bad as I'd dreamed, the constant tremors and quakes had taken down a few of the stone walls that encircled the garden's gravel paths. What was once a verdant paradise of blooms on the edge of the forest had become a messy tangle of weeds and broken stone. Restoring the garden was on my to-do scroll, but with every week that passed, I felt less and less motivation to face the mess I'd made of things.

It had taken me almost a month to realize that the flower beds were being weeded and refreshed by someone else's hands. After I ruled out brownies, I knew who was responsible.

"You're doing me a favor, sweet pea," my dad said, waving my words away like a fly. "I've been bored and need a new project."

"You have your own garden—"

"A garden that the Witchdale Horticultural Society has already deemed *Exceptional* three years running. I need a new challenge."

I snorted and took a sip of tea. Even in my half-asleep state, I knew I wasn't winning this argument.

"I keep meaning to dig out those rose bushes in the back..." I said, the spoiled scent of my own wounded pride heavy in the early morning air. "Time just keeps getting away from me."

My father pulled a second pair of work gloves from his overalls and threw them to me. "Then let's get to work. Four hands make the work go twice as fast."

"Please, it's much too early for math," I grumbled, but I put on the gloves anyways.

We cleared out some tall grass and invasive weeds in pleasant, companionable silence, but my dad can't help but stick his nose in my emotional garbage, like a therapeutic raccoon. "How's Antoine doing? He keeps beating my score on Swordle."

"He's fine," I said noncommittally. "He has a lot of time to play mirror games in…wherever he is."

"Can't be easy, the two of you being separated so soon after getting together…" I cringed for what came next. Advice that I should cut my losses and find a boyfriend in my own dimension? Recriminations for letting Antoine step through the portal to the Mirror Mainframe in the first place? "But good for you for sticking it out and going after what you want, even if it's hard."

His response caught me off guard, and I realized all the critical, judgmental ways I'd finished his sentence were said in my own voice. My own doubts and insecurities worked me over yet again, saying things that my saintly father would never utter in a million years. "Thanks, I…it can be hard, sometimes. But I think it's worth it?"

My father looked up from the stubborn shrub he was uprooting. "Briar, I've seen you give up on instant oatmeal for having too many steps. A year ago you never would have admitted your feelings, never mind fight for them. That's a good thing."

I groaned and hacked at a weed with my trowel. "Then why does it feel so bad?"

"Good things can be really frustrating at times. Gardens. Relationships. Daughters." He cracked a grin at me as I threw a clump of roots at him.

"Point taken," I said, laughter releasing the tension in my shoulders. "I'm sorry if I've been a disaster lately. Thanks for helping me weed."

"There's still good dirt underneath the thorns and the rubble," my dad said. "I'm looking forward to seeing what blooms next."

I realized too slowly he wasn't just talking about the garden. Something about my dream the night before played at the edges of my mind, but I was too tired to psychoanalyze it.

"Your friend Alice stopped by for lunch the other week," he continued. Somehow my dad was better at making plans with my friends than I was.

"Alice came all the way out to Witchdale to see you?"

"Don't act so surprised! I'm cool. I'm down with all the hip things you kids like. WitchTok. Fanny packs. Billie Elvish."

I smiled despite myself. "I'm glad you get along with my friends, Dad."

"They're your family, so that makes them my family too. It's as simple as that." He paused, and I saw his eyes flick over to mine. I might have the magic emotion-sensing powers in my family, but my dad comes in at a close second. "Are you doing okay? Alice mentioned you were struggling…with everything going on, and finding out about your background."

My background as a descendant of alien, reality-shaping tree beings.

"I'm…coping. It's been a lot, all at once, so it's hard to figure out where one existential crisis stops and another begins."

I said this with a sardonic smile, but my dad didn't take the bait to swim in the shallow waters.

"I hope this isn't overstepping, but I thought maybe part of your problem is a lack of information. I feel bad that I wasn't able to give you more answers, about your past—"

"I was left on your doorstep and you raised me as your own. How is any of that your fault?"

"I know, it's just—" He set down his trowel and turned to

face me fully. Without a shared activity to pull our attention and our focus, I suddenly felt vulnerable and exposed. "I can't imagine what all of this has been like for you. I can love you to the moon and back, but I know I can't completely walk in your shoes. So I just wondered—what if your biological parents could? What if they could provide some sort of...I don't know, guidance, or closure, that I couldn't?"

He withdrew a small scroll, tied with golden string. "I know maybe I should have asked you, but...I consulted with a genomancer."

"What? You didn't have to. They're so expensive—"

"I know, honey, but I've got the money. I can't think of a better way to spend it than to help you figure things out. Or if you don't want to, that's totally alright."

I took the scroll from him, its small size belying its emotional weight. Would opening it relieve some of the tension I'd felt since discovering the Fata, or would it just be another landmine ready for me to stumble onto?

"I...thanks, Dad. I need to think about it." I stood up and dusted the soil from my sweats. "Actually, I have to go see some friends. Are you going to be okay finishing up here?"

My father's face flashed between concern and hurt as I collected our empty tea mugs. I went over and placed a hand on his shoulder. "And...thanks. For the weeding, and...everything."

He placed his hand over mine and I could smell the fresh scent of his mood lightening, like a breeze through an opened window. "Anytime, pumpkin. Anytime."

"WHY DO YOU WANT to see my sister?" Tarris Grimmour asked over a mimosa, perched on an overstuffed green stool. His boyfriend Rick was shoveling the last cockatrice-egg crepe onto my plate with a smile in their immaculately decorated two-bedroom apartment.

It was a Thursday morning (I'm pretty sure), and yet these two gems were having a delicious homemade brunch. Living their best lives.

We were ensconced in *their* elegant breakfast nook, in front of a trio of tall, lead-paned windows looking out onto the hippest section of Havmercy. A canopy of ferns and succulents hung from macrame holders, giving the overflowing brunch spread the feel of a garden party. All their white-and-turquoise flatware was filled with a ridiculous amount of carbs, booze, and fresh fruit.

Basically, their breakfast nook was happily-ever-after Cinderella, while our breakfast nook was ol' Cindy getting her face rubbed in the ashes by the wicked stepsisters.

"I don't really have a choice," I said after swallowing some juicy pomegranate. I tried not to worry too much that the container said Persephone Farms. "Isaak Krakelev is cashing in his debt, so I've got to deliver."

"I can't believe he's still carrying a torch for Miranda," Rick chimed in. Even though I'd only called Tarris half an hour ago, they were both polished and presentable. Rick's spiky brown hair was tousled with the perfect amount of texture, and his shiny green shirt hung closely to his wide wrestler's body. "I get it, she's hot, but hot enough to overlook the kidnapping and terrorism?" I'm pretty sure I heard him mutter *"straight dudes"* disapprovingly under his breath.

Tarris took a moment to cut up his crepes, his brilliant blue eyes going down to the table. His lips were pressed thin, forming a straight line across his pale oval face. The tension of his silence was eased by the tinkling of jazz piano from their record player in the living room. "I can get you on the list," he said finally. "I'll make some calls."

"Thank you," I said quickly. "I know this isn't—this might bring up some shit for you. For both of you."

I couldn't help looking over at Rick, who kept a wide grin on his face even though his eyes winced. Rick had spent three days held captive by mountain giants hired by Miranda. She claimed that the kidnapping was just a ruse to sow division in the Multiarchy, but Rick hadn't known that when she and her co-conspirators had snatched him from his normal, non-magical life as a Columbia undergraduate.

But his grip was strong as he placed a hand over mine. "And for you, too. We were all at Grimmour Tower that day." He looked over at his boyfriend, who nodded stiffly.

When Miranda had been cornered and we'd been about to expose her plot, she'd used the spells contained in the stonework of Grimmour Tower to animate the statuary along the roof, trying to capture the three of us and Antoine. Luckily, the magic was hereditary, so Tarris was able to access it too and fight her off. But it still wasn't my most pleasant memory.

"Are you in touch with her at all?" I asked Tarris softly.

He shook his head, his bright blue eyes darkening to the stormy navy of his waistcoat. "I don't have anything to say to her. Maybe when she's released...*if* she's released." Rick reached over and grabbed his hand, forming a bridge between the two of us, and Tarris looked up with appreciation. "Now I'm more focused on looking forward. Trying to enjoy the happy ending she nearly took away from us—"

The tableware in front of us chittered as a tremor shook the floor, all three of us jumping out of our seats as the Shudder intensified. My instincts took over, and I grabbed a falling spider plant as it tumbled off their windowsill. By the time the pot was in my hands, the shaking was starting to subside, and the room went still.

My heart pounded as my mind caught up to my body, and I put the plant gently back in place. "Nice catch, Ms. Pryce," Tarris said. His tone was casual, but he gripped the back of his chair so hard his knuckles were paper white.

"Everyone okay?" Rick said, corralling some vegan sausages that had gone rogue during the Shudder. Tarris and I nodded. This Shudder wasn't even one of the worst, not by far. Their record player had somehow managed to keep playing, the smooth modern jazz unbroken, like nothing had even happened.

We settled back into our seats, but the lavender scent of brunch-time relaxation was gone. Instead, we were all wary, wondering if this small Shudder was just a preview of a more devastating one to come. By this point, most of us in the Apple were used to bracing for the next Shudder. Trying to figure out a way to live our lives in the space between the bad things.

It kept getting harder and harder.

"I just never knew a happy ending still had so much chaos in it," Tarris muttered, more to himself than to either of us sitting at the table with him.

"I think that's where some of the stories are wrong," Rick said, his face twisted in concentration, like he was thinking up the ideas as he said them. "Usually all the fighting happens, and then the hero gets a happy ending as a reward. But in the real world…it feels like we're all fighting to preserve our happily ever afters. Or at least the chance of them."

There was a moment of silence while Tarris and I absorbed what he'd said. "Grimmsdamn," I said. "This kid hasn't even lived in the Apple for a full year and he's already figured out this much?"

"Yeah, he's incredibly insightful," Tarris said warmly, raising Rick's hand to his mouth and kissing the knuckles. "Makes it really hard to win an argument against him."

"Which is why I keep telling you to stop trying," Rick said

with a smile before he popped a deviled phoenix egg in his mouth, exhaling a little around the spice.

Tarris looked like he was about to say something when his mirror chirped from where it rested on the table. He looked at the message on it and rolled his eyes.

"Ugh, I should take this. It's my dad."

"Everything okay?" I asked. Count Grimmour could be a very scary guy when he was worked up.

"It's fine. He probably just wants to rant about 'the youth of today.' There was some vandalism at Grimmour Tower and now he's gone full Boomer."

Rick made no attempt to hide his smile. "Someone broke the horns off of the statue of Oberon and reattached one of them on his...*you know*."

Tarris stood and drained the last of his mimosa before giving me a smile. "After, I'll call the White Tower. They should be able to fit you in for a visit tomorrow."

"Thanks, Tarris," I said to my departing friend. "Do you— do you want me to tell her anything for you?"

His perfectly arched blond eyebrows furrowed, and he shook his head. "She made her choices. I don't owe her a Grimmsdamn thing."

I SHADED MY EYES as I looked up the slope of Chopper's Green towards the White Tower. The Poisoned Apple's magical detention center reflected the day's sun off its white bricks, as blinding as the Royal self-righteousness that built it. Arrow slits ringed the squat tower and the small buildings clustered at its base, and I knew from experience what kind of spells lurked inside for those who made it past the front door. Security was tight, and some of the guards along the perimeter seemed to notice me at the bottom of the hill gawking, so I walked up the wide, stone stairs on the lawn's edge as nonchalantly as I could. In the center of Chopper's Green, a stone platform with rusty brown stains sat to remind us of the mercy of Royal justice. Or warn us of what awaited criminals if the Nobility stopped playing nice.

I didn't recognize the guard who was waiting by the arched stone entrance to the tower, which is probably for the best. The last time I was here, I'd had to bullshit my way in by pretending to be a wizard's apprentice, and my friend Tamsin had caused a *minor* explosion, so I didn't exactly want my reputation to precede me.

"Briar Pryce, I should be on the list," I said as I walked up, trying to cover my nerves with the bluster of an overpaid executive. Somehow, even when I hadn't done anything wrong, the guards made me nervous. It might have been the battle-axes.

"Arms out," the bored lieutenant in front of me said, before waving a wand with a large crystal back and forth over my outstretched limbs. The only things in my pockets were Isaak's flower and a few emergency roses; my dagger was affixed to my back with enchanted duct tape that my wizard friend Ravenna swore would make it undetectable. A drop of sweat traced its way down my back as the guard waved his divining rod up and down.

After a moment of pure terror, the crystal on the tip glowed green.

Satisfied by my apparent lack of weaponry, the guard jerked his head over to an armored woman with a long scroll. "Briar Pryce, here for Rosalind Farthings?" she asked. The Grimmours were keeping Miranda here under a (honestly very suspicious) pseudonym, trying to protect their tarnished reputation as much as they could. After I nodded, the guard's eyebrows raised.

"Good luck. That one is a pain in the ass."

I thanked her and went in the door. I was about to have a sit-down with the dangerous mastermind I'd put in prison a year earlier. Truly, I could use all the luck I could get.

Tarris had apparently pulled some strings and gotten us a private visitation room in one of the buildings outside the main tower, which I had plenty of time to inspect as I sat waiting for Miranda. I gazed out the barred window, looking at one of the side turrets looming above us. The endless halls of the Tower were a bleak future, but not even the worst punishment the Apple had to offer. The most heinous villains were exiled from the Apple altogether, stripped of their magic and trapped in the Otherworld forever, forced to live in a bleak world of tax returns and Toyota Camrys.

I shivered, knotting my fingers together under the large oak table in the center of the room. Isaak's black daffodil dug against my collarbone from where it sat in my breast pocket. I'd borrowed one of Jacqui's grey blazers in an effort to look respectable, but my black jeans and striped blue blouse still had wrinkles from the pile of laundry I'd dug them from that morning.

Part of me, beyond worrying that Miranda was going to play some sort of *Silence of the Lambs* head game with me, was really concerned that she was going to make fun of my outfit. High-school habits die hard.

After a solid twenty minutes of waiting, the door opened and a guard stepped in, scanning the room in case I'd gotten so bored I'd become a security risk. He nodded into the hallway, and another two guards brought in the lithe form of Miranda Grimmour.

My sartorial concerns melted away as I saw the frayed red shift that made up her prison uniform. Her wild mane of blonde hair was longer and more tangled than the last time I'd seen it, while the muscles in her arms had gained an almost predatory tone. The carefully polished princess persona that she had used to deflect suspicion had been utterly discarded; the young woman in front of me was feral, untamed, and unbroken.

And to be honest, she was pulling it off.

The two guards chained her shackled hands to the table between us before leaving. The first guy who'd opened the door looked at me, as if wondering if I'd be able to stand up to Miranda. "We'll be right outside," he told me. "Knock if you need anything."

And they shut the heavy wooden door, leaving us alone with the heavy scent of history to air out.

I cleared my throat, hoping I could just get in, deliver the flower, and get out before the Second Breakfast stopped serving lunch. "Miranda, I have something for you—"

"Miss Briar Pryce," Miranda purred, lounging back in her chair with a wide grin. "It must be my lucky day."

I shifted uncomfortably, just as she wanted. "I'm just here to—"

"What's the rush, girl?" Her tone brimmed with the stale bubbles of poisoned champagne. "It's not every day they let me out to talk to the savior of the Multiarchy. So let's chat. Aren't you curious to hear what I've been up to?"

I sighed. There was no way I was getting out to the Second Breakfast in time.

"Big update," Miranda chattered on, her eyes sharp as razor blades. "I've taken up cardio kickboxing, cut out sugar, and, *oh*, the prison I'm trapped in is constantly on the verge of collapse from the earthquakes about to tear the Apple apart." Her eyes narrowed, angry black circles underscoring their hateful blue sear. "Plus I've been journaling."

I didn't fall for her faux party-girl act for a minute. Miranda was brutally intelligent and manipulative, and if I let her know how disconcerted I was by being alone with her, she might never let me regain my balance.

So I stayed silent, hoping she'd tire herself out and I could get a word in.

"It's the funniest thing," she continued, "that the Shudders started…gosh, not too long after I last saw you. When you were all hopped up on trying to stop the princesses from screaming. As I recall, you did get them to shut up, but then…hmmmm, like a week later, the ground started moving. *What a coincidence.*"

I ground my teeth so hard I bet it made the Tooth Fairy twitch, but I tried to keep my emotions off my face. "You done?" I said as icily as I could.

Miranda fake pouted. "You continue to be zero fun." But at least she finished her villain monologue.

The best way to get her to listen was most likely to hook her curiosity, so instead of saying anything, I took out Isaak's black flower and placed it on the oak desk between us, within reach of her shackled hands.

"Guess Krakelev still has a soft spot for me," she said quietly, but something was off. Her face was still twisted into a superior scowl, but her eyes—her eyes looked at the flower with undisguised need.

"And apparently you still recognize flowers from his family's garden."

That earned me a quick snort of a laugh. "He has a very particular aesthetic."

"He sent a message, too," I said carefully, watching Miranda roll the flower between her fingers. "Our future blooms out of the stone our parents left us."

The words seemed to confuse Miranda for a moment, until recognition dawned on her face along with a wicked smile. Suddenly, my stomach filled with acid that had nothing to do with the bacon-and-cheddar pretzel I'd grabbed from a dwarven food cart that morning. The last time Miranda Grimmour had kept a secret from me, it'd almost gotten me killed.

I sniffed the air, and the emotion that I felt filling the room was…relief?

"I'd love to hear it set to music," I said as casually as I could.

"What?"

"Isaak's message. He said it was a song lyric he wrote."

There. Just for a moment, Miranda wasn't able to hide her confusion. Isaak must have been lying when he said that, meaning there was something else in the message I'd delivered. I leaned back in my chair smugly, proud that, just for a second, I'd managed to throw Miranda Grimmour off balance.

My victory was short lived, however, as my chair's legs pulled out from underneath me when the entire floor tilted with a cacophonous crash.

Looking over, I saw Miranda still upright, but the table to which she was shackled had skidded as well, pulling her forward onto her feet. The shock on her face told me that she wasn't responsible.

This was a Shudder. The biggest I'd ever felt.

More rumbling underscored the screams and shouts echoing through the White Tower, but it didn't drown out the sound of a great crack from outside the window. I turned just in time to see—

The side turret I'd noticed earlier split off from the main tower, the whole mass of stone and brickwork almost hovering in the air for an awful, terrible moment, and then crashing into the courtyard beneath with a terrible, apocalyptic roar.

Billows of dust and smoke crashed against our window, blocking out our view of the outside world. The shaking had decreased to a slight tremor, but it wasn't going away. More aftershocks would come, maybe even worse than the first. Plate tectonics couldn't predict the movements of a sleepy underground giant.

Miranda and I turned to each other, eyes wide.

We needed to get out of here.

It's funny how a crisis can make people band together. The enemy of my enemy is my friend, and currently our shared enemy was "being crushed by falling rocks."

The wild-eyed princess in front of me recovered from her shock sooner than I did. My ears were still ringing from the blast, but I thought I heard her mutter, "Might as well get this party started." Working deftly despite the shackles on her wrists, Miranda twisted the black daffodil's flower off and tapped a small amount of grey powder out of the stem and onto the floor. Then she kicked off her prison-issued sneakers and placed her bare feet on the stone beneath her.

Immediately, a stalactite of rock shot out of the ceiling and pierced the table, cracking it in half and severing the chain connecting Miranda's shackles. I scrambled backwards on the ground as Miranda stood, rising above me, unchained.

As her bright blue eyes crackled down at me, I wondered if she felt the same disaster-induced camaraderie I'd experienced. The sheath of my dagger dug into my back, and I held my breath, wondering if I should reach for it before she came at me. But my better angels said I shouldn't draw my blade unless she made it necessary.

A creaking in the floor beneath us broke the moment, and the tension dissipated like a wave. Miranda rolled her eyes and turned to the door. "C'mon, Pryce, let's move. We don't have much time to get everyone out."

"Get them out?" I sputtered as I got to my feet. "Miranda, we can't—"

She pointed out the window to where the main tower was listing dangerously. "This whole place could come down any second. If we don't free the prisoners, they'll be trapped inside when it does."

"But the guards—"

Her chin dipped to look away from the tower. As I followed her gaze, I saw them: dozens of armored guards fleeing to escape the destruction of the Shudder. Abandoning their posts to save their own skin.

"I've been here almost a full year," she said, a flinty hardness in her voice. "There was no doubt in my mind they'd leave us here to rot the first chance they had." My indecision must have shown on my face, because her voice softened as she looked me in the eye. "Whatever the other prisoners have done, Briar, we need to save them. Unless you're willing to make their imprisonment a death sentence?"

My heart twinged, and I knew she was right.

I spoke up, raising my voice to be heard above the noise of everything falling apart. "Let's go, princess."

MIRANDA STEPPED FORWARD and placed her palm on the wall next to the door. With a wrenching sound, the door jamb expanded six inches in all directions, snapping the hinges and lock as it grew. Miranda pushed the now-disconnected door over and stepped into the hallway outside.

"How are you doing that with the stone?" I asked as I followed her outside. None of the guards had stuck around to make sure either of us made it out safely. *The Poisoned Apple's finest*, I thought bitterly.

"I'll explain later," Miranda huffed, leading me down the corridor. "We need to get to the security nexus. From there, we can deactivate the spells keeping the prisoners locked up."

"And you know where it is?"

"Briar, please," Miranda said as we turned a corner, "I've been in here for almost a year. Did you really think I wouldn't have memorized the layout and identified weaknesses in their security?"

"I thought you said you took up kickboxing—" I said, stopping as a pair of guards clambered down a stairway in front of us and ground to a halt.

The taller of the two, a slender man with a scar across one eye, pointed at Miranda and drew his sword. "Back in your cell!" he barked with the aggressive tone of someone not used to having to repeat himself.

Miranda ignored him and turned to me. "Do you want to take them out with your magic, or shall I use mine?" She tapped her bare foot impatiently on the ground, and I swore I saw little shockwaves ripple through the stonework beneath us. My magic would definitely be a softer touch.

With a flicker of thought, I conjured one of the roses tucked into my boots to my outstretched hand. Given my garden's…difficulties in the months since I'd woken the princesses, this rose was just barely out of its bud, mauve petals peeking out from its tight blossom. A little harder to work with, but it would do the trick.

I recalled the crash of the tower I'd seen just minutes before, the world-cracking sound of it, the electric shock of my body realizing that this place was not safe, would never be safe again. The overwhelming, primal desire to *run*. I coaxed those feelings of terror down my arm, slowly filling the incipient rose with my power—

"She's got some sort of weapon!" the shorter guard shouted, bull-rushing me just as soon as I was putting the final touches on my rose. I had about six inches of height on him, which meant he was able to get under my arms and shove me bodily up against the wall behind me, knocking the wind from my lungs and the rose from my fingers. His gauntlets pressed my shoulders up and back, preventing me from getting any leverage to break his hold.

"Hand me your cu—*UFF!*" the man in front of me started, before Miranda's outstretched foot connected with his ribs, right in the gap in his armor underneath his armpits. Twisting closer to us, Miranda brought the same leg behind the man's, buckling his knee and tossing him easily to the ground. Before I could thank her, the taller guard dashed towards us, sword raised to deliver a killing blow to Miranda's outstretched neck.

I gulped in a breath and reached out with my magic, pushing everything I had into the rose by my feet. The mauve petals exploded into a fiery umber and shot like a rocket at the upright guard. Just as he was about to give Miranda a very final haircut, the petals hit him full-on in the face (I'm pretty sure one went up his nose, which would've been much more hilarious in other contexts). The instant they did, he staggered back, eyes wide with all the fear I'd put into the petals. Ignoring his partner's struggles to get up, the taller guard pushed off the wall and ran for the exit.

Not finished with their task, the rose petals turned around and dive-bombed the guard Miranda had laid out. As they took effect, he flopped onto his stomach and started to army crawl away. Miranda gave him one more kick in the side for good measure, after which he made it to his feet and ran as if his life depended on it.

Miranda pushed her wild hair out of her eyes and looked at me with grudging respect. "Not bad, Pryce."

A smile tugged at my lips. "Thanks. Guess you weren't lying about the kickboxing."

"I wanted to spear him with some stone, but I thought I might accidentally get you too. And you're more useful to me un-impaled."

This time I grinned sardonically. "I'm touched. Now where's this security nexus?"

The two of us jogged down a few more hallways before coming to a pair of double doors. In an instant, Miranda shot a stone battering ram from the opposite wall, smashing the doors off their hinges. Inside was a dark, windowless chamber, the obsidian walls traced with lines of glowing blue runes. Whoever normally manned this station had fled, leaving a floating, foot-long black cube in the center, glowing with its own symbols.

Miranda laid her hand against the dark wall. "Grimsdammit. It's made of some kind of metal—I can't do anything in here. Can you bring this down?"

Watching the band of runes running across the walls reminded me of something, but I couldn't place it. "I've got this," I said, drawing my dagger from its duct-tape sheath behind my back.

The cool metal of the hilt felt familiar in my hand, and my fingers curled around the scrollwork crafted to resemble twisting vines. A faint glow surrounded the edges of the thorn-shaped blade, hinting at the disenchantment charms laid into the dwarf-forged steel.

It's the rose motif, and definitely not my puerile sense of humor, that earned my dagger the name Prick.

With a flick of my wrist, I flipped to an underhanded grip and stabbed Prick's blade straight down into the center of the cube.

Usually, just the slightest scratch from Prick is enough to scramble any magic. But as I pressed the dagger's point down, I felt resistance, an invisible force field pressing up and away from the surface.

I gritted my teeth and grabbed the hilt with my other hand, pressing all my bodyweight into the stroke. Millimeter by millimeter, the blade edged closer to the cube, but still the lights of the Tower's security system blinked happily around me.

"Briar?" Miranda said as another shockwave rippled underneath our feet. "Any time now—"

A frustrated groan escaped my lips as my muscles started to seize up. This couldn't be happening—I'd never met a spell that Prick couldn't unravel.

Except—

Before I could finish that thought, a rose I'd been carrying floated up of its own accord, the petals unspooling like a miniature whirlwind. As they began to glow an electric pink, they pasted themselves to my dagger's blade.

With one final push, I pierced the shield surrounding the cube and the room exploded with blue light.

A MOMENT LATER, my eyes adjusted to the darkness that filled the room now that the runes were all gone. A rush of cheers went up as the spellocks and Daedalus Charms trapping the prisoners of the White Tower deactivated. I let out a ragged, shaky breath, just in time for the next round of Shudders to start.

We'd done what we could to get people out; now we had to save ourselves.

Miranda was already racing through the door, but my longer legs carried me forward to match speed with her. Trusting that she had also memorized where the nearest exit was, I followed her as she flew through the identical hallways and down a stairwell to the ground floor. I caught a glimpse of the main entrance just in time for a large wooden beam to fall, crossing the hallway diagonally and blocking our way forward.

Miranda stepped forward, and for the first time I noticed the strain she was under; she was panting, an un-princessly number of sweat stains dotting her shift. Still, she planted her feet and raised her arms, sending a pair of stone columns up from the floor to lift the beam just high enough for me to duck under.

"Go!" she gritted out.

"Miranda—" I said, torn between her command and wanting to make sure she got out.

"If I go first, this will drop as soon as I'm not touching stone. *Go!*"

I ran forward, my legs burning from all the unexpected apocalypse cardio, and soon I was pushing through the door, out into the sun—

—when a crash and the splintering sound of wood came from behind me.

"*Miranda!*" I yelled, whirling to go back through the doors and losing my footing on the constantly shifting ground. I recovered and yanked the double doors open, but my eyes had adjusted to the light and couldn't see her in the dust-filled dark.

Luckily my knees held as Miranda threw herself out of the collapsing hallway and right into my arms. Together, we stumbled forward, clear of any crumbling stone from the unstable building. By unspoken agreement, we gave ourselves a few precious moments of wheezing before continuing on.

Prisoners in the red uniform of the White Tower were still pouring out of the main structure, and my gut roiled to think that, without Miranda's quick thinking, they'd still be trapped inside. A few shouting guards seemed to have stuck around, but no one paid them much attention as the prisoners scattered, some towards town, others into the edges of the Afterwoods.

Whatever came next, they were alive.

Miranda's gaze was uncharacteristically satisfied as she also watched the prisoners. "C'mon, Pryce. We'd better get going."

"What do you mean *we*?" I sputtered. "I agreed to save the prisoners, but *we* aren't going anywhere."

"We," Miranda repeated, "are going to go save the Apple."

MY NEW PRINCESS-IN-CRIME WAS frustratingly tight-lipped on our way back through the city, wearing *my* cloak with the hood up to avoid detection. Yes, she looked great in it, but I did enjoy that, on her shorter frame, the hem nearly brushed the ground.

The Shudders were over, for the moment, and the streets were drowning in the scent of nerves and relief. The damage to the Tower seemed to be the worst of it, luckily. As we walked through Liars' Square, merchants from the wooden stalls nearby swept up broken glass and chased lost fruit, some of which mewled plaintively.

We'd survived another one. But how many more lucky breaks did the Apple have left?

Jacqui hit me like a rocket as soon as I opened the door to our cottage, wrapping her arms around me and crushing my body to hers. "Good Grimms, Bri. You didn't answer my messages. We thought you were—" She straightened up as she saw the cloaked figure enter behind me. "Who—?"

I had been dreading this all the way here. "Look, things happened really quickly—"

Alice looked over from where she sat on our couch, stress-eating sugary cereal and watching our mirror, where a news report replayed the White Tower crumbling. "Wait, is that—?"

Miranda swept off her hood and gave them both a strychnine-sweet smile. "I'm going to go freshen up."

"Bathroom is at the top of the stairs," Alice said blankly,

still a good hostess even though her eyebrows had gone as high as a beanstalk.

"If you need clothes, my room is at the end of the hall," I added as the princess left, leaving me alone with my two stunned roommates.

"Briar, you can't be serious," Jacqui stammered. "She *can't* be here."

"Yeah, I'm with Jacqui on this one," Alice added. "She kidnapped Rick and almost started a Grimmsdamn war. This is even worse than the time Cade brought home a libertarian."

"Guys," I said, "I know. I didn't want to spring this on you. But Miranda says she knows something—something that can stop the Shudders and save the Apple."

"That's convenient," Jacqui snapped. "Or is she just saying whatever she thinks will convince you to harbor a criminal?"

I groaned and ran my hands through my thick, black hair. The points they were making weren't bad ones. "I know. I get it. But what if she's telling the truth?" I swallowed, and my voice lowered. "Even if it's a long shot...I have to give it a try."

My roommates looked at each other and did that imperceptible couple telepathy trick they'd picked up recently. Their resolve seemed to be wavering, so I pressed on. "She was in the White Tower under a fake name. And the guards are going to have a hard time tracking down all the prisoners who escaped." Sharing that Miranda and I were the ones who engineered the full-scale prison break could be left for a later time.

Alice looked me up and down, a smile starting to soften her scowl. "This is the most enthusiastic I've seen you in months," she muttered, "but did it have to about Miranda elfin' Grimmour?"

"I promise," I said quickly, sensing an opening, "I'll feed her, and walk her, and clean up after her."

Even Jacqui cracked a grin at that, despite herself. "Just

don't get us *all* thrown in the White Tower for aiding and abetting a known terrorist, Bri."

"I'll do my best. But I think…I dunno, despite how she went about things, I think Miranda has always cared about the Apple. Maybe her evil genius will be what makes the difference in trying to save it."

Before they could respond to my possibly misguided optimism, there was a perfunctory knock on our front door before it opened and Tarris breezed in. "Hello? Briar, oh thank the Blue Fairy. I saw what happened on the news, and I was so worried—" He must have seen the looks on all of our faces, because he stopped in his tracks. "What? Did I get pesto on my vest?"

All of our heads turned towards a creak on the stairs, where Miranda was walking down in one of my robes, toweling her wet face. When Tarris came into view, her mouth dropped. "Tarris?" Her voice sounded younger all of a sudden, stripped of the blasé bitchiness that she'd donned as armor.

"What—what is she doing here?" Tarris turned on me. His blue eyes were ablaze with anger, which only made his resemblance to his twin more striking.

"The Tower was collapsing," I said simply. "She had nowhere else to go."

"I—I can't do this right now," Tarris stuttered hollowly, turning towards the door.

"Tarris, wait," his sister said, nearly stumbling down the stairs in her desperation to get to him. Tarris paused but didn't turn around.

"I'm sorry," Miranda said softly. "I'm so, so sorry. I didn't think about what my plan would do to you, to Rick…I wanted to build a new world, but I didn't think of who would get hurt in the process." She swallowed, and her hand shook as it clutched the banister. "I chose my beliefs over my own brother, and…I regret it every day."

Her apology hung in the air like an offering of incense, and for a moment all was still. I noticed a tremor in Tarris's hands, but he didn't turn around. Instead, he marched silently through the door and closed it with a final thud.

Miranda's slight frame shuddered, and she let out a single, heart-wrenching sob. She took a few shaky, steadying breaths, rubbing the tears out of her eyes with a fierce sense of authority. It was at once frightening and impressive to watch as she mastered herself, bringing every piece of her body under control, reshaping her features just as easily as she'd reformed the stone of the White Tower.

When she turned back around to face the rest of us in the living room, her eyes were moist, but her jaw was set. "I'm going to get dressed. Then I promise I'll tell you everything I know—about the Shudders. And how I think we can stop them."

"Not yet," I said. "If you know something useful, we're not going to keep it to ourselves. We're going to share it with some of the brightest minds in the Apple." I paused. "And my cousin."

THE WOOD-PANELED HALLS of the Academy of the Iron Wand were relatively empty in the late-afternoon light as Miranda, Jacqui, Alice, and I trekked through them. After the Shudders began, a suspicious number of senior wizards had taken simultaneous sabbaticals. The remaining staff had tried to figure out if there was anything to do to save the Apple, but beyond refreshing the reinforcement charms on the older Academy buildings, they'd been mostly useless.

"Hey, you ruffians can't be in here!" a familiar voice called out with mock seriousness. Linden came out from behind a long desk in front of us, grinning. The Department of Magiphysics' newest research assistant had gone business casual by way of a Bushwick rave, somehow making a baggy sweater vest, peacock-printed polo, and torn grey shorts into schoolboy chic. His dark coiled hair and amber eyes still surprised me with their similarity to my own.

I call Linden my cousin, but in reality we had no idea how closely we were related. I was a foundling, and no one in Linden's family knew anything about me or who'd left me on my dad's doorstep. But not long after we'd first met, we found out we were both part of the bloodline of the Fata: uncanny, primordial creatures who were responsible for creating the Poisoned Apple. It was just as strange as it sounded, but mostly I was just thrilled to have found family.

I leaned against one of the few parts of his desk that wasn't covered in LaCroix cans. "Heya, cuz. How's the new job going?"

"Eh, you know how it is. You finally get a job with health insurance just as the world goes to shit."

"Is Tamsin in?"

My eyes went to her closed office door. After I forced her to take the credit for saving the screaming princesses, Tamsin had been promoted out of her basement office and into a swanky suite on the second floor. They'd even allowed her to take on Linden as an assistant-slash-test-subject.

Like me, Linden was a Free Spell: someone with inborn magic abilities well outside the officially sanctioned magic of the Academy. His gift (or curse) was to go into the dreams of anyone who slept near him. Somehow, being exposed to the unfiltered subconscious of humanity hadn't completely melted his brain.

"The good professor is just coming back from a staff meeting," Linden reported. "She said you can wait inside—I'll put the kettle on." He opened the office door for us and bustled off to the nearby kitchenette.

Tamsin's office was much larger than her previous one, but that just gave the eccentric wizard more room for her experiments. Built-in bookshelves held everything from ancient grimoires to whirring clockwork devices, while she'd cleared the center of the room for a set of couches and armchairs that looked like they'd been stolen from a Victorian smoking room. Most of the horizontal surfaces were covered in empty mugs and scraps of parchment.

Currently, the armchair farthest from the door held the reclining form of Ravenna Singh, Tamsin's former apprentice and overall magical powerhouse. Her chic black dress had a feathered Medici collar, like something Maleficent would wear to the Met Gala. Her raven-black hair and russet skin glowed in the light streaming in Tamsin's picture windows, although I noticed, like most of us in the time of Shudders, Ravenna had dark circles underneath her eyes.

"I got your message and came as quickly as I could," Ravenna said warmly as she rose to greet us. "Is everything okay?"

I gave her a big hug. Ravenna had been an old flame of Antoine's, but somehow his absence had drawn us closer, the shared loss burying any lingering jealousy I'd felt when I first met her. And her brilliant magical mind would be crucial to determine if whatever revelations Miranda had to share were absolute kelpie shit.

"Everything's fine," I said by reflex. "Well, I mean, no, obviously everything is falling apart. But no more than usual."

Ravenna arched a perfect eyebrow, but I could tell from her smile that her curiosity was piqued. She turned to Miranda and extended a hand. "Ravenna Singh, lovely to meet you."

Miranda flashed a predatory smile. "Miranda Grimmour." If Ravenna had heard the rumors surrounding that name, she kept the knowledge from showing on her face as the two women shook hands.

Linden returned with a tray full of tea in mismatched mugs, all with corny phrases like *Avalon's #1 Boss* and *Stop Bustin' My Fireballs*. My eyes meandered around the office as he handed out the mugs, finally landing on a nearby display case. Inside, a single thorn floated in a protective blue shimmer.

"Holy basilisk balls," I muttered to myself. The thorn had been part of the spell that infected the sleeping princesses—and it was also the only other thing I'd encountered that Prick had been unable to dispel. Because both the dagger and the thorn were made by the Fata.

"What is it, Bri?" Alice said, blowing on her mug covered in common Welsh swearwords.

"The security system at the White Tower. Prick wasn't able to dispel it until I used my powers to help me." Luckily, I'd told the entire story of the prison break on our walk over here; I wasn't sure whether to be grateful or insulted that neither Jacqui nor Alice were that surprised by my actions. "That's only ever happened one other time—when I tried to dispel the Fata magic on the princesses."

"Don't the White Tower's security spells come from the Academy of the Iron Wand?" Jacqui asked Ravenna.

Ravenna shook her head. "The Academy maintains them, but I don't know who originally enchanted the White Tower. It's one of the oldest structures in the Apple."

"Or at least the parts of it still standing are," Miranda purred.

The history of the Poisoned Apple is vague at best, shrouded in the stories and folklore that power the city itself. Only my friends and I were even aware of the Fata and their role in creating the Apple out of threads of story hundreds of years ago. But my arboreal ancestors weren't exactly forthcoming about the details.

Before we could discuss further, the door opened and Professor Tamsin Davies scampered in. A hint of steam fogged up her cat's-eye glasses, which she immediately took off to clean on her green sweater. Her bushy brown hair was actively rebelling against the braid into which it had been press-ganged. "Ah! You're all here. Welcome, welcome," she said in her musical Welsh accent as she hung her trench coat on a nearby coat tree. "Now what's this all about?"

Now that the brain trust had gathered, I caught everyone up on the day's events—I didn't go into a deep explanation of Miranda's past, but otherwise I trusted everyone in the room completely, and none of them batted an eye when I mentioned Miranda had broken out of the White Tower.

"And then we came over here," I finished lamely. Alice was the storyteller in the household; my talent was just getting into a lot of dangerous situations.

"One question," Ravenna said as she finished one of the scones Linden had brought out during my story. She turned to Miranda with equal parts suspicion and curiosity. "How did you manage to shape the stone of the White Tower during your escape?"

The grin Miranda gave her was positively wolfish. "My father enchanted the stones of Grimmour Tower to respond to anyone of the Grimmour bloodline, allowing us to alter them as we saw fit. But over time, repairs were made, statues were replaced...the stones weren't all the same. So he updated the spell to respond even if the masonry wasn't one hundred percent original."

"A standard Ship of Theseus ensorcellment," Ravenna said as if that made any sense to non-wizards.

I ran over the events of the morning in my head, still confused. "So how does that give you control over other buildings?"

In response, she pulled out a vial from her pocket. Inside was the same dark grey powder I'd seen her sprinkle on the floor of the White Tower. "Isaak, the sweet dear, ground up some stone from Grimmour Tower to smuggle inside his silly flower."

Something in my memory clicked. "I'm guessing he was behind the vandalism your brother mentioned?" I asked.

The princess merely grinned in response. "As soon as I mixed it into the floor of the prison, the spell saw it as part of Grimmour Tower, and I was able to shape it as I saw fit."

"That's quite a loophole." Ravenna's voice held a begrudging respect that I knew she didn't dole out easily.

"It's not my fault the wizards made their spell so easy to exploit," Miranda said. A small shudder ran down my spine. This was exactly what made her so powerful—and dangerous. She cut through the assumptions and traditions of the Apple like a hot vorpal blade through butter.

"Now that we're all up to speed," I said, "we're here to share what we know, to see if we can figure something out to stop the Shudders."

Tamsin frowned as she sipped her tea. "You're not the only one trying to figure out a way to avert what's happening. The best historians at the Academy are delving through the earliest accounts of the Apple, trying to find some mention of the giant. So far, nothing."

Miranda straightened from where she had been slumped against the wood-paneled wall. "That's where I think I can help. Do you have a map of the Apple?"

Tamsin hooked an eyebrow at the presumptuous princess but waved her hand. A shimmering illusion of the Apple appeared in the center of the room, rotating lazily. I caught my breath, gazing down at the intricate maze of thatched roofs and stone battlements. The trendy boutiques of Looking Glass Lane.

The sprawling industrial warehouses of the Cast-Iron District. The laundry lines hanging between the graham-cracker spires of the Gingerbread Tenements. At this scale, it all looked so small, and yet…

It was my entire world.

"Fancy map spell," Miranda deadpanned. "You just happened to have that prepared?"

"I'll have you know," Tamsin said with a hint of prickliness, "that I get lost fairly frequently."

Miranda smirked, not entirely unkindly. "Well, can you zoom out? So we can see Drake Mountain?"

Tamsin twiddled her fingers once more, and the perspective pulled back, showing the gentle hills of the Afterwoods, leading to the protrusion of Drake Mountain. From this high up, it was easy to see what generations of geographers had missed: if you looked at the peak, as well as the craggy ridges nearby, it formed the rough but unmistakable face of the giant underneath us all.

"I've been thinking of this map ever since the Shudders started," Miranda continued. "It made me think of something I saw in the library of Elias Clewd. Remember him?"

I nodded with as much hostility as I could muster. Elias was a smoke magus Free Spell who had aided Miranda in Rick's kidnapping. Because of him, one of my cloaks still smelled like a 1970s East Village dive bar.

"He had this hand-drawn map of the Apple's ley lines. One night, he had a little too much sherry and talked about how he felt like they could be harnessed, could be turned into a weapon."

"Ley lines?" Ravenna scoffed. "Did he keep a tinfoil helm nearby, too? Every magic user knows they're not something you can mess with."

Tamsin nodded in agreement with her former student.

"Messy stuff, ley lines. A source of deep primal magic, sure. But trying to use it for spells would be like lighting a lightbulb by holding it in your hand and sticking your tongue in the Large Hadron Collider."

"Regardless," Miranda continued, "Elias thought there was an untapped potential to them. Do you have any maps that show the Apple's ley lines?"

Tamsin hummed in uncertainty and turned to the towering wooden bookshelves around her fireplace. After a few minutes of trailing her fingers along spines, she pulled out a heavy, leather-bound tome that looked like it predated the Constitution. "Here we are," she said, sweeping aside a few empty mugs so she could lay the book open on her desk. As she traced her finger along the yellowed pages, matching red lines appeared above the illusion of the Apple. After a few minutes of this, a swooping network of red hovered throughout the map, drawing out from the city through the countryside in broad arcs that branched into smaller and smaller offshoots.

Something about it did look familiar, but I couldn't place it. Miranda, on the other hand, had a satisfied grin on her face. "Now move it down a little, under the ground," she asked Tamsin.

As soon as it settled into place, my memory caught up to me. "They're veins. The ley lines form a whole cardiovascular system."

Miranda nodded, impressed I'd caught up to her. "And look where the heart is." Tamsin zoomed in, locating where all the lines of magic coalesced on the map.

Right under Castle Fortnight.

"The White Tower is also connected," I said, tracing what I thought was the carotid artery up towards Drake Mountain. "So the giant's heart is…what, powering the Apple's magic?"

"The Apple Core," Tamsin whispered under her breath.

"What's that?" I turned to her, where she had the vacant look she always got when her brain was going fast enough to break the sound barrier.

"It was a theory that gained some traction in magiphysics a few years back," she muttered, pacing over to the leaded window looking out onto the Academy's quad. "That there was a single source, the Apple Core, from which all our magic flowed. There were pulses, rhythms to the flow of ley lines that never quite made sense, but if we look at them as part of a living thing…"

"Cool that we're finally figuring out how the Apple works just in time for it be destroyed," murmured Linden.

Ravenna had also popped out of her chair and was leaning into the illusory map of the Apple. Her wide brown eyes twinkled as they reflected the loops of the giant's magic veins. "This isn't just about the theory," she said. "The Academy hasn't been able to do anything about the giant because none of our magic seems to affect him. But if the ley lines are a direct link into his heart…we could use them to bypass his defenses."

"Woah," I said, "we're not talking about like, killing the giant, are we?"

"If the giant dies, the magic of the Apple dies," Tamsin said absentmindedly as she started scribbling runes on a giant whiteboard. "Also, murder is wrong."

"Phew, as long as we're on the same page. The no-murder page."

Her whiteboard started levitating and smoking a little, but that didn't seem to concern Tamsin as she continued to write magic formulae. "Linden, I'm going to need a fresh pot of tea and a pentagram made entirely of unicorn hair, please and thank you."

"On it, boss," Linden said as he swung his legs up from the arm of the couch he'd been perched on.

It was enough of a break in the conversation that Jacqui, Alice, and I all looked down at our mirrors. And all immediately looked up at each other.

The concern I felt was reflected in my friends' faces. "Does anyone else have a lot of missed calls from Cade?"

THE RED HOODS' HEADQUARTERS was a large, squat log cabin surrounded by dirt trails and towering pines. It had the sort of rustic charm that would've made it a great vacation rental, if it weren't for all the axes and halberds dotting the walls. Alice and Jacqui had escorted Miranda back to the house, so it was just me and Cade in the dingy kitchen for off-duty Hoods.

"Aren't there usually more of you?" I said, perched against a scratched, second-hand dining table while Cade mixed up a protein potion. The HQ was almost empty, a skeleton crew of haggard rangers where normally it was bustling.

Cade himself looked the worse for wear, coming off an all-day shift. His usually bright complexion was greyish, and his square jaw flexed with tension. The bandage circling one of his large biceps had a pair of bloody dots where a feral chimera had lodged a complaint about the Hoods' trap-neuter-release program.

"It's been a rough one," Cade rasped. "It always is after a big Shudder. The Afterwoods are precariously balanced at the best of times, but now it's like…every big bad beastie out there is spooked, and they think that their best possible migratory route heads straight into the Apple."

I didn't need magic emotion powers to tell that my friend was stressed, his hands shaking as he poured his protein potion into a thermos. The endless struggle of surviving the Shudders was wearing on us all, but the Hoods were fighting that battle more literally than most. "Is that why you called? Need me to take a shift?" I reached out and gave his uninjured shoulder a squeeze. "Anything you need."

Cade shook his head. "Thanks, but it's not that. We had some strange reports. Stuff I wanted to tell you in person."

My heart thudded in my chest as I sat up straighter. "Okay. Hit me."

"Some of the younger Hoods—there's a rumor going around that the attacks in the Afterwoods are coordinated. That the reason we're running so ragged is because someone or some*thing* has memorized our patrol schedules, identified weaknesses in the Apple's perimeter, and is making all of the Things That Go Bump work together. I thought it was all talk, but a patrol came back this morning. They drove off a pack of barghests near the Cast-Iron District and they said they saw a woman in the distance. A very tree-like woman."

He didn't have to say her name.

Caesura.

I'd only met her once, in a dream. But the Fata-human hybrid had made an impression. It was her magic that had hurt the princesses, but only as a side effect to her real goal: waking and empowering the giant underneath the Apple, so our whole world would be swept away, making room for something new. She'd offered to let me join her, to help her build a new world from the ashes.

I hadn't seen her since I'd told her to go straight to hell. I have that effect on people.

"Maybe it's not her," I asked, my words tinny with hollow hope. "Maybe it's just some dryad wandering the Afterwoods on bath salts."

Cade's eyebrows did a skeptical dance. "I thought you should know either way. I'll keep an—"

The sound of breaking glass cut him off.

Our eyes met for a single moment before we both moved in adrenaline-fueled unison. There was something about living with the Shudders for this long, something about the constant expectation that something was going to *happen,* that it almost felt like a relief when that anxiety could be transformed into action. I had Prick in one hand and a rose in the other as we barreled towards the back of the building where the noise came from.

As we got to the large, two-story common room, the rest of Cade's Red Hood squad joined us. Anya Koronik's hair was still wet from a shower in the barracks, and her thin dressing gown did little to hide her lean muscles as she loaded her signature crossbow. Martin 'Scuff' McCorryn had bits of brownie in his beard, and knowing the medic's reputation, I just hoped they didn't kick in until well after we'd dealt with…whatever this was.

I followed in their wake as they moved forward with silent efficiency, inspecting every angle until they were sure the common room was clear. A single broken window let a gust of cool spring air into the room as the Hoods fanned out. Shards of windowpane twinkled in the light from the chandelier above, a monstrosity of elk horns and torchstones. To my untrained eye, nothing seemed to be out of place, and only the shattered window suggested anything sinister.

Just as we started to relax from high alert, a board creaked from the wraparound porch outside. Anya and Cade pressed themselves against the door jamb, took a breath, and whirled outside, with Scuff and me following close behind. As soon as I stepped out, a plank groaned underneath my feet. Everyone looked down as my face burned with embarrassment. Apparently the others had memorized where the creaky spots were in the porch.

When we all looked back up, Scuff was gone.

My heart hammered as the three of us pressed our backs against each other, trying to keep a full view of the scene around us. The twilit woods beyond the porch were still and ominous, and only the ragged breaths of my companions broke the silence.

Screw this scary-movie bullshit of waiting to get dragged off one by one.

My magic surged down my arm, carrying the dampness of abandoned cellars, the menacing murmur of unfamiliar voices in dark rooms, and all the fear and terror that I was fighting back. The petals of my rose turned an ashen grey with blood-red edges before floating off the stalk in an unseen wind. The petals spiraled to the floor, still thrumming with power, sending it out in pulses. Anything that tried to rush us would have to get through those waves of horror first.

As if sensing that their prey was inaccessible, three massive shapes emerged out of the brush beyond the porch and rose nearly eight feet in the air. Any features that would identify the vaguely humanoid shapes were covered by their masses of thick, tangled brown hair, covering all parts of their body. One of the creatures moved its head, and for a brief moment, I saw a flash of a hungry yellow eye visible behind its pelt.

And then, as if choreographed, all three of the monsters turned their heads towards the back of the clearing.

Maybe she'd already been there, or maybe she appeared in that moment. Her bark-like grey skin made it hard to distinguish her from the trees around her, and her midnight blue dress seemed to be made from the gathering shadows of dusk. Her root-like hair had been gathered in an elegant bun at the top of her narrow head, showing off the alien curve of her long neck and pointed face.

But even in the dark, I could tell that Caesura's ink-black

eyes were boring into mine.

"Hello, little cousin," she purred, the quiet sound somehow filling the clearing. Her voice had the timbre of something not entirely of this world, like her vocal chords were made for a language far older than any spoken by human lips.

"Where is Scuff? What did you do to him?" I sputtered, orienting myself to face her, dagger first.

In response, she gestured languidly to a tree nearby, where Scuff was unconscious, but stirring softly. Twisted black roots bound the Little Person to the trunk, with more thorn-covered branches poised nearby, ready to tear into him.

"What do you want?" growled Cade.

"Quiet, little Red Hood. This doesn't concern you."

Cade began to step forward, but I put my hand on his arm before he could cross the circle of petals surrounding us. We exchanged a look, and while I could see Cade was apoplectic with rage, his nod showed that he would let me handle it.

"Release my friend," I said with as much firmness as I could muster while staring down a sylvan demigoddess and her trio of hirsute bodyguards.

"Briar," Caesura said with a mock pout, "is that all you have to say to me, after all these months?"

"Let him go," I pressed on. "Let them all go. Like you said, this doesn't concern them." I was pretty sure Caesura wouldn't hurt me, but I couldn't be sure the Hoods would be safe.

"This obsession with humans isn't healthy. Maybe I should help you break the habit." The vines surrounding Scuff writhed, black thorns the size of my dagger rearing up to strike.

"Wait!" I shouted, sheathing Prick and holding my hands in front of me. "We can talk. I'll listen to whatever you have to say." To show I was serious, I stepped over the protective ring of petals at our feet.

"Briar!" Cade yelled, grabbing my arm before I could move

any closer to Caesura. I turned to him, hoping my face conveyed a confidence I didn't fully feel. I laid my hand over his much larger one gripping my forearm and gave it a little squeeze.

Cade's hazel eyes widened with fear, but he let me go.

Caesura's whole pitch to me was to become her right hand, to embrace my powers and go full Fata.

So it was time I showed her what I could do.

I let a rose slide into my hand from my sleeve with the theatricality of a Central Park street performer, rolling it twice between my fingers and lightening the blossom from purple to a glowing cream. A flick of my wrist sent the petals spiraling towards Scuff. As soon as they brushed the black briars surrounding him, the plants softened, becoming green and pliant once more.

Their effect on Scuff was harder to describe. Usually, I just dumped emotions on someone like a drunk Tinder date. But sometimes, I'd felt something more—I'd felt almost connected.

Almost in control.

I pulled at those strings as hard as I could, picturing my very real desire to get the hell out of this situation and transmitting that feeling to Scuff's semi-conscious form. With a blast of effort, I saw Scuff rise to his feet, head still lolling to the side, and take a step forward.

Most of me was horrified, seeing his body move jerkily like a puppet. I'd never intentionally *pushed* someone like this.

But a small part of me—a small, twisted part—enjoyed flexing my power. And that part knew that I was barely scratching the surface of what I could do.

Caesura made no effort to stop me, and soon Scuff reached Cade and Anya. I couldn't turn to face them, because I had to keep my eyes on Caesura and her monsters.

And because I couldn't bear to look at Cade after what I'd just done.

"There we go," I said with forced nonchalance. "I've gotten rid of the problem. Now let's talk."

"That's my girl," Caesura murmured. She looked over my shoulder. "You three can go."

"Briar—" Cade started.

I turned as much as I dared, just so he could see in my face that I had a plan. "*Go*," I echoed.

They didn't even hit the creaky boards as they left me alone with the force of nature I called family.

MY DISPLAY HAD CLEARLY won me some points with Caesura, as she had a wide, world-eating grin when I walked up to her. To add to the effect, I paused and made a show of inspecting one of the hairy, towering creatures.

"They're fenodyree, aren't they?" I said, trying to sound unconcerned. "They look tough, but they're actually peaceful creatures. Helpful, even."

In response, the one I'd been inspecting gave a horrible grin, pointed teeth glinting from behind the curtains of its hair. I fought the urge to step back.

"Indeed," said Caesura. "But you're not the only one who can get others to act against their nature."

"Why go through all the theatrics, then? You could've just sent me a mirror message. Or showed up in my dreams uninvited. Again."

Caesura stalked forward, moving gracefully through the forest like the predator I knew she was. Plants seemed to move aside in front of her, bending away from the inexorable sway of her dress. "I needed your attention. Your *undivided* attention."

"So, what? You allowed some Red Hoods to spot you this

morning, in the hopes that I'd come along?"

"Hope is for the powerless. I pulled the strings, I pushed the dominoes—I made this moment happen, and now here we are." She began to circle me, ever so causally, as if I were a particularly unimpressive sculpture at MoMA.

"So you've been coordinating monster attacks for weeks, just for one conversation? Seems a little desperate."

Caesura laughed, a violent sound somewhere between a cackle and a tree trunk breaking. "Not everything I do is about you, little cousin. The encouragement I've been giving to the Afterwoods' creatures is a kindness."

"I have a cabin full of Red Hoods who would disagree with you."

"There's still time, you know. Before the giant wakes. Before this world gives its life to make way for something new. My kindness is sending these messages to the people here. The cannier residents have already listened and left."

Fierce tears came unbidden to my eyes. "This is our *home*," I said with an unwise amount of anger. "Sending us an eviction notice before you tear it down isn't a kindness. And what about the creatures you're manipulating? They have nowhere else to go."

Caesura stopped her circling and shrugged. "Death is an unavoidable part of life, sweetheart. The question is, will you do yourself the kindness of delaying it? Those of us with Fata blood can live a very, very long time. It'd be a shame to cut your story short before it truly begins."

Her perspective became so utterly clear in that moment— that my life, my friends, the people I'd tried to help—all of it was the meaningless preamble to my true life as…whatever she was.

"As long as my story has more chapters," I said, my voice calm—somehow my anger, my fear, didn't seem to matter in that moment, because I knew so clearly what I had to say, "as long as I've got more life in me, I'll spend it trying to stop you. So if you still think there's a snowball's chance in Smaug that I'd help you, you should just kill me now and get it over with."

"You know," she said with the warmth of a schoolgirl giving a bathroom-stall confession, "I was kind of hoping you'd say that."

"Then fine. Do it. But I'm not going to die without a fight." I clenched my fists and began to feel my magic singing through my veins. The underbrush nearby began to twist and lengthen, thorns weaving themselves into existence as my fingernails dug into my palms.

"No," Caesura said, and even though her eyes were completely black, I could tell she was rolling them, "not the killing part. That you'd oppose me. You would be vaguely useful as an ally, but as an enemy…I haven't had this much fun in decades. Maybe opposing me will be a brief but amusing climax to your short life."

I knew there was a dirty joke in the phrase "brief but amusing climax," but I was also sure she wouldn't get it, so why throw away good material?

"Then let's do this," I said simply, throwing my hands out to my side. "Fata vs. Fata. Winner take all."

"Don't worry. I will," Caesura said, stepping backwards but not taking her eyes off me. She then turned and walked slowly into the woods, her haunting voice echoing with a final, "I will take it *all*."

"AND THEN SHE JUST DISAPPEARED, but it was like, super ominous," I said around a mouthful of Jackalope Tracks fudge ice cream. I was curled up in the turret window of my room, wearing the coziest clean pajamas I could find. My mirror sat on my knees, giving Antoine a view of my face mostly unobstructed by the pint of ice cream I was cradling like a newborn kitten.

Antoine had been doing his best listening face, the one he makes when I tell him something ridiculous and he has to process before telling me what he thinks. He started when I told him about the prison break and held tight to his impassivity through the confrontation with Caesura. But I could tell his true thoughts were coming soon.

"Got it. Honestly, Bri, I'm so, so—" I flinched for the inevitable disapproval. "—proud of you," he finished.

"Sorry, what? I think I misheard you."

"I know you've been down lately, and I would've been excited to see you just pick yourself up. But you're back in the saddle. You're fighting the good fight. I just hope you're proud of yourself."

"Wow, I've never heard that phrase from anyone but a disappointed school principal."

He laughed, and the sound was sweeter than any chocolate-filled ice cream. "I'm serious. This can't have been easy. My only wish is that I could be there for you."

My cheeks warmed, and I stroked a finger down the side of the mirror. "You are," I said softly. "You've always been here for me."

Despite all my frustration at our situation, Antoine's grin felt like summer skies opening up before me. "Well, get used to it, Pryce."

I grinned but the pixies in my stomach made me look away for a moment, and my smile faded as my eyes landed on the small scroll by my bedside table.

"What's wrong?" Antoine asked, immediately in tune with

my apprehension even from a dimension away.

"Oh, it's nothing. My dad…" With everything going on, I hadn't filled Antoine in on his visit the other morning. "He apparently consulted a genomancer to figure out who my biological parents are."

Antoine blinked and buffered for a moment. "Oh. Wow."

"Yeah, I think he's been worried about me, with all the Fata stuff and…I haven't looked at the info yet."

"Do you want to?"

I sighed. "I'm not sure. Part of me definitely wonders."

"I was curious how you felt about your parents…it is a pretty big mystery, and we are detectives sometimes."

I snorted and put on my best prime-time drama commercial voice. "She solves crimes for a living, but the one mystery she can't solve is her own past."

Antoine chuckled. "I would probably watch that."

The uncertainty I felt around the scroll didn't go away, but it felt good to talk about it. "When I was younger, I was fed all those stories…every tale of a young orphan discovering their part in a magical legacy, the twist that someone who thought they had nothing actually had everything." Antoine nodded along, letting me figure out what the hell I was saying as I was saying it. "But as I got older, I guess I realized…I am not an orphan with nothing. I won the friggin' lottery when it came to my dad, and the family that I've built around me is all the magic I need. Is it weird that I'm worried figuring out about my biological parents might somehow take that away?"

"It's not weird," Antoine said. "You're allowed to feel however you feel about it. I'll back you up whatever you choose."

Before I could come up with a snappy response, my mirror thrummed in my hand. "It's Ravenna," I said, watching her name appear under Antoine's face in wispy script. "I can call her back."

"Want me to patch her in? I'd love to say hi," Antoine said.

"You can do that? My mirror can do three-ways?" My cheeks burned as I listened to what I'd just said. "Er…mirror conference calls."

Antoine just chuckled. "Yeah, most mirrors in the post-MySpace era can. Give me a second."

He closed his eyes, using whatever connection he had to the Mirror Mainframe to take control of the call. After a second, Ravenna's face appeared on the other side of the image.

"Hey, Briar," she started, before noticing Antoine. "How's it going, Boy Scout?" A tinge of sadness passed through the magician's face—a hint of her regret. It was Ravenna's spell that had gone awry and stranded Antoine between worlds, and although no one blamed her, I knew she still carried that guilt with her.

"Good to see you, Ravenna," Antoine said. "You back in the world-saving game?"

"Eh, tenure gets boring." She shrugged. "That's what I was calling about, if now is a good time. I'm not interrupting anything?"

I tried to nudge the pint of ice cream out of her line of sight. "Not at all."

Her dark eyes sparkled with mirth. "I'm more of a Minotaur Mint gal myself. Anyways, Tamsin and I finished our analysis of the ley lines, and I figured you would want to know what we found. Miranda was right, annoyingly. The lines do seem to form the giant's cardiovascular system, and the core of the magic is in his heart, right below Castle Fortnight. I'm going to guess that whoever built the original structure knew that and wanted to control access to the giant's magic. To the Apple Core."

Most of that wasn't a surprise. The Nobles of the Apple,

hoarding power for themselves? What else is new.

"But we think with a little finagling, we might be able to use the heart to access the giant. And hopefully get him to go back to sleep."

"Wasn't I able to affect him when I broke his sleeping curse in the first place?" I said.

"You were, but now that he's awakening, we don't think it will be so simple. If we're thinking of his magic as sort of like a body—now that he's in a more active state, we have to worry about his immune system. In addition to using Castle Fortnight to tap into the ley lines, we're going to need something to fool the giant into thinking we're part of his own magic system."

"Why do I feel like this is leading to a fetch quest?" I groaned.

"Because you've got good instincts," Ravenna confirmed. "The giant is the source of all of the Apple's magic. We need to find something equally as powerful so we can access his magic without immediately being pushed out by his defenses."

"You said this plan would require finagling," I said. "How is tracking down a piece of ancient, world-generating magic your definition of *finagling*?!"

"This is still good news, Bri," Antoine chimed in. "At least now we know what we're looking for."

"I know it's a lot," said Ravenna. "We're going to try to figure something out, but we're just the wizards. You two are the detectives."

"Only when it involves being nosy and wearing trench coats," I grumbled.

"Let me take a look," Antoine said. This time, when he closed his eyes, a faint, blue glow emanated from under his eyelids as he sent his consciousness out into the magical version of cyberspace. Part of me wondered what it must be like, having that sort of access to all the information of the supernatural world.

Part of me wondered if he would be the same when he came back to our world. If he came back.

Before I could follow that thread of ideas too far, his eyes snapped open, back to their usual human look. "I might have something," he said, but there was hesitance in his tone that made me squeamish.

"Where is it?" I asked. "*What* is it?"

He gave me a smile that said he'd explain it all, eventually. But first, he asked, "Is your passport up to date?"

YOU WON'T FIND IT in the history books, but Dorothy Parker was once quoted as saying, "There's no place on Earth quite like the Poisoned Apple. And thank the King in the Mountain for that." And while the illustrious Ms. Parker was very right, there are a few places that are similar—other magic, in-between places. The lands that people tell stories about, where people might disappear for a night or for the rest of their lives. There are still a handful that have survived the age of GPS and Google Maps, lurking in the bright meadows and the dark alleys, waiting for the right person to come along. We call these realms World Slips.

So when Antoine said I'd need my passport, he was being facetious. There are still places that don't answer to the lines humans have drawn in the dirt.

I did, however, insist on bringing one of those ridiculous neck pillows.

"I just want to state for the record that I'm embarrassed on your behalf," Jacqui said, scowling at the fluffy pink monstrosity circling my neck as we waited in Tamsin's office at the

Academy of the Iron Wand.

"It's okay, girl," I said, patting the neck pillow on the side. "At least I know you'll always support me."

Jacqui grinned and looked heavenward, as if something up there would save her from being seen with me. Cade tried not to laugh but let a couple of rumbly snickers escape from his covered mouth. "Don't encourage her," Jacqui sighed. "You know this spell is going to transport us instantly, right?"

"C'mon, Jacqs," I said. "I've never been to another World Slip. Can't we at least have a little bit of a vacation vibe underneath the apocalypse-averting quest?"

"I'm with Briar," Alice said from behind a big pair of bug-eye sunglasses. "If you can't relax and enjoy the ride, what's the point of even adventuring?"

The door opened, and Ravenna came in, carrying a chic leather valise and a black, eldritch staff. "Ugh, sorry. I got caught up with some slimy donors." The scent of frustration cut through her chic floral perfume. "But after I was able to escape, I got the head of the department to let down the wards. We're cleared for inter-dimensional takeoff."

Now that the moment had come, a slight sense of uneasiness took root in my stomach. "You're sure this is safe?" I asked for the dozenth time.

Ravenna nodded. "The Academy has conferences all over, and they never pay for us to fly. These portals are totally stable. We're much more likely to die after we arrive."

Alice lowered her glasses and gave Ravenna a look. "I'm not sure that came across as comforting as you intended."

I stood, cracking my neck and fluffing my pillow. "Alright, let's get this over with."

The five of us stood in the middle of the office, four of us with absolutely no idea how this portal stuff worked. "Oh crap," Alice said. "I have sunscreen in my bag. Am I allowed to have liquids?"

Ravenna smiled. "Unless your sunscreen is haunted by ghosts or inter-dimensional beings, it shouldn't affect the spell."

"Nope. It is SPF 70 though, so it's basically magical."

"No haunted stuff?" I asked. "Then we better hope Cade didn't bring that creepy toy bugbear he slept with until high school."

Cade whirled towards me. "Sir Tum-Tum was not *haunted*, he just had a unique look—"

"Briar's right," Jacqui added. "Those hollow, soulless eyes…" She gave a theatrical shiver that I knew was inspired by real events.

"Remind me why I volunteered to quest with them?" Cade asked Ravenna as the rest of us did our best Sir Tum-Tum impressions. The familiar banter with my best friends had the welcome effect of dulling my nerves better than any enchanted rose could. I hadn't had anywhere near enough laughter these past six months.

"Are you all quite finished?" Ravenna said with the beleaguered air of someone who teaches undergraduates. She walked to the center of the room, her black traveling cloak billowing dramatically. I should have known she'd be one of those people who looks flawless even when they travel.

I choked back my giggles and focused on the task at hand. It felt good to forget everything that was happening, just for a moment—to lay down our burdens for a brief laugh—but we had a robbery to commit.

After we quieted down, Ravenna spread her arms wide and raised her staff, beginning to chant something guttural. A ring of green runes formed on the floor, glowing through the scattered sheets of parchment that had fueled Tamsin and Ravenna's research spree. As Ravenna continued to intone, the runes flowed forward into the center of the circle, forming a patch of pulsing green quicksilver, arcane and bubbling. In an instant, it split into two prongs, shooting up through the air to form a hovering oval frame. Ravenna's chanting reached a climax, and she pointed her staff forward, the clear gem on its tip turning a dusty yellow-green. An arc of lighting shot forward, striking the center of the portal and bouncing through it, until the bright afterimages of its passage resolved into a picture of a sandy mountain path.

Ravenna cricked her neck and looked over her handiwork. The rest of us stared, mouths slightly agape at the *hole in spacetime* that she had casually ripped in the middle of the room.

Alice recovered fastest, shouting, "Dibs on going first!" With a quick look to Ravenna for permission, she bolted forward and jumped into the portal. There was a short sizzling noise as she passed through the barrier and disappeared.

Jacqui shook her head but couldn't hide the smitten grin at her girlfriend's antics. She and Cade passed through next, leaving me with Ravenna, who nodded me through.

I tried to put Antoine's experience with portals out of my mind as I stepped forward. The quivering magical energy pulsed outwards, raising the hairs on my arms and smelling faintly of ozone. I swallowed, held my duffel bag close, and stepped through the gap between World Slips.

As my head passed the portal, I found myself in a woodland not dissimilar from the Afterwoods. Something about the golden, syrupy quality of the light told me that I wasn't in a physical space as much as a Passway between worlds, a way for us to acclimate from the magic of one pocket universe to another. I couldn't see my friends ahead of me, but Ravenna had warned us we'd be separated for the short trip—right after I'd unsuccessfully begged her to explain how teleportation worked in a Scottish accent, for *Star Trek*-related reasons.

The air began to change as I walked down the forest path,

the damp humidity of a dark forest beginning to lighten to a dry heat. Soon my boots were no longer sinking into moist loam, instead skidding along a sandy topsoil interspersed with tall beige grass. The path began to wind up a slope, the forest giving way to a few twisty fir trees. As a warm breeze caught my cloak, I could smell the salt of an ocean hidden somewhere nearby.

The path neared the top of the hill, and I noticed fallen columns dotting the landscape, their intricate designs painted in bright colors. An ancient statue beckoned from beside the path, the figure's flowing robes still caked with red paint, even though her head and one arm had cracked off long ago. At the slope's peak, a stone archway stood, and the sky beyond was a dark, saturated blue, as opposed to the unnatural gold of this in-between place. The landscape beyond the portal also didn't match, although it shared the rolling, coastal hills.

I clomped up the path, adjusted my neck pillow, and stepped through the gap between worlds.

There wasn't much more than a tingling sensation as the magic washed over me, but the scorching heat of the other realm felt like stepping into the world's most scenic hair dryer. The cry of distant gulls underscored the bustling vista laid out before us: a terraced city of marble and stone with forests of columns and pediments that grew into each other in a chaotic harmony. At the foot of the mountain was a vast market, as bustling as any I'd ever seen. Boisterous satyr shopkeepers yelled out over the hubbub while hulking minotaurs worked security, some in traditional tunics, some in XXXL leather jackets. Harpies roosted on the clay roof tiles, gossiping and shrieking with laughter in the blazing afternoon sun.

After months huddled in the snowy Poisoned Apple, the slopes of Mount Olympus looked pretty close to heaven.

Our group took a moment to look around in awe (and in Alice's case, take as many pictures as she could) before dragging our luggage down the slope. The path led down to a small gate guarded by a few nonchalant hoplites. Outside, leaning against a large cypress tree, was one of the largest men I'd ever seen. Upon seeing us, he pushed himself upright with a grin and a wave of his massively muscled arms.

"Hello there!" he boomed out, moving up the slope with surprising speed. "You must be Antoine's friends. I'm Leander. Welcome to Olympus!" Despite its volume, Leander's voice was warm and throaty, his Greek accent adding texture to each word.

In the space it took us to greet him and introduce ourselves, Leander somehow insisted he carry the majority of our bags; Alice's carry-on luggage looked like a shopping bag in his hubcap-sized hands. His shoulder-length black hair waved in the warm breeze, just brushing his wide, tan shoulders. Something in the grace of Leander's movements under his knee-length red chiton told me he knew how to handle himself in combat, but something else in his wide smile told me he wasn't one to start fights—only end them.

"Come, come," he said generously. "Our place isn't that far. Is this your first time in Olympus?"

All of us nodded, except Jacqui. "I did a horseback riding camp here one summer when I was young," she explained. "Centaurs know a thing or two about dressage."

"Well, my wife and I are excited to have you all," Leander continued.

"I didn't realize you were hosting us so last minute," I explained. "Antoine made all the arrangements. I hope it isn't too much trouble—"

"Nonsense!" Leander boomed, scaring a nearby family of squirrels. "Antoine is an old friend. He's saved my life enough times that this is the least I can do."

As we passed the guards at the gate, Leander called out

something to them in Greek that made them all laugh good-naturedly before waving us through.

"We don't need to check in with them or anything?" Ravenna asked.

"I told them you were coming earlier," Leander explained. "Olympus is always open to travelers—a holdover from the days when mysterious strangers were usually some god in disguise, ready to make your life a living Tartarus if you offended them." He cocked a bushy eyebrow at us. "You're not, right?"

"Not what?" Ravenna said.

"Gods in disguise," he clarified. "If one of you is going to turn into a swan and seduce my wife, I'd at least like to know in advance."

He paused a moment before breaking into a peal of laughter at the befuddled looks on our faces, just as he began to part the crowds of the marketplace. We followed in his wake through the winding rows of food stalls; it was all I could do to stay close and not be lured away by the fragrant smells of spiced lamb, fried halloumi, licorice-scented ouzo…

Grimmsdamn, if I was having this much trouble resisting with the food, I was gonna be screwed if we met actual sirens.

I clocked movement over my shoulder, in the direction of one of the high mountain peaks, and soon we were covered in shadow. I stared up at the sky for as long as I dared in the crowd, then hustled forward to tap Leander on his solid shoulder.

"Hey Leander, are those mountains… flying?"

He looked up and rolled his eyes. "They're floating islands, made of Aeolian limestone. It's not enough for the Midases to have their own private islands, they have to make them fly above the rest of us."

"Ahh, you have rich assholes here, too?"

"Such is the way of the world," he said with a shrug that

flexed more muscles in his shoulder than I have in my whole body.

We peeled off from the market and wound our way up another incline, climbing a precarious stone staircase until we reached a rounded wooden gate. Leander unlocked it and shouldered it open, and if traipsing up the hill with most of our luggage tired him out, he didn't let it show.

Leander's hillside villa was a light, creamy sandstone paradise. We stepped onto a wraparound porch that treated us to a panorama of the temples and colonnades of the city, framed by wooden trellises bursting with bright pink bougainvillea blossoms. Geometric mosaics in green and yellow traced the square outlines of the terraced levels, with the repeated motif of lions and owls.

Just as we got used to our surroundings, the front door opened, and a striking woman in bronze armor stepped out, cleaning her hands on a towel. "Ahh, welcome, welcome! So good to see you. Sorry I couldn't help pick you up, I had some work things to take care of." She noticed a spot of blood on one ornate bracer and wiped it off. "The erinyes have bad timing. I'm Athena."

I looked over at Leander at the mention of her name, eyebrows raised. The big man chuckled. "After ten years of marriage, I still suspect she's at least a demigoddess."

Athena smirked and punched his arm lovingly before turning to me. "And you must be Briar. Antoine's reports of your beauty precede you."

She grabbed my forearm in a warrior's greeting, and I smiled at her in return. "Thank you for hosting us. Antoine spoke highly of you both. Said you're the best mercenaries in all of Olympus."

Leander actually blushed like a schoolboy. "He's too kind. Antoine is a mighty warrior himself. For a little guy."

"Now please, get yourself settled, and then we're taking you out for dinner," Athena said, just in time for my stomach to rumble like Zeus's thunder.

OUR FIRST MEAL IN OLYMPUS was at a delicious hole-in-the-wall seafood place run by a pair of naiads who immediately gave Leander and Athena their best table. Course after course of hydra calamari, lemon-kissed orzo with feta, and fried Cetus tail were laid out before us, until I was fuller than a kid in a gingerbread cottage. With the time change, it was only lunchtime for us, but I didn't complain.

Over a round of baklava, Athena and Leander strong-armed us into drinks at P@N, a nearby spot frequented by the mercenaries of Olympus. When I offered to at least pick up the check for dinner, Athena whipped her dark braid over her shoulder like a weapon and gave me a glare she must have picked up from a Gorgon. Apparently the Olympian duties of hospitality were no joke.

After settling the tab, they led us to a large, temple-like structure, its stone pediment festooned with a frieze of satyrs, dryads, harpies, and all other manner of creatures dancing together. The thump of music and flashes of colored lights spilled out between the columns surrounding the entrance, and as I'd come to expect from traveling around with our mercenary hosts, the cyclops working the door ushered us past the line outside with a nod of her head.

The interior reminded me of the origins of the word "bacchanal." Throngs of people covered the floor of the dark, two-story space, a few gyrating nymphs and satyrs elevated on columns spread throughout the dance floor. Leander took us upstairs to the balcony that ringed the room before leaving to get us all drinks. Athena secured a long table before stalking over to a nearby column. She placed her hand on a small carving of a woman, and immediately the ear-splitting sounds of debauchery faded to a distant thrum.

"One of the reasons mercenaries love this place is for its Echo Chambers," she said in the newfound quiet. "We won't be distracted by the noise, and more importantly, no one will be able to hear us in here."

My friends and I all exchanged looks, impressed with the magic and the mercenary. Apparently this wasn't just a social occasion.

Leander returned with a tray of clay cups filled with glowing golden liquid. As he passed through the entrance between the columns around us, a trickle of blue light danced over his skin, which I assumed was the Echo Chamber taking effect. "Alright, first things first: a toast. Everyone, have some ambrosia." As he handed the cup to me, I caught a sweet, floral scent wafting from the drink inside. "To new friends and old treasures," Leander said, holding his cup aloft and arching a bushy eyebrow.

"Yamas," Athena toasted, as we all repeated and clinked our cups together.

"Now, let's plan our robbery, yes?" Leander grinned and pulled out a plastic lighter. At the center of the table was a small bronze censer, with some sort of leafy incense inside. It lit quickly, filling the small space with the savory scent of rosemary. The long plumes of smoke began to dance before becoming the figure of a reclining woman on a pedestal.

"We've tracked down what Antoine was asking about, but it wasn't easy. All we knew were the legends—rumors that the great sculptor Phidias made a statue of Gaia so lifelike that it was blessed by the goddess herself. From what Antoine told me, you need something with Gaia's power to save the Poisoned Apple, no?"

Ravenna nodded. "We need something imbued with world-generating power."

"Well, Gaia gave birth to half of the beings in our cosmos," Athena said. "No wonder Phidias sculpted her lying down."

Leander grinned at his wife's quip. "It turns out the statue has been making its way through private owners for centuries, handed from Midas to Midas. Luckily, a friend of ours saw it while running security at a recent symposium in the house of this man." Leander pressed his fingers onto the handle of the censer, and the smoke reformed itself into a haughty-looking nobleman in a cravat and a high collar.

"Lord Elton Wallace, an expatriate from Avalon with an affinity for buying up historical Greek art for his private collection. Among the plunder at his compound, Gaia sits waiting to be rescued."

I looked at my companions, who had all switched from vacation mode to heist mode without a thought. Jacqui gave me a nod, and I turned back to our hosts. "Doesn't seem like someone I'll feel bad about robbing. Just point us at him, and we'll do the rest."

Athena scoffed. "We're coming with you, naturally."

"You don't have to risk—"

"We're getting something out of the deal, too, "Athena continued. "We're not just going to liberate Gaia from his collection. We're going to clean him out of all his stolen statues. Give them back to the people whose ancestors made them. Besides, we have the best chance of pulling this off if we all work together. Now let's get back to how we're going to get inside Wallace's fortifications."

"Fortifications?" Alice said with raised eyebrows.

"Of course," Leander said. "How else do you expect him to defend his floating island?"

THE SUNRISE BROKE SLOWLY over the rooftops of Mount Olympus, warming the clay tile roofs for the day to come. Even after rounds and rounds of ambrosia at P@N, I was unable to sleep, so I'd padded out to Leander and Athena's balcony to see the night turn into day. The lemony-blue dawn sky brightened as the city lulled, the streets emptying of revelers and just beginning to fill with commuters.

This was one of the few times it was nice to have a boyfriend trapped in a dimension where he didn't need to sleep.

I'd angled my mirror on the stone balcony so that Antoine's SparkleCast form projected up beside me, almost as if we were watching the sunrise together.

"Look there," Antoine murmured, a shining blue hand projecting up from the mirror. "Just in front of the sun."

I squinted, just making out a small speck moving across the lightening sky. "What in Rapunzel's split ends is that?" I asked.

"Helios's chariot, pulling the sun across the sky."

"I thought no one had seen any of the Greek gods in decades," I said, furrowing my brow. Was it my imagination, or could I see the tiny team of horses running ahead of the chariot?

"It's just his chariot," Antoine explained. "It's operated by teamsters now."

"It's beautiful," I muttered, more to myself than him. More and more, I found myself saying what I was thinking around Antoine, without a thought or a filter. Surprisingly, he still hadn't run away.

"You look happy," Antoine observed as I watched a god's chariot trace slowly across the sky.

"Really? I didn't think the ambrosia had much of an effect."

He smirked. "Look at your hands."

I brought my hand up to my face. Just beneath the skin, tiny motes of golden light trickled through my veins, lighting my cardiovascular system like the Christmas tree at Rockefeller Center. My veins glowed with the faint echo of the power of gods and goddesses.

"Huh. Would ya look at that." I kept turning my hands over in the dawn light, watching the gold sparks flow through them. "Well, if ambrosia is good enough for Zeus, it's good enough for me."

"I don't know a lot about Greek mythology, but I'm pretty sure we're not supposed to use Zeus as a standard for moral decisions."

"Fair enough." I smiled at Antoine's hazy blue form. "I guess I am happy. Is that bad? I feel like I shouldn't be, given everything that's in front of us. With the Apple teetering on the brink of destruction. But I can't help feeling a little joy." *When I'm around you*, I was too chicken to say out loud.

"Of course it's okay," Antoine said. "It's what you're feeling. In fact, I think you *have* to find moments of happiness, especially when things are the absolute worst. You remember my old fencing master, Halvern?"

Maybe it was the ambrosia or the jetlag, but my mind struggled to keep up with his change of subject. "Yeah, grumpy old gnome warrior. You introduced me at your birthday party."

"When I was younger, training for my Knight Trials, I was having a tough time. It was all I ever wanted, but no matter how hard I practiced, I couldn't get over the fear that I'd fail."

"Antoine, you're one of the most brilliant swordsmen I've ever seen. Of course you were going to pass your Trials."

"I wasn't always brilliant," he said quietly. "I got so in my head, I started to think I'd be happier not trying. Just letting all the stress and pressure go, finding something else to do. I was miserable. And Halvern, as much as he's a tough old goat, could see I was struggling."

"Did he tell you to relax and take a day off?"

Antoine shook his head, and a few blue sparkles tumbled out of his projection and fell towards the alley below us. "Self-care wasn't really his style. Halvern started doing these absolutely terrible gags when I showed up for training each morning. I'd walk in and find him picking his teeth with a spear, or pretending his sickle was a mustache. And every time he'd make this big show of acting surprised, like I'd caught him in the act. It was incredibly dumb." Even though he wasn't looking at me, I could hear the smile in Antoine's voice as he described his master's antics.

"Just starting the day with a little laugh, something to take me out of my head, made all the difference. Soon I was enjoying our sparring, remembering why I actually liked training in the first place. And even though it was still demanding and challenging, I wasn't dreading the coming Trials.

"That lesson didn't always stick with me. When I finally became a Knight, it was easy to devote myself solely to the next quest, righting the next wrong, and forget that there was more to life. I might've continued on like that, pushing myself until there was nothing left of me underneath my armor." He tilted his narrow face down, but I could see his eyes search for mine behind the curls of dark auburn dangling over his brow. "If I hadn't met you."

A glowing warmth not unlike the Mount Olympus sun filled my chest, and for once I didn't push it down or lock it behind a wall of guilt. Even knowing it was a futile gesture, I placed my hand on top of his where it rested on the balustrade, imagining I could feel his fingers underneath mine.

"Briar," he said, his voice strained in a way that made my heart clench, "I can't keep asking you to stay with me, can't keep promising things I have no idea if I'll be able to deliver…it's not fair to you."

Once again, his change of topic threw me through a loop, but I recovered more quickly this time. In a minute my hands were cupping his face, as if I could reach through the endless ether between us and bring his head up straight and tall. "Nonsense," I said, my voice firm. "Antoine, I know there are no guarantees. Being together is a risk, and I'm here anyways. You make me feel so, so good and—I'm willing to put up with this shittiness in the present for a chance at a future together."

My knight took the cue and raised his head just as if I'd been able to touch him. "Are you sure?" he whispered.

"I'm sure," I said, and I was. "Take your own advice, Du-Carr. We've got to savor this, even alongside the struggle."

Antoine wiped a tear from his eye and put an illusory arm around my shoulder. "Thank you," he breathed into my ear, and together we watched the light return to the world.

THE NEXT AFTERNOON, still scrubbing sleep from my eyes, I followed Athena down a white stone staircase into the lowest level of her villa. As she walked into the cavernous room at the bottom of her home, torches flickered into life around the walls, their wavering light glinting off a constellation of polished metal around us. Spears, blades, and a multitude of more unfamiliar death-dealing devices waited, ready for battle. The rich golden paint of the walls was barely visible, as any space not covered in armaments held trophies of battle: taxidermied hydra heads, dented armor, and a tattered banner with a stylized cyclops.

Athena stepped into the center of the room, a large clear area with straw-filled mats to cushion the hard floor. Her long limbs moved with grace and economy, not a single wasted movement as she propelled herself over to a barrel full of wooden spears and took one of the longest ones. "Nice set-up, right?" she asked rhetorically as she casually threw the seven feet of wood across the room with Olympian grace, burying it into the chest of a cloth practice dummy.

I trailed along the wall, trying to identify even half of the esoteric weapons laid out in front of me. "This is amazing," I answered, my gaze moving from a bident to a piece of craggy stone plating on the wall. "What's that from?" I asked. It looked like a pauldron made of pocked limestone, much too heavy for a human shoulder.

"A little souvenir from the rock titan attacks a few years back," Athena said. Her voice carried in the large room, but something about her tone made me turn to face her. Her sharp grey eyes looked vacant for once, as if a veil of mist had blotted out a sunny day in the Grecian hills. "They fought hard, and there were so many—I wasn't sure if Mount Olympus would make it through." Her focus shifted from the trophy on the wall to me.

Something about the way Athena moved, powerful but never predatory, made me trust her. "How did you keep going?" I asked softly. "How did you keep fighting when everything was crashing down around you?"

Athena shrugged and offered a ghost of a smile. "Stubbornness, I guess. The titans weren't like anything else I'd fought— they wanted to raze everything we had to the ground. There was no negotiation, no compromise, no coexistence with them. So it came down to whether we could hang on longer than they did and drive them out of our home. I decided I would, no matter what." Her words were simple, unselfconscious, but some sort of timbre in them revealed the heroism at Athena's core. "So I get what you're dealing with in the Apple," she continued. "It's hard to feel like your world is ending when no one else seems to notice."

I had read a few headlines about the rock titans carrying out an invasion of Olympus, but all I'd done was skim a couple *Teen Vogre* articles and move on. It wasn't happening to me or anyone I knew, so it was hard to keep it in the front of my mind. A deep sense of guilt took root in my stomach.

"That's why I was so glad Antoine reached out," Athena continued. "Things are so much better now—the rock titans are back in Tartarus, and fighting them off brought all the different Olympian factions together. Not all of us get along here, but there are definitely worse monsters out there. So I just feel…lucky, I guess. And helping you with your quest is making it feel like, whatever we went through, it was worth it."

"Thank you," I said, crossing to where she stood by a table full of swords of various lengths. "I don't know what we would do without you…and if you ever need our help, we'll be there."

She winked and grasped my shoulder with a warrior's grip. "That's how it works, yeah? The phalanx is only as strong as its weakest shield. Now let me see your weapon."

I pulled Prick out of its sheath and handed it over to her. As much as it felt strangely intimate to let her hold the dagger, I was able to let go of that weirdly maternal instinct as Athena twirled the weapon around in her hands. I was going to have to get used to working without Prick if our plan was going to work. "Well balanced," she remarked. "You keep the blade sharp. I bet we can find something similar."

Athena gave the blade back to me and let her hands float across the smorgasbord of swords (smorgasword?) in front of us. Finally, her fingers alighted on a short sword not too dissimilar to Prick. "This should do. We call it a *xiphos*. Give her a spin."

The double-edged sword was a bit heavier than I was used to, but it felt steady in my hands. I nodded and stepped into the middle of the floor. My attention zoomed into my body completely, noticing the subtle shift of weight as I took the *xiphos* through a series of practice cuts and stabs. My arms protested against the extra weight at first, but soon I was able to compensate for the unfamiliar heft of the haft.

"Nice," Athena said, circling around the outside of the floor to face me. She'd picked up a blade of her own, with a curving single-edge and a grip that bent up towards her hand like the guard of brass knuckles. Her other arm boasted a small round buckler with the design of an owl etched in bronze. "The guards we've been able to observe at Lord Wallace's compound are using shields and *kopides*. Want to get a little practice in?"

I grinned and sank into a fighting stance. "I'm still a little portal-lagged, so go easy on me, okay?"

Athena winked, and a moment later she was lunging towards me, the curve of her blade whipping down like a metal snake. My instincts brought my unfamiliar dagger up in a clumsy parry, the heavy blade providing a little cushion as I deflected her blow and danced out of her reach.

"You'll never match a *kopis* for reach," Athena said as we circled each other. "You'll have to be quick to get in close."

I feinted once towards her side, but she didn't take the bait, grey eyes trained on mine, the hint of a playful smile on her lips. Next I copied Athena's arcing, overhand strike, her curved sword instantly coming up to meet mine. I could feel the steely strength in each of her movements, and I knew there was no way I could overpower her blade-to-blade.

I could, however, get a knee up into her side while she was looking at my dagger.

The noise Athena made as my kneecap connected to her ribs was something between a grunt and an impressed laugh. Her shield arm pushed forward in a brutal sweep, pushing me off balance and back a few steps.

"You're getting creative," she said warmly. "Good. Now let's go again."

Many, many bouts later, the *xiphos* finally felt at ease in my hand, although its grip was slick with sweat. Athena seemed to have boundless energy and enthusiasm, but even her lithe movements had slowed down to an almost human level.

"Let's call it a day, no?" she said as I wheezed air. "No sense in pushing you too hard your first full day in Olympus. There will be plenty of time for that later."

I groaned, but in some ways I felt better than I had in weeks. Here in the training room, I was able to forget everything going on in the outside world and get back to listening to my body. Even if most of what my body was saying at the moment was a Greek chorus of *ow ow ow ow ow ow*.

"You feel it, right?" Athena said, her eyes crinkling at the sides. "There's nothing more relaxing than the feeling of a battle well fought."

"That sounds both wise and violent. Your parents knew what they were doing when they named you."

Athena's usually languid movements made it pretty obvious when her posture stiffened, and I could immediately tell I'd said something wrong. For a moment, she seemed to weigh a decision before waiving off my look of concern. "I gave myself the name Athena about ten years back, when I transitioned. But I appreciate the compliment nonetheless—I always thought Athena was the best of what a woman can be: intelligent, judicious, and deadly with a spear."

I felt my face get warm at my blunder. "I'm sorry, I didn't mean to—"

Athena lightly punched my arm as we started up the stairs. "Briar, please. You didn't do any harm." Her smile twisted up at the side with mischief. "Just like that last thrust of yours."

I chuckled and stuck my tongue out at her. "Was Athena also such a bully?"

She turned and looked at me over her shoulder, long braid dangling down her back. "Goddesses get called a lot of things," she said. "Guess it just comes with the territory."

I LEANED DOWN TO FIX the strap on my borrowed sandals, placing a hand against the white-stuccoed wall of a tunic shop as my friends went on ahead. We were winding our way up a narrow staircase that kept doubling back on itself, the stone steps made gritty with Olympian sand. I made sure my calf-length sandals were tight before I jogged to catch up with the others.

I wasn't going to be the girl from the Apple who pulled a Cinderella on her first night among Mount Olympus's high society.

Catching up to Jacqui, I gestured for the skewer of souvlaki that we'd been handing back and forth on our journey from Leander and Athena's place. I'd never been to a rich person's party that had decent serving sizes, and the delicious grilled chicken and vegetables were hitting the spot. Jacqui had somehow managed to avoid getting a single stain on her cream pantsuit, and her makeup was still flawless despite her licking delicious, garlic-filled marinade off of her fingers.

Not as graceful, I stuck my neck out awkwardly to take a bite, very conscious of the finery Athena had let me borrow. "I'm still not sure why I had to be assigned to the fancy party mission," I complained, not for the first time, around a bite of souvlaki.

"Well, Leander and Athena are too well known here for undercover work," Jacqui explained with saintlike patience, "and Alice somehow got herself invited to an underground pankration match with some cleaners from Lord Wallace's compound."

"Also you have the power to manipulate emotions with roses, remember?" Ravenna added.

"Yeah but it doesn't help with *small talk*." I kicked sullenly at the sandy ground underneath my feet. The sandals, while a little too big for me, were pretty cool, with leather straps laced in a braided pattern up my ankles. They ended just at the hem of the flowing yellow dress that Athena had wrapped me in, a waterfall of amber cloth that she'd twisted into a flattering flow that hugged my figure and dangled over my left arm, leaving my arms bare in the evening's light chill.

"No magic is that powerful," Ravenna said with a smirk. Her kohl-rimmed eyes gleamed in the carnation-colored light of the sunset sliding between the nearby buildings. Like Jacqui, she'd also brought her own formalwear: a midnight-blue sari embroidered with actual starlight, the haunting forms of galaxies and nebulae twinkling across the draped fabric. In a display of magic as impressive as any of her spellcraft, Ravenna had tied and twisted the fabric in a matter of minutes, trading pleating tips with Athena as the warrior wrapped her Grecian-style dress around me. Ravenna's ebony hair cascaded in expertly arranged waves down her back, drifting easily in the cool breeze.

We turned a corner at the top of the stairwell and came out onto a street dominated by Lord Wallace's estate. Even in a city where space was at a premium, the Midas's compound took up half the street. Slightly taller than its neighbors, the marble building had a green tile roof and more columns than *Ask Abbey*. At the back of the structure, a small balcony led to a metal bridge, which connected to Lord Wallace's floating island above.

The mass of light grey earth hovered in place, bobbing placidly in the windy night air. A circlet of stone, covered in Greek lettering as tall as I was, surrounded the flat top, about an acre in diameter. Another towering villa topped the island, a complement to the terrestrial compound on the other side of the bridge.

I looked down at the city on the slope underneath us. "So what do those people do when Wallace decides to park his island above them for a month? *Literally* live in his shadow?"

Jacqui shrugged. "Apparently the Midases float around on their islands wherever they like. They're basically magical yachts."

"Gross."

A trickle of rich people streamed into Wallace's gatehouse, and I begrudgingly let Ravenna finish the skewer of souvlaki before we went inside. The giant stone doors were left open, and the tinkling of champagne flutes and brittle conversation spread out onto the street. What's the use of the good life if you can't shove it in the faces of those not on the invite list?

Most of the glitterati entering were merely nodded in by the two hoplites standing near the door, but the one nearest us made sure to wave us over. There was no way we were going to pass for locals, so we had decided to try to depend on the famous Olympian hospitality.

I hung back while Ravenna presented our doctored invitation and scroll of introduction, naming us as visiting academics from the Academy of the Iron Wand. Instead, I decided to method act our role of tourists and gawk at the building around us. We were in a large, two-story foyer, the result of some tasteless fusion of classic Olympian architecture and Avalonian modernism. The colorful mosaics I'd begun to expect from Olympus here were replaced with a cold checkerboard of black-and-white marble. At the opposite end of the room, a large archway spilled out into a square central courtyard, where most of the guests had gathered. Twin staircases split from the back of the entrance hall leading to a second-floor balcony that ran along the perimeter of the garden.

Our cover story seemed to be good enough for the guard, who waved us forward, where we were swept up with the attendees into the central courtyard. We stuck out less than I thought; the crowd was a swirl of Olympians in chic chitons and expatriates from other World Slips. A pair of yōkai in blood-red kimonos took shots with a group of imposing Aziza in flowing blue caftans. The visitors from Avalon were the easiest to pick out, with their ridiculously ornamented formalwear, gleaming with gold brocade and shoulder pads.

Ravenna guided us to a small pocket of empty space in the corner. "Alright, let's split up, try to cover as much ground as possible, and see if we can get the layout of this place and any decent intel on their defenses."

"Remind me," I said, "what are we looking for again? Good places to knock people out and hide their bodies?"

"What?" Jacqui asked. "No, Bri. You've been playing too many video games. If all goes according to plan, the guards will never even know we were here."

"Well, that potted fern over there looks like a great place to hide an unconscious guard, just saying."

Ravenna rolled her eyes and looked heavenward, an expression I get a lot. "Athena said to look for access points and security measures, and see if we can determine the location of the statue of Gaia. Anything else we can find is a bonus. But just remember, keep a low profile. We don't want to give anyone an excuse to remember us."

"Yeah, yeah," I said, waving over a caterer with a tray full of bacon-wrapped dates. "Low profile. I'll be as quiet as a mouse."

As I thanked the waiter, he looked at the three of us through his long blond hair. "Excuse me, are you from the Apple?" The three of us shared a quick look of panic before he turned to Jacqui, his voice raising in volume. "Princess D'Lucien Ardor, ohmygosh I'm a big fan. My name is Corey, it's so good to meet you. Can I introduce you to my friend? We just moved here from the Apple and—"

Just as he was about to wave over another waiter, my rose petals hit him in the face and knocked him out.

Reacting quickly, Ravenna and Jacqui caught the slim guy by the armpits and pressed him against a nearby pillar. Jacqui even managed to save the tray of dates.

"I'm sorry, I'm sorry," I whispered, trying my best to block the unconscious servant from view with my body. "He was going to blow our cover, and I had a sleepy feeling from eating all that souvlaki—"

Jacqui adjusted her grip to keep Corey upright. "No, it's fine. We'll just—"

"Excuse me, ladies," a clipped, posh voice from behind us said. My heart dropped down somewhere near my appendix, and I turned to see Lord Elton Wallace approaching us. He looked exactly like the picture Leander had shown us, except he was wearing an old-fashioned burgundy dinner jacket and an honest-to-goodness Elizabethan ruff. The collar, combined with his aristocratic, up-turned nose, gave me the distinct impression of a Boston Terrier who'd just gotten home from the vet.

"Lord Wallace," I said through my suddenly dry throat. I gave a curtsy and did my best to draw my dress as wide as possible to hide the incriminating tableau behind me.

"My guards approached me about you three," he continued imperiously. I drew another rose from the folds of my dress and got ready to spell him. If I could distract him long enough, maybe we could make it across the courtyard before anyone noticed. My fingers shook slightly as I grasped the stem, waiting for an opportunity—

"They told me you're professors. And one of you is an art historian? I just knew I had to come bend your ears."

I glanced back at Ravenna and Jacqui, my eyes wide. There was nothing subtle about them pinning a comatose caterer to a pillar. But it seemed like Wallace had just overlooked the boy's existence altogether, as if he couldn't be bothered to concern himself with the help.

Jacqui seemed to have come to the same conclusion. "Why, yes, Lord Wallace. May I introduce Professor Lily d'Lis, our art history expert?" She gestured to me, which made me glare and made Corey slip a few inches towards the ground.

"Pleased to make your acquaintance," I said to our host, silently cursing my luck.

"I was wondering, Miss d'Lis, if I might take you on a tour of my collection? Always wonderful to have an expert's perspective." He offered the crook of his bony arm with a flourish, and I could smell the cloying scent of his self-congratulations. It smelled almost like true generosity but gone sour.

I had spent the afternoon cramming art history talking points with Rick over my mirror, but I hadn't expected this. I slowly withdrew my hand from my rose and plastered on a smile. "It would be a pleasure, sir. My friends were just going to take a turn around your lovely garden."

As I took Elton Wallace's arm, I made eye contact with Jacqui and jerked my head in the direction of the potted fern I'd found earlier. I just hoped they'd be able to *Weekend at Bernie's* poor Corey over there and hide him without anyone noticing.

This is why I hate parties.

I SHOULDN'T HAVE EVEN BOTHERED preparing my art history knowledge. It turns out, like most rich idiots, all Lord Wallace wanted to do was hear himself talk. Besides chiming in with the expected sounds of approval and agreement, I was free to take in the sights as he led me up to the second floor.

Just as we crested the pretentious marble staircase, I heard a crash from below. If I had to bet, I'd guess it was the clatter from a tray of bacon-wrapped dates, dropped by an unconscious caterer. But who's to say?

Lord Wallace started to turn towards the noise, so I had to pull out the big guns. Something guaranteed to get his focus back on our conversation.

"You're so right," I responded to whatever inane thing he'd just said. "Can you explain that again?" I even patted his arm where it twisted with mine. Lightly, because I was pretty sure with sustained effort I could snap his ulna. And probably make it look like an accident...

My flattery worked like a charm. He puffed up and started chattering about art auction strategy or something without a further thought to the scene unfolding below us.

A pair of guards waited at the end of the mezzanine overlooking the courtyard, keeping the general party guests inside. As soon as they saw Wallace, they stepped back, revealing a small circular balcony outside with more of those hideous black-and-white tiles. At the end of the balcony, a thin bridge of dark metal extended up into the sky, connecting the earthbound estate to the island floating above us. With its grated steps and wooden handrails, it gave off sort of a "Brooklyn fire escape meets old-timey elevator" vibe, but it looked stable as Wallace stepped in front of me and began to climb.

Not for the first time that night, I was glad I wasn't in heels as I clambered up the bridge's steps. They were deep enough that it was a bit of a calf workout, and I was so focused on not slipping that I reached the midway point before I even realized it.

A solitary barn owl whirled in my peripheral vision, making

lazy circles against the stars, and suddenly I realized how far up I was. Instinctively my hands gripped the handrails as I drew to a pause, but somehow the bridge felt steady. Taking a breath, I turned to look over the side.

There's a reason Mount Olympus had been home to the gods. From way up high, the slopes of the hills underneath me opened like the petals of a lotus, cradling the structures below as they flickered in the torchlight. I couldn't hear much from the city at this height, but I could trace the way people and carts flowed through its streets, like dew drops drifting down leaves. My gaze lifted heavenward, where the clear skies offered a deep purple backdrop to the stars that danced in front of them. It felt like I was practically suspended up there among the cosmos, the cloud-like glows of galaxies and nebulae close enough to touch. If I looked long enough, I swear I could see the twirl of shapes among the stars, a glimpse of a tail here or the swirl of a skirt there. The skies above Olympus had always been the gods' menagerie, there to catch the various monsters and maidens of mythology who had slipped away from earth, transfigured to starstuff.

Then I looked down again, to the entire neighborhood that sat in the shadow of Wallace's island.

He'd taken this beautiful sky from them.

Speaking of the asshole, he cleared his throat from a few steps up, obviously annoyed at my unscheduled break. I bared my teeth at him in what I hoped came across as a smile. "It's beautiful up here," I said. My tone sounded brittle in my own ears.

"Yes, well," he said, turning back to start up the staircase, "just wait until you get to my actual collection." Then he made some sort of wheezing noise that could've either been a chuckle or the beginnings of a respiratory event.

All my time racing up and down stairs to the subway

must've paid off, because I was barely out of breath as we reached the top of the stairs. The handrails led onto a little stone dais on the side of the island.

Once I'd made it up and looked around, I could see why the railings were there. The island was like an infinity pool, but with land instead of water. Ground that was there and then… precipitously gone. I took a few steps towards the center of the island, just to be safe.

Wallace had bustled ahead, towards the large, column-strewn estate in front of us. I know I was only pretending to be an art historian but honestly, it looked pretty much the same as his home below in the city. Like he just had one idea and had it built twice.

Imagine having all the money to own a floating island and so little imagination.

I shook my head and hurried to catch up with him. I had to stay on mission: case the joint, identify security weaknesses, and find the statue of Gaia. And while it made my skin crawl, I had to keep up a conversation with Wallace while I did it.

We passed the row of columns surrounding the villa's entrance and entered a familiar foyer. The courtyard here, however, had been cleared of plants and turned into an open-air statuary. A dozen statues sat atop pedestals in rows, depicting gods, goddesses, heroes, and everyday people. Besides the marble, we were alone; apparently guards were few and far between once you made it to the floating island. Scanning the tiled roof-tops surrounding the courtyard, I didn't catch any other security measures, but I smelled the faint whiff of magic lingering just beyond the realm of everyday perception. If we were able to make it this far during the actual heist, we'd still need to be on our guard.

I tried to linger near the entrance, to see if I could catch a glimpse of our target, but Wallace quickly ushered me to a large statue in the middle. I knew enough to recognize the winged helmet and sandals of Hermes, but I was taken aback at the expression of abject grief on the carving's face. Kneeling, he held another man in his arms whom I didn't recognize, but I could tell from his limp, twisted body that the second figure was dead. I was shocked by the cascade of grief that seemed to emanate from Hermes as he cradled the corpse of the other man.

"Wow," I said involuntarily as I walked around the central statue, lost in the powerful story that had been hewn from stone. The two men looked real enough that I could reach out and feel a pulse underneath Herme's muscled neck.

"Hermes and Krokos," Wallace said proudly. "The gem of my collection. The god clutches his dead lover after accidentally killing him with a discus. This statue has great personal significance for me."

I looked sideways at him, confused. Wallace didn't seem like an expert in love or the discus, so what was the connection?

Sensing my question, Wallace smiled. "The Greeks believed after Krokos's death, Hermes was so distraught that he turned the man into a flower. The crocus, or saffron." He left the sentence there, half finished, as if I would automatically jump to the conclusion he wanted.

I was still lost.

Wallace's smile faded. "Saffron tea? The basis of the Wallace shipping empire? I've been exporting saffron from the slopes of Mount Olympus to all the other World Slips for decades." His voice had turned curt and sour, as if I should already know all of this.

"Ah," I said, unsure of what to do to soothe his ego. "Well, it's a beautiful sculpture."

"Yes," he said, recovering his pomp with remarkable celerity, "a testament to both my shipping empire and Classical Greek sculpture."

"It's Hellenistic," I blurted out before I could stop myself.

"Excuse me?"

"It's not from the Classical period, clearly," I continued. Apparently Rick's Greek art history lessons had taken. Or I just really wanted an excuse to correct this asshole. "The pose, the melodramatic emotion—this is definitely Hellenistic."

Lord Wallace opened and closed his mouth a few times, apparently unused to being corrected. Before he could get too whiny about it, I looked around for a change of subject.

"What's that?" I asked, pointing to a sculpture in the corner. Without waiting for him, I walked forward to inspect it. Wallace followed and confirmed what I already knew.

"A sculpture of Gaia by the great Phidias. One of a kind," he boasted.

She looked much more imposing in person than she had in the smoke image Leander had shown us on our first night in Olympus. This statue was pure Classical, a regal posture, butter-smooth skin. Gaia looked every inch a goddess as she reclined, full-figured and awash in flowing fabric so lifelike I expected it to drift in the breeze. Where she touched the ground, small stone plants tangled around her fingers.

I circled the sculpture, awed. Even the pedestal was beautiful, traced with a geometric border design and a phrase in carved Greek letters. "What does the inscription say?" I asked.

"Something rather inane, to be honest," Wallace said. "'*Those who meander do not get lost,*' or some rubbish along those lines."

I looked at Gaia one final time, her chin raised proudly from where she lounged on the ground. Unbothered. Proud. And really hydrated if her skin was any clue.

"I like it," I said defiantly. "Now, if you would be so kind, could you lead me back to the party?"

I'll be back soon, I said silently to the statues as we walked to the exit. And when I returned, I'd liberate Gaia, Hermes, Krokus, and all their companions from their tasteless prison in the sky.

NOBODY SEEMED TO FIND the unconscious caterer in the fern, so the rest of the party was uneventful. The next few days, however, were a flurry of planning and stakeouts—I volunteered to keep tabs on the entrance to Lord Wallace's compound, carefully tracking the guards' rotations.

If the best vantage point just happened to be a delicious rooftop gyro place, it was purely coincidence.

That's where Alice joined me the afternoon before our heist, just as I was licking the tzatziki sauce off my fingers. So far, all of the security measures were running just as we expected, but an aura of tension had settled over our planning sessions as the actual event drew near.

Alice crossed her legs and sipped a rich black coffee. Her short turquoise sundress showed off the new leather sandals she'd found in the marketplace, with little embossed wings on the heel. So far, they hadn't allowed her to fly, but they did show off her glossy purple pedicure.

"You're stressed," she observed with her usual level of filter. Her big sunglasses sat low on her nose, allowing her the space to give me a knowing glance over their edge.

"Yeah," I admitted. "Aren't you? The stakes for this quest are pretty high, even for us."

"C'mon, Bri, you've pulled the Apple back from the brink of destruction before. Doesn't it get easier with practice?"

I shrugged and looked out over the balcony, observing the flow of Olympians on a warm spring day. "I guess…every time something like this happens, I learn how close our world is to completely collapsing. When Miranda nearly started a war, when the princesses started screaming…things came so close."

"And both times you saved the day," Alice said. "Why don't you think you'll do it again?"

"Because I'm not going to keep getting lucky!" I said, the frustration I'd been feeling with every Shudder coming to the surface. "When I was younger, I always thought heroes got some sort of destined prophecy, some guarantee that they were going to beat back the forces of darkness and save the day. Now, it feels like we're barely keeping ahead of each new crisis. How can I not worry that this one is going to be the one that sinks us?"

Alice gave my outburst a moment to settle, actually weighing my words as she swirled her coffee. When she spoke, she was a little quieter, a little sadder than her usual vivacious self. "When *I* was younger, the idea of destiny terrified me. My parents had me prepping for law school by age ten, and I already felt the white-picket fangs of suburban conformity closing in on me. I'd get my degree, a mortgage, a husband, all the parts of my life preordained like a paint-by-number set. But all I really wanted was a life that surprised me."

I nodded, closing my Hawaiian shirt a little more tightly around me, even though the day was spectacularly sunny. "I get that. I guess things were different growing up in the Apple. Everyone wanted some heroic destiny, some prophecy that their story was going to end happily ever after."

"Sure," Alice said smiling. "I see the appeal. But isn't it better to write your own ending? Not wait for some white-bearded old geezer to hand you a prepackaged fate?" I laughed, and she continued. "Think about the Oracles of Delphi. Athena was telling me how basically the old priests, all dudes, would get some young girl high on volcanic fumes, and then decipher

her ramblings based on whatever they wanted to happen."

I cocked my head to the side. "Okay, I'm not sure I follow."

"What I'm saying is, *let's cut out the middlemen*. I'm still a little buzzed from my morning joint on the balcony, so let's make some mothergoosin' prophecies. No priests required."

"Alright, alright," I chuckled, starting to feel the weight of anxiety lift off my shoulders. "Do we need to light a candle or something? Get some goat entrails?"

"Ew," Alice said simply. Instead, she took off her sunglasses and shook out her shoulders before taking my hand. "Here's your prophecy: we're gonna make this work. We're gonna figure out how to save the Apple, one way or another. If our first plan doesn't work, we'll try again. I don't care if we have to go to Alfheim, or Yomi-no-kuni, or Secaucus. We're going to fix things. And then you know what?"

"What?"

"We're going to eat *pancakes*. We're going to get Antoine back, and then we'll get everyone together, rent out the Second Breakfast, and have so many pancakes that we'll cause a widespread syrup shortage. The Canadian economy will never be the same."

"I feel like your prophecy might be a little influenced by your munchies."

"Blasphemy!" Alice flicked a bit of pita at me. "Your oracle has spoken. Now go forth and save the world."

Her smile brought me up out of the whirlwind of my thoughts, and I laughed, imagining her and all the rest of my friends having our breakfast in some distant, Shudder-less future. I could picture it so easily, the image of all of us laughing and eating at long tables laden with brunch food, that it seemed both mundane and extraordinary. But I couldn't fully see the path forward from where I was. There was still so much for us to face, so many unknowns. Still, somehow, out from under all the ambiguities, I caught the faint, airy smell of hope.

"Thanks, Alice," I said, grabbing her hand on the table and giving it a squeeze. "I needed that."

"I knew you were going to say that," she quipped, but the slight sheen in her eyes told me she understood how important her pep talk was to me.

"So, do you find your life surprising now? More unpredictable than what your parents had planned for you?"

"You mean ever since I discovered a portal to a fairy-tale fantasy world in Central Park?" She sipped her coffee and gave me a look that said I should know better. "I had a Greek omelette this morning made by a *frickin' sphinx*. I never could've anticipated that, no matter how much LSAT prep I did. All I'm saying, Briar, is there are going to be a lot of surprises coming up. But let's not forget that some of them might be good."

Movement caught my eye from across the street. Wallace's guards were changing shifts, exactly on schedule. I made a tick in my notebook.

"I hope so. Maybe Wallace's guards will surprise us by calling out sick tomorrow."

"Unlikely," Alice said. "But I think they have a lot of surprises coming to them, too." She waggled her eyebrows prophetically. "Your soothsayer has foreseen it."

MY STOMACH GURGLED UNPLEASANTLY throughout the morning of the heist, and it wasn't just because my gyro-based diet had basically turned my blood into watered down tzatziki sauce. Even after all of the planning and working through possible outcomes, we were rushing into a veritable fortress full of guards and security magic with the fate of the Apple hanging in the balance.

So there were plenty of reasons for my tummy to hurt.

Ravenna and I were currently sheltered in an alley, casually loitering in the shade as we peered at her mirror. Ideally, passers-by would just see a couple of American tourists watching a cat video or something.

Little did they know the cat part wasn't coming until later.

Antoine, Athena, and Ravenna had rigged some sort of complicated mirror network between our phones, magic ear cuffs, and a set of brass owl necklaces that allowed us to stay in contact with each other and see how the other parts of the plan were going. So I was only a little spooked when I heard Antoine's voice whisper in my ear. "You doing okay?"

Even from a dimension away, he could see right through me.

I took a steady inhale, held it, and pushed it out of my lungs. "I'll be okay. I'm just anxious to get started."

"Cade and Leander are on their way. Just hang tight," Antoine said. Knowing he was looking over my shoulder made this all feel a bit better.

I snuck a glance upward, where Alice was sitting at a table in the rooftop gyro place, another level of surveillance in case things went sideways. She saw me looking and saluted me with her milkshake. She too spoke over my enchanted ear cuff, trying to give her voice oracular gravitas as she said, "May the pancake prophecy commence."

Indigestion or not, at least I wasn't doing this alone.

The image in our mirror shifted as Antoine patched in the feed from what must have been Leander's necklace. He was walking down the dusty street on his way to the Wallace compound's main entrance, Cade a few steps in front of him. The Red Hood was dressed in an olive-green jumpsuit and carrying a large crate in front of him. I could easily see the tension in my childhood friend's posture, and it had nothing to do with the mostly empty box he was carrying.

The image on our mirror flared for a moment as Leander and Cade stepped into Wallace's estate, and the lighting changed from the sunny streets of Olympus to the cool dimness of the foyer. I heard Leander greet the guards stationed there warmly, holding out a clipboard. Whatever he said seemed not to register with them, as they shook their heads and tried to wave him off. Leander answered back in rapid-fire Greek as he stepped forward to show them something on his doctored order form.

Meanwhile, Cade had set down the box and stepped in front of it, looking to all observers like a bored deliveryman taking a break.

Then the feed in our mirrors shifted to darkness, finally broken by the sight of Jacqui's paws as she pushed open the hidden cat door in the package that Cade had just put down.

Honestly, I couldn't believe anyone in Mount Olympus would fall for such a classic Trojan Horse.

Jacqui had been cursed once, by a magic muffin basket that I'd only recently learned was sent by Caesura. My friend had spent over a year in the body of a cat, and even with regular treatment by the Academy of the Iron Wand's Curse Reversal and Removal Department, she still had a few remaining magical loopholes that made her sprout fur. Overall, she manages her condition, and it doesn't impact her life much.

Here, it was essential. We'd rigged a cat collar with enchanted moonstone, suffusing her in the moonlight that triggered her transformation. No one in the room noticed the small, grey-striped cat slink from the foyer and up the stairs.

There weren't many guards on the second floor, so Jacqui nimbly raced down carpeted corridors until she got to the room she was looking for. Alice had met a cleaner who just happened to live in the neighborhood underneath Wallace's floating island who was happy to give up the floorplan of her former employer's estate; unfortunately, she had been correct in assuming the security office was guarded.

Jacqui lurked around the corner from the room; there was no way to sneak past the burly armored guard in front of the doorway, even as an adorable cat.

"We're going to need you to escalate things, Leander," Antoine said over our magic comms.

"Don't worry, he'll love that," Athena added snidely.

Our image stuck with Jacqui, but we could hear Leander's booming voice from the entrance, along with the sound of scuffling. The guard Jacqui was watching heard it too, and he rushed down the hallway towards the foyer.

Cat Jacqui waited a moment before darting forward. As she reached the closed door, her paw reached up and batted at her collar, spinning the moonstone in its casing so it no longer faced her skin. In a pop of magic, our perspective changed to her usual height, and her now-human hands reached forward to open the door.

Luckily, Jacqui's transformation is instantaneous and lets her keep her clothes intact—our werewolf friends are super jealous.

The security office inside was nothing too impressive—it looked more like a storage closet than anything else. A desk littered with scrolls of security logs, a cheap gas-station pin-up calendar featuring scantily clad harpies, and a few enchanted bowls of water that displayed live feeds of the entrances. Wallace favored guards over fancy security spells, but still, if we were going to make this work, we needed his systems down.

In between the magic bowls, a pedestal held a small, pockmarked sculpture that looked almost like a stone pineapple. Whenever Jacqui's amulet turned to face it directly, the image fuzzed out a little around the edges, making me think it must be radiating all kinds of magic.

"There it is," Athena said in my ear. "The Omphalos. The center of all the compound's magic. Take it out and all of their defenses—Daedalus Charms, Janus Wards, Odysseus Auras—go down."

"On it," whispered Jacqui. From the sheath at her side, she drew the familiar shape of Prick. Without hesitating, she spun the dagger in her hand and drove it down overhand at the Omphalos.

Sparks flew out from where the dagger nicked the stone (I'd have to sharpen it when we got back to Athena's place), but that was all it took. Instantly the images in the bowls around the Omphalos blurred and faded into the water.

I turned from the image in my mirror and saw a quick green flash behind us, tracing around the outline of the side door into Wallace's compound. The Janus Ward was down, leaving the door unlocked and unprotected.

Ravenna put the mirror away and looked at me. "Guess it's our turn," she said. Somehow I felt better that even my brilliant friend looked a little nervous.

"After you," I said, pulling open the door and letting her slip inside to start robbing the compound of one of Olympus's most powerful men.

LIKE ANY SWANKY HOUSE, the Wallace estate put absolutely no effort into making the servants' back hallways pleasant. But the narrow, dimly lit corridors were perfect for moving about undetected. I could still hear shouting from the entranceway, but pretty soon Cade and Leander's diversion would run its course, and the guards would be back on patrol.

"I made it out," Jacqui panted over our comms. "The wards on the back entrance were down, so it seems like the Omphalos truly was at the heart of everything."

"Well done, Jacqs," I whispered. "Thanks."

"The rest is up to you, ladies," my friend said. "Give 'em hell. Or, er, Hades."

Ravenna muttered a few magic words and thrust her hands out in front of her, a wavering wall of blurred air forming from her fingertips. As she'd explained in our planning sessions, she couldn't make us truly invisible while we were running around the compound, but she could give us a little camouflage cloak. With a bit of luck, and a lack of Odysseus Auras, none of Wallace's guards would have the sharp eyes to catch our blurred-out forms.

We ran up a dilapidated stairwell with a few steps missing (I had a complaint for whoever was the Greek god of unsafe working conditions) and made it to the second floor, on the mezzanine surrounding the courtyard. I knew my way from the night of the party, but a pair of guards stood outside the exterior balcony that led up to the floating island.

Ravenna and I crouched beneath the balustrade. Antoine chimed in from our earpieces. "You got this, Bri?"

"No problem," I said, drawing a rose. Athena had introduced me to a nice dryad couple with a gorgeous garden on the outskirts of town, and I'd spent a pleasant afternoon wandering the slopes of their terraced garden and stocking up on roses. For some reason, the roses I'd taken from the Apple didn't work in Olympus.

The only emotions I felt rattling around inside me were panic and adrenaline-induced nausea, so I took a second to breathe, letting the feeling of the stem cradled in my fingers ground me. It took me back to the sun-soaked afternoon when I'd picked it, exploring the garden in the dry Olympian heat. Going where my whims took me as I gathered roses by feel, letting my conscious, detail-oriented brain go silent.

With a push of will, I sent those feelings into the rose, turning the cream-colored blossom a vivid indigo. I took one more deep breath and, on my exhale, let the blossoms drift lazily over to the guards.

The purplish petals fluttered like butterflies, circling the two men in a sedate whirl. Their pointed helmets hid their faces, but I could tell when the magic took effect by their posture; both warriors went from military attention to lackadaisical leans in a matter of seconds. As the whimsy filled them, I let a little more magic flow out of me, and the petals started to spin and drift away down the other side of the mezzanine.

The two guards, filled with the carefree curiosity of schoolchildren, followed the magic petals, giggling like kids chasing fireflies.

I smiled as I stood up behind the balustrade. Nothing like giving a couple working stiffs a little magical R&R.

Ravenna, always thinking ten steps ahead, kept our cloak pointed in the direction of the retreating guards as we crossed to the exit. The small balcony on the other side was just as I remembered it. Ravenna balked at the thin bridge drifting in the wind, connecting us to the island floating above.

"It's not as bad as it looks," I said. "Do you want to go first or second?"

I saw her neck tighten as she swallowed her fear and grit her teeth. "Let's get it over with." With a swirl of her thin, gauzy-black cloak, she began to go up the bridge, with me a few steps behind her.

It was a struggle not to get absorbed by the stunning views of Olympus in the daytime, but the threat of immediate discovery and execution kept us climbing at a quick pace. As we got further from the city below, the sounds of urban life were replaced by the rushing of wind. Wallace lived within the city limits, but it was clear that he didn't consider himself a part of the community below.

Ravenna's hands were a little jittery as she hauled herself up the last few feet of the bridge, but she didn't miss a step as we hurried across the airborne island towards Wallace's second estate. Just like the night of the party, there were no people here, but Ravenna kept her spell active nonetheless.

I let out a quiet sigh of relief that we'd made it up to the island undetected. Dashing across the courtyard towards the main entrance, alone on a piece of rock floating through the sky, it felt like Ravenna and I moved through our own private world. Even the patter of our footsteps floated through the empty air and then died away, with nothing around us to summon Echo's answering call.

My thoughts got much less poetic when we reached the entrance.

As soon as Ravenna's boot passed the open threshold, angry red Greek letters spread out from the door and swirled like snakes along the floor. The high trumpet of a salpinx sounded throughout the foyer, but the room seemed empty. I didn't hear any shouts of alarm or footsteps of approaching soldiers.

Still, I grabbed Ravenna's arm and pulled us both behind a large pillar. The two of us stared at each other, hearts pounding, as we waited for the other shoe to drop.

"Legolas' lipstick," Antoine swore over our earpieces. "The security up here must run through a different system. I thought taking out the Omphalos would shut down everything—"

Ravenna stretched her arms, spreading her invisibility field as wide as she could to cover us. I peeked around the edge of the column, where the ribbons of Greek writing were writhing up the walls. "I think we're alone up here, but something is happening—"

The threads of security magic wound their way to the top of the room, twining across the coffered ceiling to the center. There, they swirled around a particular panel, circling like a pack of wolves. Their glow intensified until the square panel pulled open and a spray of tiny white stones fell out, falling to the middle of the floor.

No, not stones. *Teeth.*

As soon as they clattered to the stone, the teeth began to shudder and swell, quickly quadrupling in size. Their growth was haphazard and messy, bloating and lurching about the ground until they were the size of small dogs. As they continued to grow, bands of metal began to emerge out of the dull, white enamel. Soon, the dozen teeth had taken on vaguely humanoid forms, with jagged blades and bronze armor wrapped around their almost-human shapes.

Where their helmets should have shown a face, there was only the flat, shiny surface of a bicuspid, and what's worse, each had a mouth full of perfect, toothpaste-ad teeth of their own.

My blood ran cold.

The horrors began to organize themselves into four squads, seemingly communicating to each other in some sort of chittering language that sounded like teeth gnashing. Luckily, they split off to search the perimeter, leaving Ravenna and me shivering behind a column.

"They're *spartoi*," Athena said hollowly in our ears. "The Sown Men. Originally created by Cadmus sowing a dragon's teeth. But these modern iterations are...different. Nigh indestructible. And, if I must say, really, *really* creepy."

Wallace didn't need to house guards up in his private demesne when he had a magic alarm system that could spawn inhuman soldiers at a moment's notice.

"The guards at the gate threw us out, finally," Leander

chimed in, the sound of a busy street behind his voice. "The full contingent of guards are in play, and it's only a matter of time before they realize their security is down. And once they get it back up and running, I imagine they will see that the wards on the floating island have been triggered."

We had to move quickly. And hope we weren't found by these things that could give the Tooth Fairy nightmares.

Ravenna and I looked at each other and nodded, too shaken to risk talking. Staying low to the ground, we rushed through the foyer and out into the statue garden. I didn't see any of the patrols in here, but every pearly white statue made my heart jolt. Winding through the pedestals, I led Ravenna towards the back, where Gaia waited for us.

"Alright, Briar, you keep lookout while Ravenna takes down the invisibility and starts laying reduction charms to shrink the statues," Antoine guided us. "Start with Gaia and then—"

"Wait," Ravenna said, a frown coming to her face. She slipped a hand inside her pocket and came out with a pair of small metal opera glasses. I knew from previous adventures that the handy little things let her see magical auras and analyze spells.

Putting them to her eyes, Ravenna twisted the lenses this way and that, and each time she did, I saw her posture deflate a little. My own stomach tightened empathetically. Finally, she withdrew them from her eyes and shook her head.

"I'm not getting anything," she said quietly. "No magic. It's a reproduction."

I don't remember my hands hitting the pedestal, only that I just barely kept myself from collapsing completely as I felt the world give away.

It began to sink in. All of this, everything was for nothing. This wouldn't help us save the Apple.

Heedless of the dental death squads patrolling the corridors, I covered my head with my hands and slumped against the base that held Gaia's useless reproduction. We'd come halfway around the world, spent weeks preparing for this heist, and now...

The Shudders would continue until the Apple was torn apart from the inside out. It was inevitable.

Tears stung my eyes as I sank my head back with a thud.

So this was defeat.

"That sounded hollow," Ravenna whispered.

"Hey, I know I don't have a half-dozen degrees like you, Rav, but I wouldn't say my head is empty—"

"Not your skull. The pedestal."

I uncovered my face and looked at her. While I didn't have much hope, something about the brightness in her eyes made me reach up and rap the stone pedestal with my fist.

She was right.

My eyes caught on the lettering along the edge of the pedestal. I cast my mind back, trying to remember what Wallace had said the Greek lettering meant. "*Those who meander do not get lost,*" I muttered.

The clanking of Sown Men armor let us know that we were seconds away from a patrol coming into the courtyard. I pressed my palms into my forehead, willing my brain to work faster, to fully unravel the beginnings of an idea.

"Meander," I repeated, something from Rick's art history lesson surfacing from the silt of my mind. "*Meandros.* These decorative border patterns along the top of the pedestal." I began to trace my hand along the labyrinthine pattern of repeated lines, folding in on themselves. "Also known as key patterns."

The boots of the Sown Men were just about to round the corner when my finger caught on an edge of the pattern jutting out slightly further than the rest of the design. It pressed into the stone with a satisfying *clonk*, and the entire pedestal began to move, pivoting smoothly across the floor. Cool, humid air arose from the hole, and moss-caked stone stairs beckoned us downwards.

"You don't have to ask me twice, mysterious secret staircase," I mumbled.

Ravenna and I nearly tumbled in our haste to throw ourselves into the inky blackness below. The pedestal fastened back into place above us, leaving the stairs in complete darkness. Whether the Sown Men heard us or not, I couldn't tell. Wherever we were, it was as silent as a grave.

Ravenna muttered an incantation and summoned a mote of lavender light that flitted around her face. Its illumination revealed a narrow staircase hewn from the rock around us. It felt like a total shift from the posh house above—the carvings felt old, ancient. And the steps seemed a little too tall for most legs. Or at least most *human* legs.

"Well, nowhere to go but down," Ravenna said after a moment of looking around.

"That's the spirit," I said, following her and her light deeper into the cavern. "Do you think Wallace knows this place is under his house?"

Ravenna shook her head. The farther down we went, the more moss and lichen began to hang from the walls. "I don't think we're under Wallace's house anymore."

"What do you mean?"

The wizard brushed a pair of hanging vines away from her face. "This feels like an entropic causeway." Before I could ask her what the Hecate that meant, she explained. "Like the Doors or Passways to the Apple. Strong magic builds up and starts to push its way through the barriers of reality, like lava through the opening in a tectonic plate."

"Wait, you're saying we're entering another World Slip?"

"Maybe." Ravenna shrugged. "Maybe just a little pocket of magic connected to the statue. But I'd rather be down here than up there with those…things."

"Same," I muttered, picturing the Sown Men's uncanny faces. I was never going to be able to floss again.

"Antoine? Jacqui? Athena?" Ravenna tried into her earpiece, but there was no response. "Wherever we are, we're out of range of our comms."

The lush flora began to thicken as the stairwell leveled out and opened into a large cavern. Ravenna's small light brightened and flew towards the ceiling, but it barely made a dent in the encompassing darkness. After a moment, a faint greenish-blue light began to issue from the walls. Bioluminescent moss shimmered through the gloom with a liquid grace. Somewhere in the twilight of the cavern, a small trickle of water provided a calming serenity to the scene before us.

The moss's glow danced over a collection of figures, and I began to reach for a rose until I realized all the silhouettes in front of us were stock still.

Another statuary.

This one, however, was as diverse as it was beautiful. The artworks were from all different time periods, materials, and colors: some hewn from shining black volcanic rock, some carved from bone-white wood. A curving, stone Venus of Willendorf sat next to a few pop art prints leaning against the wall. The pieces were arranged haphazardly but aesthetically, like the lair of a magpie with impeccable taste.

All were pictures of women, all of different colors, sizes, and shapes, but somehow, I knew they were all one divine feminine essence, wearing dozens of faces. Something about her gentle kindness, her motherly mischief, carried from face to face, whether she was garbed in a hijab or hanbok.

We were in the being-sometimes-known-as-Gaia's personal

gallery. And judging by the Banksy spraypainted on the side of the cavern wall, it was still very much in use.

Neither of us spoke as we circled the chamber, awestruck by the art. For someone with the spiritual leanings of a footstool, even I felt the otherworldly holiness of this place.

Seeing the many fractal faces of the goddess around me, I began to notice the twining leaves and barklike skin of some of her incarnations. "Ravenna," I said softly as I circled a portrait that might've been a Vermeer, "do you think Gaia is one of the Fata?"

Ravenna came up behind me and put a hand on my shoulder. She knew my relationship with my plantlike relatives was fraught; the term "family tree" hits different when your ancestors have literal roots.

"Maybe," she said. "Maybe she is something similar. A world creator. The soil from which all of Olympus grew."

"And other worlds too," I mused. Drifting through the gallery was like going through a hall of mirrors—every so often I caught a nose that seemed to echo the width of mine, or a pair of dark eyes would stare into mine like they knew me.

I followed my instincts towards the center of the cavern, where I could see a column of stone that reached down from the top of the cave to the bottom. Upon approaching, I felt whatever had been pulling me in this direction intensify. The roses that I'd hidden in my boots were glowing, their watery light pulsing in time with the moss of the cavern.

The sculpture at the base of the column was in many ways identical to the forgery that sat in Lord Wallace's statuary. The seated pose, the measured folds of the tunic, and the staid facial expression all matched, although no one had put this Gaia on a pedestal. But something wild and ineffable lurked within this version's eyes, something authentic and indescribable, revealing that this was Phidias' true masterpiece. Without thinking, I reached out and took the statue's extended stone hand.

The carving remained the same, still and implacable. But as soon as my fingers grazed the stone, the world around me twisted into a kaleidoscope of greens and yellows. Flashes of sunlight filtered through leaves, humid morning mist, and tall grasses all layered on top of each other, lighting the white marble in front of me with splashes of color. The strobe of verdant scenes buffeted me for a second, and I felt my knees start to slacken. It felt like there was no stable ground beneath me, just an endless void of greenery and forests. Only my firm grip on Gaia's hand kept me from drifting off to join the growing chaos around me.

As my mind started to process, I inhaled deeply and was greeted with the loamy smell of freshly turned earth. Even the quality of the air had changed, no longer the dank oxygen of a subterranean enclosure but a clear, alpine freshness with just the hint of pine. The air had a spark within, a blank canvas of breath charged with possibility. As soon as my lungs filled with it, my feet felt grounded, sinking into soft soil beneath me. I held onto Gaia with both hands now, fighting to steady my breath as the world cartwheeled around me. As I centered myself with steady inhales and exhales, the changes in the leafy scenes around me began to slow to a dull throb, each scene of growth and peace settling down until they felt like the murmur of a heartbeat.

Closing my eyes, I felt the earth underneath me, the richness and grit of the soil seeming to seep through my boots and straight into my veins. Soon it felt like I was breathing in through my feet (which were beginning to feel disconcertingly like roots) and drawing strength from the nutrients beneath me. The endless cycle of growth and decay, life and death, churned within the dark depths of the ground, accelerated by each step I took in the world above. For once I didn't feel separate, a lone wanderer in a chaotic world; instead, I was a small, integral, *beautiful* strand of a network that encircled the globe. My life, with all its struggles, was a firework of biology, blood pumping and synapses firing, but before I knew it, I would join back joyfully into the ecological dance of decomposition, making way for something new to grow.

The sound of fluttering leaves surrounded me, and a gentle gust of wind traced its way down my forehead, brushing my hair back behind my ears with an almost motherly tenderness. If I listened less with my ears and more with the rest of me, I could feel a kindly laughter within the breeze, indulgent and proud.

I opened my eyes to the rush of nature before me, an answering laugh of my own playing across my lips.

Then with a plunge, I was back in the cave, still holding onto the statue of Gaia. The world around me didn't seem any different. But I felt changed.

Withdrawing my hand, I found a seed pod the size of a large apple in my hand, its casing the weathered brown of old bark. Looking closer, I swear I could see the ridges of mountains, coastlines, and entire tiny continents tracing the circumference of the seed. Even as it sat motionless in my hand, I felt a thrumming from within it, a quiet heartbeat of dormant magic.

Ravenna rushed forward to put her hand on my arm. "Bri, what happened? You disappeared for maybe thirty seconds and I thought—"

"I'm good," I said wonderingly as I inspected the seed. "Gaia must have wanted me to have this."

Now that she was sure I was okay, Ravenna went into full professor mode. In a moment her opera glasses were pressed against her face, and she swore impressively as she examined the seed pod. After a moment, she pulled her eyes away. "These readings are—*something else*," she said, blinking as if she'd just stared at a bright light. "But whatever it is, it's definitely got a metric buttload of magical potential."

"Enough to access the giant's magic back in the Poisoned Apple?"

Ravenna shrugged and gathered her black cloak around herself. "If this can't, I don't think anything else in the world will be powerful enough."

Before I could react, a clank of boots echoed through the cavern, and from behind us we heard the click-clacking of the Sown Men speaking through their perfect, chattering teeth.

RAVENNA AND I DUCKED behind an ornate paper screen, listening to the steps of a pair of Sown Men. I drew the thick steel dagger that Athena had loaned me and gripped it tight. Now that we had the seed, we just had to get home to the Apple.

Alive, preferably.

I stole a glance over at Ravenna, who was silently mouthing an incantation and wreathing circles of runes in the air. As she sculpted hovering symbols of power, her hands shook. Ravenna was a brilliant magic theorist, but she was no battlemage. She wasn't used to the chaos of combat, where you had to be ready for anything.

Like, to pull an example out of nowhere, a terrifying tooth man busting through a painted paper screen and trying to gut you.

Luckily, battle-hardened veteran that I was, I rolled out of the way with minimal screaming. My warning shrieks gave Ravenna enough time to finish her spell, and a purple vortex lifted our attacker off his feet and threw him backwards into the cave wall. I gave her a nod and readied my *xiphos*.

The Sown Man's partner came rushing over the remains of the paper screen, aiming to decapitate me before I was able to get off my knees. Instead, I dove to the side and whipped my boot out, taking his leg out from under him. The creature stumbled but didn't go down. That gave me enough time to find my footing and draw a single rose into my offhand.

I wasn't sure if these things could feel—even if they could, what emotion would disable a nightmare? So I took the easy route, and channeled into the rose all the fear and repulsion that I felt gazing at their enameled faces. The flower turned a very goth blue-black that reminded me of Isaak's black daffodil.

Squaring up with the Sown Man, I tried to remember everything Athena had taught me. Get in quick, dance around the enemy's sword, and get out with the same number of holes you went in with. Easy.

Wielding my rose like a second dagger, I twirled around to my opponent's side, feinting forward with my blade. As his sword rose to meet my blow, I lunged forward, stabbing my rose into his side, where his armor was thinnest.

An azure explosion erupted from the blossom of my rose as it hit the Sown Man, and I felt the emotions within it discharge like a firecracker. The creature stumbled back, raising its sword to protect itself from a blow from my dagger.

I held my breath, waiting for the magic to take hold. The aberration tilted its head to the side, and then advanced, fearless.

My stomach dropped. "My magic is no good," I gritted as I maneuvered in between the dental demon and Ravenna. The monster that she had tossed into the wall slowly got up. If it felt the pain from its arm bending the wrong way, it didn't show it.

Apparently these things weren't the touchy-feely type.

"We've got what we need," Ravenna said breathlessly. "Do you think we should just—"

"RUN!" I agreed, spinning in place and following Ravenna as we scrambled towards the staircase. I felt extremely guilty as I knocked a bronze Art Deco statue of a woman in a flapper dress into the path behind us. It slowed down the Sown Men just enough for us to beat them to the staircase. I half-ran, half-stumbled up the large stone steps, keeping a hair's breadth ahead of the serrated blades and grasping gauntlets of our pursuers. A few of the petals that I'd unleashed in the cavern floated in front of us, glowing softly. When they reached the top of the stairs, I heard the clunk of the pedestal in Wallace's statuary starting to open again.

Having rose petals open doors for me was weird, even for my life. But I didn't have time to worry too much about it as one of the Sown Men grabbed my ankle and I face planted on the stairs.

Ravenna made it to the top of the staircase before she realized I wasn't behind her. She turned and called out my name, but she was too far, and there was nothing for me to grab onto as the Sown Man pulled me down, banging me painfully against the hard stone of each step.

The light from Wallace's statuary was so close, if only I could reach it.

With a surge of strength, I lashed my legs around wildly like a relentless Final Girl in an '80s slasher flick, and I managed to wriggle out of my attacker's grip just as he brought his sword down where my legs had been a few seconds before. With a final kick, I pushed myself forward on all fours, clambering up the stairs heedless of the scrapes on my palms and knees, just trying to get away from the monstrosities behind me.

Ravenna reached down to pull me the last few feet and shouted some sort of ward that froze the Sown Men just long enough for the pedestal to click back into place, trapping them in the subterranean art gallery. Hopefully they wouldn't do too much damage before Gaia came by to clean house.

Together, we collapsed onto the floor of the statuary. I could still feel the seed pod pulsing with magic, zipped into the bag around my waist, safe. It felt good to pause, just for a moment, and soak in the sense of stillness. Somehow it almost felt like we were still surging up the stairwell.

"Briar," Ravenna panted from beside me, "are we…moving?"

My eyes widened. "We're not," I whispered. "But the island is."

Looking at the clouds above us, we were rising slowly but steadily into the air. Away from Olympus. Away from our friends.

"The island must disconnect from the ground as a security measure," Ravenna muttered, her brain practically whirring behind her eyeballs. "If I had some time, I could try to scrounge up the ingredients for an incantation of Galandriel's Glorious Glide, but that's only for one person—"

"Briar?" Antoine's voice came through our comms. "Please, come in—"

I pressed my finger to the rune on my ear cuff. "Hey, we're back."

"Bri, the island's bridge retracted and started floating off."

"We know," I said glumly. "Any ideas?"

"Athena's working on it. Did you get what we came for?"

"We got the seed," Ravenna chimed in, "but we haven't had time to get the statues, and—"

Her voice caught as Sown Men began advancing into the courtyard from all sides, closing us off from the rest of the compound. My stomach lurched; even if we could get out of the villa, we were on an island hundreds of feet in the air.

My limbs felt heavy as we scrambled to our feet, back-to-back in the center of the swords. Honestly, it was exhausting: the running, the fighting, the last stands. Grief threatened to overtake me, but something felt…off.

The Sown Men began to circle closer, making a spiral

around us. I could feel Ravenna shaking behind me, her voice catching as she murmured defensive spells under her breath. I wondered if Lord Wallace had instructed his horrific guard dogs to bring us to him alive.

A single tear ran down my cheek, and all of a sudden I knew what I was feeling didn't belong to me. I could never cry that aesthetically—I'm either making snide remarks or ugly sobbing, there is no in-between.

I followed the thread of unknown emotion, feeling the pull of it through the tendrils of my magic. When I took the time to stop and examine it, the room was filled with the scent of feelings, but they weren't like anything I'd smelled before. There was a certain restraint to them, a dry faintness like the scent of flowers pressed between old books.

Just as the Sown Men got within striking distance, and without being even a little sure of what I was doing, I poured as much of my magic as I could into the ambient emotions around us, hoping that I could pull off one more unexpected magic miracle—betting on the wild card that was my power, one last time.

From where we were in the center of the courtyard, nothing seemed to change. Then, suddenly, a Sown Man to my left was swept off his feet and dragged away. Before any of us could react, another went down hard, his gauntlets scraping on the marble as he was flung backwards.

All of us, Sown Men included, turned to see what was behind them.

At the center of the courtyard was a statue. *Laocoön and His Sons*, if my art history knowledge was correct. A man and his two boys writhing while being attacked by snakes, sent by the gods as punishment for some sort of heretical offense—or maybe because the gods were bored, I don't remember. What caught my attention was growing around the statue.

Twice as large as the sculpture, a twining topiary of roses

and vines grew, an animated copy of the three men circled by rootlike snakes. All the drama and anguish of the statues poured out of them as they reenacted their battle, fighting tirelessly against the snakes and still managing to snag the Sown Men in their verdant fists. Even as the nearest Sown Men hacked at their leafy legs, Laocoön and his sons never gave up the fight.

My jaw was hanging open, but I pressed my lips into a line and assumed a fighting stance. Existential questions could wait. At least now Ravenna and I weren't fighting alone. However I'd done it, I'd set the stories in these statues free. They didn't deserve to be trapped here in some sterile, private gallery when there was still so much passion in them.

"Ravenna," I panted after exerting my magic, "do you still have those reduction charms prepped?"

"Yes, but—"

"Start shrinking the statues. I'll hold off the bicuspid brigade."

Ravenna looked skeptical, but nodded and began tracing runes in the air.

Putting myself between the wizard and our adversaries, I sent another wave of magic out into the room, and then felt a surge of confidence answer back from the corner. In a moment, a twelve-foot-tall woman of briars and leaves lifted off her pedestal, felling two Sown Men with thorny arrows. Atalanta tossed her tresses of thorns over one shoulder and nocked another arrow, but not before giving me a cocky, petal-filled grin.

Distracted by the mythic figures made of flora, the Sown Men broke ranks and skirmished across the statuary, no longer pinning Ravenna and me down. I stole a glance at my friend, who had shrunk a half dozen statues and placed them reverently in her bag.

Given how fiercely these Greek heroes were fighting, I was glad we could return the favor.

A pair of Sown Men broke loose from the pack and rushed towards us, swords raised. As intimidating as they were, their heavy armor meant they couldn't react as fast as I could. If I moved quickly, I'd be able to at least keep them distracted long enough for Ravenna to finish her spells and get away.

Fighting between the pedestals was closer quarters than I'd prefer, but it meant the two Sown Men couldn't both face me at once. I hefted my dagger and tried to remind myself of all the moves Athena had shown me.

As soon as the first opponent began to thrust his sword forward, I dodged to my left (from what I could tell, all these crimes against nature were left-handed) and leapt up onto the base of a pedestal. In one motion, I bounced back behind my attacker and hurled a cross-body slash at the unsuspecting Sown Man behind him, catching my victim by surprise. My dagger slashed cleanly across his throat, just under the buckle of his iron helmet. His sword clattered to the ground while his hands pawed ineffectively at the wound as a thin, milky liquid leaked out of it. As he dropped to his knees, I reflected that these things just kept getting more and more disgusting.

I remembered they were also dangerous as soon as the sword pierced my left side.

Pain flared through me as I twisted away from the blade, but the cut was long, if not deep. Twisting around, I saw that the first Sown Man hadn't even turned to face me, instead plunging his sword behind him without looking. *Maybe their creepy chittering is some kind of echolocation,* I thought as my head went woozy.

My left arm curved instinctively around my wound as I held my dagger out in front of me. I'd lost the advantage of my speed, and if the fight went on too much longer, the blood loss would become a major problem.

The Sown Man gave me a toothy grin as he lurched forward.

I caught his first two swings easily enough, but I couldn't raise my guard quickly enough to counter his third slash. Instead, I ducked down, barely keeping my feet under me as his sword cut through the air that I'd exhaled mere seconds before.

Before I could celebrate, the creature I'd been fighting took his sword in both hands for an overhand swing. I got my dagger up to stop his blow, leaving us locked blade to blade. My arm shook as I tried to push back his sword, but it felt like I was only delaying the inevitable. More blood leaked from my side as I used my left arm to press up on the blade.

Then, through the adrenaline, I felt a puff of the same grief that I'd felt earlier.

Something moved, more quickly than my eye could track. Suddenly, the head of the Sown Man bearing down on me jerked to the side with the jagged sound of cracking teeth. His limbs spasmed for a second before he went limp and crumbled to the ground.

Behind him, a figure stood tall, from his feathered helmet tipped with fronds to his winged sandals of corded root. Branches formed an athletic torso with a tunic made of soft blue petals. As I watched, the man's leafy chest expanded, some strange amalgamation of plants and magic and myth. This floral version of Hermes nodded at me, and then sped away, knocking two Sown Men to the ground and hurling another one fifty feet, through the doors of the villa and off the edge of the island.

Even in his mourning, the god of travelers and tricksters didn't stop trying.

With a deity on our side, or at least the plantlike echo of one, we turned the tide on the Sown Men. Ravenna scooped the last statue into her bag just as a satyr made of vines drop-kicked the last of our opponents into a column with a crack. The room was scattered with empty pedestals and chips of tooth. Breathing heavily, I took a moment to tie my loose shirt tight against the cut on my side, hoping that the thrill of victory would keep me conscious long enough to receive medical attention.

Hermes and the rest of the myths who had fought beside us turned to face me. A few warrior-types saluted me with their branching spears against their leafy shields.

"Thank you," I said. No other words seemed right to speak to the stories I'd summoned. Hermes gave me a warrior's nod, before stepping back to a small grove of flowers that had grown in the center of the courtyard. Entombed in the center of the wild crocuses was their namesake, or at least a flowery copy of him. Hermes knelt down in front of his dead lover and clasped the other man to his chest.

One final moment of grief pulsed through the courtyard, and then the force animating the mythic figures dissolved, the twining leaves and branches falling to the floor, returned to the earth from which they'd grown.

"Well," Ravenna said, "that about wraps it up. Now how are we—"

We both froze at the unmistakable sound, echoing through the villa, of teeth hitting the marble floor. The security system in the foyer was spewing out more Sown Men, even more than we'd just defeated. Scattering across the floor, teeth began to grow and shape, gestating in front of our eyes, giving me nightmare fuel for years to come.

"*Run!*" I shouted, pushing Ravenna in front of me, hoping we could clear the entrance to the villa before the army of monsters finished growing. Toothy hands reached for our ankles as we skidded through the building, not moving towards anything in particular, just clearly *away* from the burgeoning horrors.

The sunlight blinded me briefly as we ran out the main entrance and down the front steps, onto the manicured grass. Already, Sown Men were pouring out of the villa—some not even waiting to fully form. One toothy torso pulled itself forward with its hands, its legs still made of the four points of a tooth's root. The creatures lurched towards us as we skidded to a stop mere feet from the edge of the island.

Ravenna and I shared a stricken look before turning to the advancing monsters. If she was anything like me, she was also bruised, bloody, and drained of magic.

But I thought of the legends we'd just fought beside, the father protecting his sons as best he could from divine snakes, the huntress refusing to shrink from danger. The god filled with grief and regret, still coming to the aid of a stranger from across time and worlds.

And I squared my feet and faced the monsters.

The adrenaline roaring in my ears almost covered the sound of beating wings behind me, and just before the first wave of Sown Men surrounded us, I heard a familiar voice ask, "Need a lift?"

Athena, golden armor gleaming in the midday sun, came riding up on a Grimmsdamn pure-white pegasus, with a pair of additional flying horses right behind her.

Ravenna and I had just enough time to throw ourselves off the ground before the blades caught us. For a terrifying moment, there was nothing underneath my boots but open air, and I wondered if this mission was my own private Icarian flight too close to the sun.

But then I landed gracelessly on the pegasus's back, and I've never been so happy to have the wind knocked out of me. I was barely able to right myself in the saddle before we were half-flying, half-falling away from the island, away from the Sown Men, and away from Wallace's compound. With a cosmically powerful seed and a fortune's worth of stolen art ready to be repatriated.

Maybe it was the blood loss, but I couldn't help but whoop

as we soared over the tile roofs and gleaming columns of Olympus, all spread out underneath the azure sky.

IT TOOK A HERCULEAN EFFORT, but we were finally able to convince Leander that we didn't want a night out on the town to toast our victory, instead opting for a quiet celebration on their villa's balcony with spiced wine around a fire pit. He probably wouldn't have accepted this outcome if I hadn't been seriously injured.

I played absentmindedly with the bandage on my side while Alice finished telling a story, something about explaining veganism to a talking pig in a Troll Foods deli line. After we'd all reconvened at Leander and Athena's house, they'd called over a healer to patch up the slice in my side. The sharp-eyed priestess didn't speak any English, but Athena translated the woman's instructions and disapproval of my general state of wellness. I tried to tell her that I didn't have health insurance, but apparently the concept didn't translate.

When Alice's performance was over, Ravenna drifted over to me and nudged my uninjured side. "You okay, Pryce? That was...*a lot*, on the island." She took a sip of wine.

I nodded. "Yeah, it's not every day a monster makes me afraid of my own teeth."

She smiled but was undeterred. "Not just the Sown Men. What you did with your power in the statuary...do you wanna talk about it?"

I took a sip of the sparkling soda I'd opted for (remember kids, alcohol and stab wounds don't mix). "I don't know if there's much to talk about. Just another weird surge of my power, doing something wacky per usual."

"Briar, you brought those things to life."

I shrugged. "I think I just brought out the life in the stories that were already there." My gaze scanned across the sun-drenched vistas of Olympus. "I guess it's not that different when you think about it. I put emotions into roses. And what's a story but an expression of feelings?"

Her dark eyebrows arched. "You're being remarkably blasé about this."

"Yeah, after the past year we've had…not much surprises me anymore."

Athena made her way over to us, looking cozy in a plum-colored wrap that was half-sweater, half-chiton. "A toast," she said, raising her wide-rimmed clay chalice to the sky, "to the heroines of the day."

"It was a group effort," Ravenna said smoothly. "We'd still be trapped on that floating island if we didn't have you watching our backs." She peeked into the other woman's cup. "Let me get you a refill, Athena."

The warrior smiled and handed over her cup. "I won't put up a fight," she chuckled before joining me at the railing. For a moment, we stared out at her city, the golden light of sunset freezing everything in amber.

"What you've done for us, for the people of Olympus…" Athena said softly, "I can't thank you enough."

"When you risked your lives to help the Poisoned Apple?" I responded, smiling. "I think you've repaid us in kind. Besides, those statues kicked a ton of toothy butt. I'm happy to get them home to the people who made them."

"That's how it always is with you Americans," she said teasingly. "It's always about payment and debt. But you and I, we're sisters-in-arms now. There's no ledger, no scorebook. My sword is yours whenever you need it, without hesitation."

She grabbed my shoulder, her grip both tender and strong,

and I returned her smile. "Likewise. I hope we can make it back to Olympus sometime soon."

"I just wish we could help you take the fight back to the Apple," Athena continued. "But Leander and I have been working our contacts, trying to get the statues to good homes where the public can appreciate them. We'll keep an eye on things here and make sure Wallace doesn't come after any of us."

"Thank you," I say to her, "truly. You've taken us in when I didn't think we had a chance."

"You're more than welcome, Briar," she said. "The phalanx is only as strong as its weakest shield, remember? If your shield is ever getting heavy, just give me a call. I'm happy to lend you my strength, as long as you require it."

The sun began to dip behind the farthest hills of Olympus, and for a second, I saw the tiny chariot pulling it across the sky, strange and impossible and beautiful. The magic of Olympus had its own frequency, a way to take my breath away even after growing up in a land of frog princes and enchanted mirrors.

Ravenna returned with drinks, and I lifted mine to the air. "To saving each other, as often as necessary," I said to my friends, both old and new. "Yamas."

RAVENNA WAS ABLE TO GET US an early-morning portal back to the Apple the next day. It was hard to say goodbye to Athena and Leander and leave the easy, sunlit days of Olympus behind, when all I had to do was focus on evading guards and pulling off an impossible heist. When we returned to the Poisoned Apple, the sky was the slate, gunmetal grey of a tired knight's armor. We stowed our luggage at home and reconvened at the Red Hoods' cabin HQ.

A steady rain trickled down through the trees outside as I nursed a strong cup of tea. Miranda and the Hoods caught us up on what we'd missed in our week away. The Shudders had held steady, still causing damage but not any worse than we'd seen. Supplies were running low, and the magic flowing through the city was down to a dribble.

But, as Alice was quick to point out, we were surviving.

Miranda had spread out a map of the Apple on the long, oak table in the center of the Hoods' great room, putting her ferocious brain to work and plotting the occurrences of monster attacks from the Afterwoods. It was now clear what we'd only suspected before: Caesura was guiding the guerrilla-style offensives. And just like the fenodyree I'd seen with her before, the more peaceful creatures of the Afterwoods were falling under the Fata hybrid's control. Nixies were sweeping Red Hood patrols away in torrential floods, Cheshire cats were leading children away from their homes and abandoning them in the woods, and brownies were stealing everyone's MetroCards. The last one was more annoying than aggressive, but still out of character.

"So, looking at all the attacks from the past few weeks, they all seem to be pushing into one point," Miranda concluded. The pins she'd placed in the map all formed a spiral with a clear center.

"Castle Fortnight," I said grimly.

The princess nodded. "It's not just about the location. Caesura is targeting anyone connected to the castle whom she can get her hands on—guards, maids, servants. There have been a few disappearances, and we worry that she might be trying to get people on the inside. Either charming them with magic or kidnapping them and replacing them with imposters wearing fleshjackets."

"Even the best fleshjackets aren't capable of producing

more than a passable likeness of someone," I countered.

"Right," Jacqui said. "But how closely do the Royals pay attention to their servants?"

She had a point.

"So you think Caesura is on to us?" I asked Miranda. "She knows that we're going to try to use whatever is in Castle Fortnight to connect us to the giant?"

Miranda nibbled on the end of a quill. Her messy bun and the dark hollows under her eyes told me she'd been working on this theory for more than one sleepless night. "Honestly? I hope that's the case. Because otherwise, she has some other motive that we don't know about, and that terrifies me."

I balked at the thought of something that scared a force of nature like Miranda Grimmour.

"So we move up our timetable," I said. "I know Ravenna and Tamsin wanted more time to examine the Gaia seed, but I think we need to get it into Castle Fortnight as soon as we can. Before Caesura has an opportunity to do more damage."

I looked around at my friends and the gathered Red Hoods and was surprised by the faith I saw in their eyes as they nodded back at me. Blue Fairy help me, they trusted what I was saying. They trusted me.

"Tomorrow?" Jacqui asked. "I can get us in the front doors. Even a disgraced princess still has privileges."

Cade spoke up. "We're barely holding the line against the denizens of the Afterwoods, but we can try to position our forces along the outskirts of the castle in case something goes wrong."

"We should keep our plans as quiet as possible," Miranda said. "If Caesura has people on the inside, then the fewer people who know, the better."

"Alright," I said, pressing my palms on the table to push myself up to my full height. "Tomorrow it is. We break into

Castle Fortnight, use an unknown magical artifact of limitless power, and save the Apple."

Two years ago, when I was a lackey for the Royals, delivering roses and pining after Cade, I would have rather danced all night in hot iron shoes than speak up in a group. Today, I was surprised to hear my voice didn't even shake.

As the meeting wrapped up and the Hoods went back on patrol, Miranda pulled me onto the back porch, right where I'd last faced Caesura. "Briar," the princess said, "I think we need to talk about what we're going to do once we get into Castle Fortnight."

"Didn't we just do that?" I asked. "Use the seed to overcome the giant's magical defenses and put him back to sleep."

There were several disturbing cracks as Miranda arched her back and let herself lean heavily against the railing. "We should discuss contingency plans."

The air around us had chilled in the early evening, but it was her tone that made me tighten my cardigan around myself. "What kind of contingency plans, Miranda?"

"There's so much we don't know about this whole situation," Miranda said. "What if we can't restore the sleeping curse? What if the giant is hostile? I just need you to be prepared if we need to make a tough call."

"Like what, slay the giant?" I sputtered. "I'm not a murderer, Miranda. We'll find a way to do this without killing him."

"You'd risk the fate of everyone in the Apple for one life?"

"From what Tamsin said, the giant is the source of all the magic in Apple. You'd kill the very wellspring our home is built on?"

"I'd rather have a home without magic than no home at all."

Her words fell into the pit opening in my stomach. I knew they made a cruel, cold sense, but I didn't want to hear it.

"I will find a way," I said, my voice edged in steel. "Not all of us can make the heartless decisions you make. Speaking of, how are Tarris and Rick doing?"

Miranda straightened, but instead of the anger I was expecting to provoke, there was only hurt and shame. Instantly I regretted taking the cheap shot at her old wounds. She ran a hand through her disheveled hair. "I don't want to hurt anyone," she said softly. "Not anymore. But I won't stand by and let the Apple get destroyed."

And the princess who nearly burnt the Apple to the ground walked away. I inhaled deeply, but I didn't smell the cool scent of the pine trees around us. I breathed in the smoky scent of Miranda's regret—the dark place where the fire of her rage had burnt clear through her subconscious.

I blinked and turned away, the fragrance of ashes all around me. I just hoped they weren't a portent of more wildfires to come.

"Fascinating," Tamsin murmured for the thirtieth time in the past twenty minutes. She was knee-deep in spellcraft, analyzing the Gaia seed through a series of increasingly convoluted rituals that had left her office looking like a cyclone had hit a Halloween store. "Look at this," she said, calling me over to where she peered through a pair of binoculars adorned with owl feathers. The seed itself floated serenely, encased in a shimmering blue orb by containment spells that Tamsin had painted on her hardwood floors.

I got up from where I'd been slumped against one of her bookshelves. So far, nothing Tamsin had said about thaumaturgic resonance and quantum rune theory had made a lick of sense, but I had always been a more visual learner anyways. I stuck my eyes into the view piece of the binoculars.

I blinked, slowly, and then stood back and looked at the seed floating in the containment circle in front of us. Then I looked at Tamsin.

My disbelief must have been evident on my face, but Tamsin only nodded, her voluminous hair shaking with the movement. "Yes, what you're looking at is the seed itself. Magnified heavily, but you're actually seeing the surface."

When I'd first glimpsed the seed in Gaia's pocket dimension art gallery, I could have sworn the ridges along its brownish-green crust looked like continents. But as I put the binoculars up against my face once more, I saw entire landscapes. Rolling hills with pine forests, a coursing river rushing to a waterfall over wild cliffs, wide plains where herds of six-legged…*somethings* grazed.

I stepped back, suddenly feeling lightheaded. Even with all the things I'd seen, this was incomprehensible.

"What…" I started. "How…Is that a world? Did I carry around an *entire world* for two days?"

Tamsin nodded, giving me time to sort my thoughts out.

"If I'd known I was keeping an entire planet in my messenger bag, I would have at least cleaned out the loose Doritos."

"I'm not sure it's a fully formed world yet," Tamsin said. She clearly could feel my growing sense of existential confusion, because she started making a pot of tea. "If I'm understanding this correctly, it's more of a…potential world. Kind of like a spell scroll is a bit of magic that exists but hasn't been activated yet."

"But instead of casting a fireball or whatever, this seed would cast an entire realm."

"Apparently," Tamsin said. She seemed incredibly unfazed by all of it as she waited for her rune-powered teapot to boil. "From everything I've researched, this seems incredibly reminiscent of the spellwork of the Fata."

I decided to sit on the overstuffed grey couch by the window, before my knees decided to buckle of their own accord.

Tamsin saw my face and frowned. "Sorry, I shouldn't bring up the Fata so casually. I know it's a…loaded issue for you."

"So Gaia was a Fata then? I had my suspicions…"

The professor was uncharacteristically quiet as she poured the tea, the smell of something woody and herbal filling the room as the water hit the leaves. She set the two mugs on her weathered coffee table and joined me on the couch.

"Briar," she started hesitantly. "I'm a wizard. I have spent my entire life trying to understand what makes the world work, how words and wands can make a person fly or make a lightning bolt fall from a clear sky. But in all of that research, I've had to constantly remind myself that the world is a lot more wonderfully complicated and frustratingly beautiful than it first appears. And the labels that we use to try to contain that wondrous complexity are only tools, only signposts that we can use to find our way. But they're never going to be exactly perfect.

"Fata, goddess, divinity…these are names we're trying to force onto a being who is greater than anything we can hope to understand."

I considered her words as I added an unhealthy amount of honey to my tea. Ever since I'd found out about my connection to the Fata, I'd been trying to figure out what it all signified. What this part of myself that I'd never chosen meant, how accepting it could change me.

Cradling the cup of tea in my hands, staring at the Gaia seed spinning peacefully in midair, I could see what Tamsin meant. There was no room in my life to keep carrying these words if they weren't helping me. The best I could do was keep trying to make my own meaning and leave the labels behind.

I blew on the tea and took a sip, the golden taste of slightly spiced honey-water tickling my throat. A knot that had been pressing into my spine for the past six months eased—not disappearing completely, but at least feeling better than it had.

"If Gaia is so powerful and ineffable, why can't she fix the Shudders herself?" I could smell the sweaty scent of petulance on my own words. "Why leave us to suffer?"

Tamsin shrugged. "I can't pretend to understand what a being like that's motivations might be. But if she is out there, watching us muck about trying to fix these problems, maybe it's because she thinks we're able to do it on our own."

"Hard to have a lot of faith in a divinity who won't lift a finger to help us," I grumbled.

"You are most likely a distant daughter of that divinity," she said with a smile. "Maybe she has faith in you."

I sat with that for a moment. It seemed unlikely, but Tamsin's steady voice made it seem that much more possible.

"Thanks, prof," I said, nudging Tamsin with my shoulder before changing the subject. "You know, Miranda thinks we might have to kill the giant."

Tamsin frowned into her mug. "Why is that?"

"If we can't figure out a way to put him back to sleep. She said it might come down to us or him."

The Welshwoman snorted. "A convenient condensation of the many, many actions we can take into a misleading binary." She sipped tea. "There's more magic in the Gaia seed than the Academy's entire Department of Evocations. If we can't find a way to resolve this without unnecessary bloodshed, it's because we aren't creative enough to see other options."

I put down my mug and started to walk a lazy circle around the Gaia seed. Was it my imagination, or was there a tingle in the air as I got closer to it? "I'm with you," I said quietly.

Tamsin got up and stood to face me on the other side of the seed that held mountains. "You get to the giant. I'll make sure we know enough about this seed that we can use it to grow a future for the Poisoned Apple."

I WIPED THE SLEEP out of my eyes while riding in the carriage-share on the way to Castle Fortnight. Even after talking to Antoine for two hours last night, he'd sent me a text first-thing this morning. I kept running my finger over the message on my mirror:

#

You've got this.

#

Here's to facing giants, my love.

#

It couldn't help but remind me of my conversation with Miranda the night before. I hoped that by the end of the day, both the giant and I would be fast asleep, dreaming of a new chapter for the Poisoned Apple and its inhabitants.

We'd decided to keep our raiding party sleek and small—it was Jacqui, Cade, Ravenna, and I. The perfect combination of knowledge of Castle Fortnight, fighting skills, wizardry, and smartassery.

Jacqui was as good as her word and was able to get us into Castle Fortnight without any issues. There was a tension in the air that made my neck muscles clench. The spacious grounds were mostly empty, with just a few servants here and there, rushing and keeping their eyes down. Castle Fortnight, the beating heart of the Poisoned Apple, had gone cold.

Ravenna referred to Tamsin's map of leylines and led us

east, towards a flat area of the castle covered in gravel paths and topiary. Nobody gave our motley group a second look. We took several wide stone staircases down towards the center of the garden, where a large Gothic cathedral of black stone dominated the surrounding towers.

"That's where all the ley lines converge," Ravenna said, looking back and forth between her map and the building. "Underneath that is the giant's heart."

"The Black Duchy?" Jacqui said, eyebrows quirking. "I guess that makes sense. The Duchess is always bragging about how it's one of the oldest structures in the Apple." We made our way across the wide courtyard leading to the Duchy's entrance but took a side path around the back. There weren't many people out and about in Castle Fortnight today, but we still probably couldn't get away with waltzing in the front door of one of the Nobles' private residences.

"So we need to get into the lower levels?" Cade asked. "Do you know the layout?"

Jacqui shook her head. "I only remember being in the ballroom on the ground floor."

"Hey, didn't Alice used to work at the Black Duchy sometimes? Maybe she knows how to get downstairs." I pressed a rune on my ear cuff. "Antoine, can you patch us through to Alice?"

"On it, boss," Antoine replied, and even through dimensions I could tell he was smiling.

Cade rolled his eyes. "You do have her on your mirror's speed dial, right?"

"I mean yeah, but this way makes me feel like a spy." I took out my mirror and held it up so the SparkleCast version of Alice's face floated where we could all see her. We had left Alice and most of our other friends at our house, ready to provide backup if needed.

"Ooooh hi guys!" Alice chirped through the mirror. "How's the quest going so far? Jacqs, did you have enough to eat this morning? I put a granola bar in Cade's scabbard for you."

Jacqui blushed. "Thanks, babe," she said while swiping the aforementioned granola bar from a pouch on Cade's waist.

"Alice, do you know a way to get into the lower floors of the Black Duchy?" I asked. "We think that's the way into the giant's heart."

Alice frowned. "There are no lower floors of the Black Duchy. I've dusted every inch of that place and it's all above ground."

Before we could react, the goofy grin of Rick Pearson leaned over Alice's shoulder. "Hey hey, what's that beautiful building behind you? Nice buttresses!"

Tarris leaned in on Alice's other side. "Darling, could you at least not compliment someone else's buttresses in front of me—"

"That's weird though," Rick continued, oblivious. "The rest of the structure is a much earlier style…looks like those buttresses are a later addition."

I turned to the soaring compound behind us. If I squinted, I could just make out what Rick was saying—the black stone of the supports wasn't as worn and pockmarked as the structure itself.

"Wait," I said, trying to keep up with everything, "so the buttresses were added on after the main structure…do you think they're blocking an entrance to whatever is underneath the Black Duchy?"

"Could be," Rick said noncommittally. "All I can tell is that this building was built in two phases in two different time periods. Maybe they had to add the reinforcements later after structural damage."

"We should go," Tarris said, looking down at his mirror.

"My dad has been calling me nonstop. I should probably see what's gotten him all worked up."

Jacqui's back straightened, a look of confusion on her face. "You know, now that you mention it, I had like ten voicemails from my mom this morning—"

After that, things happened very quickly.

Across Castle Fortnight, a chorus of alarms erupted, everything from air horns to sirens to alarum charms. The four of us immediately gathered together just as a stream of people came rushing out of the Black Duchy's entrance. For a moment, I thought we had triggered some sort of alarm, but the rest of the nearby turrets and demesnes were also emptying of their inhabitants.

"Briar? Jacqui? What's going on?" I could hear Alice shouting into the mirror as I spun around, trying to get my bearings. If I'd had a Grimmsdamn clue, I would have answered.

"Does Castle Fortnight have fire drills?" Cade shouted over the din.

Jacqui shook her head. "Where's the Black Duchess? She always loves to make an entrance. Is she stuck inside?"

I scanned the crowd—the only people gathering on the lawn were servants, and they all seemed as distressed and confused as we were.

"Abort the mission," Antoine's voice said over my earpiece. "Whatever is happening, you should just get out of there, Briar—"

A flash from behind me broke through the morning light, bright enough to cast my shadow in dark black across the gravel underneath our feet. I spun around, trying to see what had cast it, expecting the resounding boom of an explosion to catch up to the light any second.

What I saw was much stranger.

High above one of the nearby towers—a spindly spire with

a handful of side turrets perfect for isolating your daughters—a shimmering portal had opened in the sky. Rippling like quicksilver, the disc seemed to reflect a view of a mountain range I had never seen before.

Before I could make sense of what I was seeing, more and more discs flashed into existence over the nearby buildings, hovering in place like a squadron of magical UFOs. I had to shield my eyes as a portal opened right over our heads. Through the undulations and distortions, I thought I could catch the sight of a sun-soaked valley filled with Grecian architecture.

"Is that…Olympus?" I asked, rhetorically. No one around me seemed to have any more of a clue than I did. Even Ravenna looked horrified and confused, and she had more degrees than a thermometer.

Jacqui had apparently gotten a hold of her mother on her mirror. "What is this? What have you done?!" she was shouting over the confused shouts of the crowd.

And then, "What do you mean, '*goodbye*?'"

Dread, confusion, and awe fought across the planes of Jacqui's face as she let her mirror drop to her chest, staring up at the holes poking through the sky. A handful of servants had broken away from the crowds and were racing through the paths of Castle Fortnight, trying to get away from whatever these things were. Confused voices, shouts, and sobs echoed through the castle grounds, but the portals hung silently, eerily mute.

Then they started to move.

In perfect synchronicity, all the portals descended, smoothly and inescapably. Where the surface of the magic touched the roofs of Castle Fortnight, the towers and turrets disappeared. At certain angles, I could see the reflection of the structures reappearing in the vistas through the portals, sliding easily into their new homes. The Black Duchy was whisked into the reflection, appearing on a serene Olympian mountaintop, leaving behind the rows of buttresses.

The world they were leaving behind wasn't so serene.

Only the best parts of Castle Fortnight were taken through these rips in space. The barracks, the walls, the guardhouses—they were all left behind, in some cases without the towers they were built onto, mortar crumbling away from the walls they'd shared for centuries. One sleek glass tower took the attached stables but left the servant's quarters hanging in mid-air, before they plummeted to the earth with an echoing shatter. The grounds of Castle Fortnight looked like a wasteland, the dirt speckled with the bedraggled remnants of half-formed structures.

I gaped at my friends, hoping one of them had formed some sort of meaning from what we'd just witnessed. Cade was fuming, Jacqui looked heartbroken, and Ravenna had tears streaming down her face. But it was Miranda's voice that pierced through our ear cuffs.

"Caesura has been putting spies in Castle Fortnight," she said frantically. My mind was a whirling ball of hypotheses, but I couldn't put together what Miranda was saying. "Whatever *that* was, she knows. She knows that Castle Fortnight is no more."

As if to underscore her point, the ear was split with a dozen blood-chilling howls, as all around us, monsters poured out of the woods.

❦

A PACK OF WOLVES rushed through the shattered remains of Castle Fortnight, flowing around the stunted stone ruins with predatory efficiency. A flock of giant bats took to the skies, unnatural in the midday sun, and scattered across the length of the grounds. The trees ringing the castle shook as a platoon of ogres and mountain giants rose up to their full heights, knocking branches aside as they descended on the remains of the castle.

The crowd of servants and hangers-on surged around us, jostling and rushing in desperate attempts to get away from the nightmares approaching us from all sides. Everyone was pushing, moving in different directions, frantically trying to get *away* without any thought to what they were heading *towards*. A pair of valets winged me from either direction, spinning me around and further disorienting me. Cade had just been to my left, but now his comforting bulk was nowhere to be seen.

"Cade?" I screamed, trying to be heard over the cacophony around me. "Jacqui? Ravenna?" If they heard me, the response was lost over the roar of panic surrounding me like a straight-jacket.

"Briar."

I spun around, trying to find where the voice was coming from.

"Briar, it's me," Antoine's voice said in my earpiece. Tears sprung to my eyes without warning, blurring the crush of bodies around me. "These people need your help, Bri. I know this is scary, but you need to find a way to come back to yourself."

I shook my head, fear robbing me of my voice. Antoine was right. We only had a few moments before the monsters were up-on us.

Whenever I heard Antoine's voice, I felt a little tension drain out of me. His smooth, rich tones sparked a peace and a serenity that I experienced so rarely those days. It was a gift, and if I wanted any chance of surviving the next five minutes, it was a gift I was going to have to share.

Already, there was a rose in my hand. I concentrated on all the calm that Antoine brought out in me, the security of his presence at the end of a long day, ready to listen to my complaints and excitements, my bad jokes and my dark secrets. I clung to this comfort feverishly, stowing it away in the rose like a greedy chipmunk.

And then I threw the rose into the air, and the petals erupted into a soft pink torrent, encompassing the people around me.

Immediately, the screaming and shouting stopped. I could feel the crowd through my magic, and we all took a deep breath as one. Dozens of heartbeats began to slow. We were all aware of the danger but no longer letting the panic get the better of us.

"We have to move," I said, and even though I spoke at a normal volume, I knew everyone around me could hear it. A mother pulled her two dark-haired kids close, and all three nodded. As one being, we surged away from where the Black Duchy had once stood, calmly but quickly returning to the gates leading out of Castle Fortnight.

I still hadn't found my friends, but I could feel them somewhere in the crowd, eagerly lapping up the magical calm that I'd passed along. People waited patiently while the path in front of us narrowed into a stone stairwell. The two valets who had nearly trampled me were helping an older gentleman find his footing on the shallow steps.

If we could just get to the gates, maybe we could escape Caesura's clutches.

I stood guard as the crowd stepped carefully. Whatever was pursuing us wasn't in view, and I had to take another deep breath to stop myself from picturing wolves and redcaps hiding behind every bit of shrubbery or low stone wall.

A scream shattered the air.

One of the kids I'd observed earlier grabbed desperately for their mother as a giant bat lifted the screaming woman from the ground. The nearby people were still supernaturally calm, with just a thin veneer of horror as they watched the events unfold. I saw Ravenna a few feet away from the bat staring blankly, frozen in place. The kids were fighting like hell, even as the bat screeched in their faces, its scrunched face splitting open to reveal its hideously long tongue. But with a violent jerk, the monster ripped the woman from her children's hands and took off into the sky.

And then the terror broke my spell right open.

People shrieked as the woman rose higher and higher, and the panic set in, pushing the carefully controlled march into disarray. I used my magic to bring a rose into my hand, but I felt my grip on the stem go limp as a dozen more bats began to circle around us. Even if my power could do something, the first bat would soon be out of reach of even my magic.

Luckily, arrows fly farther than spells.

I've never been particularly happy to see Anya Koronik, certified mean-girl ranger, but my heart swelled as she jumped up on a nearby pedestal. "Cade, you ready?" she said, not taking her eyes off her target as she loaded a bolt in her crossbow and took aim. I heard a familiar, affirmative grunt from the crowd, and Anya let her arrow fly.

The bat made a wet keening sound as the shot pierced its flank, stuttering in mid-air as its wings clenched involuntarily. The woman wriggled one last time, escaping the beast's claws only to plummet into the arms of gravity.

There was a flash of movement, and I saw Cade break from the crowd, legs pumping towards the point where the woman was falling. But she was dropping too fast, and even if Cade could reach her, the impact would snap her neck like a matchstick.

"Ravenna!" I shouted, finding her dark hair in the crowd. *"Do something!"*

For a moment, her dark eyes caught mine, but a brittle, haunted look of shock kept her from really seeing me. After a moment, she shook her head and seemed to see the situation around her for the first time.

Ravenna pointed a single finger at the woman and said something frantically in a language I didn't understand. Black, spectral wings sprouted from the falling woman's back, not stopping her fall but at least generating enough drag to slow her descent. Those few fractions of a second gave Cade the time to throw himself forward and reach the woman. He caught her and twisted in mid-air, putting his body between her and the ground as they skidded to a stop.

Before I could check to see if they were okay, another bat swooped down towards the tail end of our group, the part that hadn't yet made it up the stairs. In a flash of petals, I thrust all the panic and terror I'd felt during the attack into a rose aimed straight for the thing's gaunt nose. The magic hit it just in time, and the monster wheeled away in the air.

I saw Cade reunite the mostly unhurt mother with her children, just as Anya yelled over the crowd, *"Run!"* People kept a tinge of their earlier calm, making it up the stone stairs without trampling anyone. Anya continued peppering the bats with arrows—they weren't enough to take any of the creatures down, but they at least kept them off our backs as we scrambled for the castle gates.

As we ran, I found myself next to Ravenna, whose eyes still had a bit of a glazed look to them. I'd been on a handful of adventures with her, and the wizard wasn't one to lose her proverbial shit easily. Although my lungs burned from exertion and fear, I was able to wheeze out, "You okay?"

Ravenna's hand shot up, covering her mouth like it was trying to hold in a sob or a scream. Her deep brown eyes, however, burned with painful shame. "I did this, Briar," she croaked out. "This is all my fault."

BEFORE I COULD ASK Ravenna anything else, Cade's booming voice echoed across the battlefield that had been a courtyard mere minutes before. *"Incoming!"* he shouted as a stream of wolves began to harry the retreating servants. I saw him grab a snarling beast by the scruff of its neck and hurl it off a porter before it could tear the poor man's throat out.

Looking over my shoulder, I saw the jarring, knifelike movements of redcaps as they wove nimbly through the remnants of Castle Fortnight, their lithe grey limbs finding purchase in the stonework. Above them, waves of banshees floated like spectral leaves, and just at the edge of hearing, their keening screams heralded the coming death.

I could've kept running. The adrenaline in my blood wanted nothing more than to propel me forward, past the slower parts of our convoy, the elderly and the young and the vulnerable, until I could get out of the gate, get to the nearest Doorway, and leave the army of monsters at my back as far behind as I could.

But I was done running away.

I skidded to a halt and turned to face them, gritting my teeth with the terror of it all. "Get everyone out!" I yelled to my friends, and then I let loose.

I could feel the stories in the soil here, the generations of fairy godmothers and long-haired princesses who had made Castle Fortnight their home. It was like a prismatic film over everything, the sugary, slightly stale scent of the narratives that everyone in the Poisoned Apple enacted and reenacted. In Olympus, the myths had found me and jumped into being more or less on their own—this time I was actively summoning them, pulling them out of the ground to place themselves between us and danger.

All around me, twining vines and branches began to grow, forming into a small regiment of knights and wizards and royalty. My magic strained as it pressed them into being, forcing the strange and unpredictable stories of the Apple into a fighting force that could hopefully match the approaching monsters. I dared a quick look behind me, where the crowd had started to funnel through the gates of Castle Fortnight. Anya and Scuff had taken positions by either end of the gate, firing crossbow bolts into the swirling mass of bats that hounded the escapees. Cade was carrying a pair of children on his broad shoulders, barely keeping them out of the jaws of the circling wolves. And Ravenna was trying to weave some sort of barrier spell, but the runes she drew in the air flickered like dying neon.

It looked like it was up to me. At least I could buy them some time.

A plantlike courtier beside me raised a flag made of billowing fronds, and it was all the signal my creations needed. The battle was on.

My feelings guided my actions as my awareness spread through the battlefield, my story soldiers spreading out to meet the forest's creatures on all sides. Thorn met tooth and claw, and my forces quite literally dug into the earth to stop the gathered monsters from getting by them. Snarls and otherworldly cries from our opponents were met with the eerie silence that my minions kept, even as some were torn apart by werewolves or carried off by wyverns. But their viny swords and branching wands took their toll on the monsters as well, and for a moment, our two forces were balanced, neither side gaining a clear advantage.

A faint sheen of sweat covered my skin as I redoubled my efforts, my magic crackling across the earth like invisible lighting. Where it struck, more stories grew, conjuring a cavalcade of wicked stepsisters, heroic princes, and jealous queens. I just needed to keep it up for a few moments longer, needed to keep replacing the plant beings as quickly as they fell. But with each new growth, the leaves seemed to droop, the brittle branches snapping, and I knew my reserves would run dry before the Afterwoods emptied of monsters.

Something told me I wouldn't be leaving the gates of Castle Fortnight.

A throbbing headache began to grow behind my eyes, and as I winced and looked upwards, movement caught my eye. A woman stood atop one of the giant, disconnected buttresses of the Black Duchy, her charcoal dress blowing in the wind. Although she was far away, I felt Caesura's awareness meet mine, and she gave a sardonic little wave.

Interesting new trick, her voice whispered in my ear. Whether it was in my mind or she had actually had the wind carry her words to me, I couldn't guess. But I didn't give her the dignity of responding. Or, if I were totally honest with myself, I knew that splitting my attention for even a second could let one of her creatures slip by me.

It's not enough, you know. Soon, your little stories will fall flat, and the Apple will give way to something glorious and new.

Out of the corner of my eye, I saw a regal queen with a crown of thorns, who moments before had been spearing banshees with twisting vines. As I watched, a curving tree grew into the shape of a mirror, and the queen turned, as if transfixed by her reflection, turning her attention from the battlefield and letting a shaggy hellhound slip by her.

With the Royals here, perhaps you stood a chance. But they've done the smart thing and abandoned the Apple.

To my side, I saw a swordsman made of birch drive off a redcap, only to be stabbed in the back by another tree man. An echo of some long-dead betrayal coursed through my mind, bringing with it all the pain as if I'd been the one attacked.

I was so used to putting my emotions into plants, but now it seemed like the connection was going the other way.

It's not too late, Briar. We can stop all this fighting. Just join me.

A regiment of guards in armor made of bark marched forward, a distant, willowy king giving them orders as they charged into battle. One by one, I felt them fall, their sparks of magic snuffed out as their monarch looked on, unfeeling.

The stone of the courtyard bit into my palms as I fell forward onto my knees, closing my eyes against the pain as the stories I'd summoned unraveled around me. I reached for more magic, for something to keep me going, but my insides felt hollowed out. Empty.

A screech above me brought me to my senses, and I looked up, only to see a mottled black bat begin to dive straight for me, its fangs as long as my forearms. I was frozen, and for a moment, it felt like Caesura would get her wish. I was going to give up and stop fighting.

"Briar!" someone was shouting, and before the giant bat could get to me, a crossbow bolt hit it in the eye, and a strong hand gripped my shoulder, jerking me to my feet. A few more crossbow bolts whizzed by my face as Cade manhandled me towards the gates. Around me, all I could see were the stunted remains of my magic, the broken stems and wilted leaves of what had been fairy tales.

My feet finally began to help push us along, and only through Cade's sheer strength did he get me to the castle gates. The portcullis had been mostly lowered, with Anya and Scuff shooting through from the other side to give us cover. We had maybe twenty feet to go.

Cade gave me a squeeze. "We got everyone out. You did it. We—"

His words turned into an animalistic snarl as a redcap landed on his back, its black serrated knife cutting deep into his shoulder. The grey-faced little gremlin snickered through pointed teeth, raising its blade for another cut.

Before I could react, a lance of purple energy struck the redcap in the chest, throwing it off Cade. Now I was dragging him forward, as he clutched his wounded shoulder, trying to staunch the bleeding. The redcap landed with preternatural agility and sprang forward, dogging our last steps as we raced for the gate.

Cade pushed me forward, and I painfully tumbled on the cobblestones. Once the world righted itself, I looked back to see him do a badass commando roll, dodging the redcap's final swipe just as Anya and Scuff shoved the portcullis all the way down.

I scrambled backwards, looking to the skies, expecting a rain of bats and banshees to fly over the castle walls and finish us off. But the swarms of flying creatures merely perched on the battlements, looking at us like living gargoyles as we retreated.

Now I understood. Caesura had exactly what she wanted. Castle Fortnight had fallen, and now she was queen of its remains, cutting off our access to the Black Duchy and the giant's heart underneath.

We might have survived the battle, but we had lost the war. Now, all she had to do was wait for the giant to finish awakening and destroy the Apple once and for all.

Checkmate.

"WHAT DID YOU MEAN, that this was all your fault?" I asked Ravenna as I bandaged Cade's shoulder. Anya had tried to push me aside to do it, but the look I'd given her had apparently given the Red Hood ranger second thoughts. We had retreated to Tarris's apartment to regroup, showing up a bloody, confused mess only to have Rick start making us scones.

Three scones later, my insides still felt empty.

Curled up on the boys' turquoise couch, Ravenna drew her fringed shawl around her and looked at the floor. "I—can we talk about this later?" Her voice sounded as hollow as I felt.

"Castle Fortnight just disappeared into thin air. Caesura and her army of monsters nearly ripped us to shreds," I said, hands shaking as I wrapped cloth around Cade's thick arm. "We need answers, Ravenna. Now."

"I—" Ravenna smoothed her hair back, trying to compose herself. I'd never seen her unravel this far. "I've been doing research, into portals. The kind that I made with the water from those ponds near the World Tree—what did you call them? Worldpools?" I nodded, because despite everything, that name was one of my better creations. "But I didn't have enough samples, so I needed an expedition to get me more of the water. And to spearhead an expedition into the Afterwoods, especially during the Shudders, I needed funding."

I remembered something she'd said just before our trip to Olympus. "Your slimy donors. They were the Royals?"

Tarris's couch creaked as Ravenna shifted forward, burying her head in her hands. "Count Grimmour connected me with some other Academy researchers, hooked me up with all the equipment and materials I needed. But to collaborate with the other wizards, I had to share my research."

The pieces clicked into place. She'd been played.

"Why didn't you come to us?" I said furiously. Even though I knew she wasn't to blame for all that had transpired, it was easier to be mad at the person I could see than the many circumstances that had forced her hand. "Any of us would have happily led a trip into the Afterwoods to get you what you needed. Why—"

"Because it's my fault!" she burst out, standing to face me. "I messed up, and we lost Antoine. I couldn't ask anyone else to take a risk to get him back. I had to do this alone."

Something like fire began to build in my belly—all of it, the self-isolation, the insistence on some heroic journey of martyrdom—was just too much. Couldn't she see she was being selfish by trying to make things right on her own? That if she'd just talked to us, told us what she needed, we could've helped? We might have been able to get Antoine back?

Out of the corner of my eye, I saw a delicate white orchid on the back of Rick's upright piano, tucked into a boxy minimalist vase. As my rage built, the petals began to shift, firetruck red beginning to flow from the center of the bloom and staining the white petals.

The image short-circuited my brain, suddenly flooding me with curiosity instead of frustration. Was I affecting other flowers besides roses now?

With conscious, painstaking effort, I unclenched my fists and took a breath. It didn't take much to see why Ravenna's behavior was pissing me off. It was exactly what I'd done during the Shudders—gotten so wrapped up in my past mistakes that I couldn't face the present, never mind the future.

And it was a lot easier to get mad at her than to get mad at myself.

"Rav, look," I said, trying to massage my temples to drain away some more of my piping-hot rage, "you didn't know what the Royals were going to do with your research. None of us could've known." A very similar conversation I'd had with Antoine flickered through my mind, nearly making me smile. "You were trying to save Antoine and it had unintended consequences. I can't fault you for that."

Ravenna's spine curved, like a bowstring ready to be released, and finally I looked up at her, my face caving into an expression of sympathy. It was all the indication she needed. She shot forward into my arms, sobbing hysterically. "I'm gonna do it, Briar. I promise. I'm going to use the water they got me and—I'm going to bring Antoine home, I swear."

I watched as the orchid on the piano faded back to white.

Before I could finish calming her down, frantic knocks jolted through the apartment. We all looked at each other apprehensively. There were still bats and other nasties swooping intermittently through the skies above the Apple. Even if most of the monsters seemed to have stayed around the former castle grounds, the streets were empty as the people of the Apple hunkered down to see what would come next.

Cade drew his axe and went to the front of the apartment, his giant frame moving silently from his many years sneaking through the paths of the Afterwoods. Just as he peered through the eye hole on the door, the tension in his posture eased.

"Uh, Tarris, it's your sister," he said quietly.

A year ago I would've said she was just a different kind of monster, but apocalypses make for strange bedfellows.

Cade waited for the prince's approval before drawing the chain and unlatching the door. In an instant, Miranda Grimmour swept in with an expression of terror and a drawn rapier, still wet with blood.

Miranda ran her shaking hands back through her hair, blurting out in an incoherent ramble, "Are you all okay? I saw what happened on the mirror-cast, and there were so many monsters, I couldn't see what happened and I just—I needed to get here." She ended her monologue staring at Tarris. "Are you okay?" she repeated, her voice tinged with a fear I'd never heard from her before.

"I'm fine," Tarris said, eyes dragged down by the sword. "Is that—?"

Miranda followed his gaze down, and seemed almost as surprised by the sword as her brother was. "There were some kobolds in my way."

"I—" Tarris shook his head, discarding whatever response he had to that. "Miranda, what's wrong? You look like shit. And you never look like shit."

I noticed, with some indignation, that she was wearing a *Trolling Stones* hoodie from my closet.

Miranda seemed to settle down a little from whatever keyed-up adrenaline high she was on. "I just saw Castle Fortnight disappear, and I guess our parents with it and—Tarris, you're my only family left, and if anything happened to you, I don't know what I'd do."

In a moment, the sword clattered to the floor, and she rushed forward to her brother, wrapping him in a feral hug. At first, Tarris stiffened, and I thought he might push her away. But then his arms came up, and he pressed her against his chest. "You're okay, sis. I'm here, and we're going to be okay."

As quickly as she pounced on him, Miranda took a step back and turned her gaze to Rick. "Rick, I am so sorry. I know nothing I can say could make up for what I've done to you—"

Rick's kind eyes narrowed as they darted between Miranda and Tarris. He put a finger up to stop her. "You get one— *exactly one*—more chance with me. Because I love your brother. Don't mess it up."

"I won't. Thank you." Miranda sniffed and wiped her eyes, looking for the first time a little embarrassed at such a public display of her emotions.

Alice swept in to redirect attention and save the princess from squirming. "So what do we do next, team? What's our next move?"

A giant bat flew by the window, close enough that I could see the slather dripping from its fangs. From a nearby apartment, a child screamed. As I looked around at my friends' shell-shocked faces, it became clear:

None of us had a mothergoosing clue.

THE NEXT FEW WEEKS passed in a blur of rain and candle-light. Much of the magic that powered the Apple was routed through Castle Fortnight, so we traded our magic lamps and enchanted chandeliers for flickering fireplaces and candles. Our main focus was keeping everyone fed and safe as Caesura kept her hands around the city's throat. Her monsters swept through the streets with enough regularity that most people stayed indoors as much as they could, trying to keep their heads down, bracing for whatever came next. Low-grade Shudders shook the ground day and night, like simmering water finally coming to a boil.

With the whole Apple falling apart, I kept my focus on Havmercy, trying to take care of our neighborhood and hoping that people across the city were doing the same for their own. With my focus narrow, the small problems seemed solvable—how to get torchstones to the local Red Hoods squads who needed them, where to find baby formula for the little old woman who lived in a sneaker. Whenever I tried to think of a way out of the present, to grapple with the vice that Caesura held us in, my brain felt foggy and the plants around me turned increasingly poisonous colors. So I stayed as focused as I could, trying to ease suffering in Havmercy whenever it was possible. We were in pure survival mode—it was too much to hope for happily ever after.

It was late evening, and I was still hunkered down in our breakfast nook, pouring over the supplies lists that Alice had gathered, trying to figure out how to stretch what few resources we had for another week. The community food pantry run out of the Second Breakfast was going to be light this week, but I didn't see any way around it. The numbers in front of me started to blur and dance in the candlelight, and I welcomed the distraction as Jacqui came in from a late-night neighborhood council meeting.

"Geez, Briar, I haven't seen you burning the midnight oil since…" She scrunched up her face. "Ever?"

I stuck my tongue out at her and kicked the table's other chair out for her to sit. "Ha, ha," I said drolly. "How was the council?"

Jacqui shrugged as she threw her raincoat onto the coat tree and took a seat. "People are hanging in there," she hedged. "But we seem to be rapidly approaching a point of no return."

Her voice was rough, matter-of-fact. We'd all gotten pretty good at these sorts of conversations lately, keeping our emotions at bay long enough to share the constant stream of bad news. "How long do we have left?" I asked, similarly flat.

"If nothing changes and we can't find ways to juice the magic supply? Probably two weeks. Then we really need to start considering full-scale evacuation."

I nodded numbly and searched around for another topic. "How's Raye holding up?"

Jacqui's sister, who had woken up from the sleeping curse with the rest of the princesses, had been at a boarding school in Switzerland for the past six months. Jacqui had been the one to tell her that their parents had abandoned the Apple and transported their home to a golf course in Cockaigne. "She's doing okay. Keeping busy. She wanted to come here but I told her to stay put."

I caught her eye. "Is there a part of you that has considered flying out and joining her?"

The princess gave a not-so-dignified snort. "Considered it? Of course. But there's no way I'm going to go relax in a Swiss ski chalet while the Apple needs me."

"Really? You love that thing with hot chocolate and booze.

What's it called? Appy ski?"

"It's pronounced *après-ski,* and yes, I do love it," she sighed wistfully. "But our home comes first."

I nodded. What else was there to do?

Alice clomped downstairs with a hint of her old enthusiasm, followed by a sheepish Linden. "Are you guys ready? It's almost midnight."

Both Jacqui and I exchanged a look of confusion. "I don't think my sweatpants are under any fairy godmother magic," I said. "And what are you doing here, cuz?"

Alice rolled her eyes and set down a long, thin candle in a silver holder onto the table. The black wax was carved with purple runes that seemed almost familiar. "C'mon, you guys haven't heard anything about this? It was all people could talk about on their mirrors today."

With the magic rationing, our mirrors were only active for an hour a day, but Alice pounced on those opportunities to connect, checking in on people across the Apple and getting all the latest updates.

"C'mon, it'll be fun," Linden said, clearing a spot on the floor in a circular shape.

"Oh Grimmsdammit, is this a ritual?" I said, rolling my eyes. Tamsin had once explained wizard magic as being made up of runes, which were arranged into spells like how words fit into sentences. But if spells were sentences, then rituals were rambling stories told by a drunk guy on a bus: overly long and usually pointless. But at least wizards usually trusted us amateurs to light a few candles and pour water in a chalice.

Alice scrambled in the kitchen's junk drawer as our grandfather clock begin to chime. "No time to explain," she said as she found a matchbook from the Woodsman's Log and ran over to the table. After a few attempts, she lit the match and pressed it to the wick of the candle.

A flame caught immediately, thick black smoke billowing out in an instant. I tried to breathe in before the smoke hit me, but instead of clogging my lungs, the cloud smelled refreshingly like woodsmoke and cedar. The small candle blossomed with smoke, and soon the room began to fill with the scent of magic.

I took a breath in, waiting for something else to happen, but the room looked unchanged. The candle's flame surged in one final flash of magic and then went out. "That was it?" I asked. Apparently this ritual wasn't much more than a tweet.

"That was it for now. Now go to sleep," Alice chided. "I'll see you soon."

WHEN I FINALLY GOT INTO BED and closed my eyes, all I could see was darkness, as expected. But the scent of magic still teased my nostrils, and beneath my lids danced an echo of the grey wisps from the candle's flame. As my mind quieted and dimmed from the pressures and stresses of the day, the smoke around me grew denser and resolved into new shapes, a world of greys and purples sprouting in my mind's eye.

Apparently the ritual wasn't done with me yet.

It no longer felt like I was curled up in my cramped bedroom on sheets I probably needed to wash. Instead, the smoke inside my mind became a dark, starless night, and plumes of vapor rose around me to form rows of skyscrapers like standing stones. The scene rippled and roiled before resolving into a full panoramic of Lower Manhattan at night. I was standing in the middle of a street in the Financial District, the columns of the Stock Exchange peering around the corner from me like the teeth of a hungry mouth. For a moment I shuddered, picturing the enameled faces of the Sown Men from Lord Wallace's estate. Blessedly, the streets were empty of those monsters or the day traders and finance bros who usually populated this part of the city—or else this truly would have been my nightmare.

A swirl of smoke kicked up, and I could see a trio of figures stepping insubstantially down the sidewalk. Two of them I recognized instantly—Alice and Jacqui wore ridiculous business outfits, but I would know their slightly drunken struts anywhere. The next figure was me, wearing a silly thrift-store pantsuit the color of a blueberry, laughing at some story Alice was telling as we stomped blissfully homeward.

I remembered this night, even though it felt like a lifetime ago. It was the night we'd all gone to FiDi on a lark, pretending to be some of Manhattan's young, rich, and tasteless. I remembered the carefree, electric feeling of our laughter, like the three of us were sharing the world's best inside joke, and nothing in the world could pierce the magic circle of our youth.

The feeling didn't last.

This was the night the princesses started screaming, and nothing was ever the same again. It didn't take long for Jacqui to discover her sister was affected by the curse. Soon, we'd learn about the Fata and their centuries of manipulation. And then, after fighting and sacrificing so much to save the Apple, I'd lose Antoine.

It was just earlier this year, and yet somehow this was the last night I felt young.

Without thinking, I began running, trying to chase after the wispy trio of girls from my memories. I called after them, wanting to—I'm not sure, hug them? Replace them? Tell them what was coming? But they couldn't seem to hear me, lost in their own time, their own world. My footsteps echoed throughout the empty street, growing louder the farther I went. A strain of laughter drifted from around the corner, but each of my steps forward got louder and louder.

Then I realized those echoing footsteps weren't entirely my own.

From somewhere uptown, a distant tread got closer and closer, each step sounding like the impact of a car into solid concrete. I'd lost sight of the younger version of myself, and each time I moved forward, the noise grew, until the glass of the windows around me shook with the echoes of each footfall.

My breaths came quickly and unevenly as I skidded to a stop, but the steps still came towards me. Giant hands grasped the side of an office building, pulling a dark shape into view. With the horrifying clarity of a nightmare, I knew that the shape towering over me was the giant under the Apple, the timeless creature who was waking up to destroy us all. But all I could see was smoke, vast and dark and flat, in the vague shape of a person hundreds of stories high. Where I expected a face or eyes was just a storm of vapor and cloud, lit by the occasional flicker of purple lighting deep within.

We stood there, looking at each other, predator and prey on the city streets, and as much as I would have liked to run away, my legs were locked in place. It wouldn't have done any good, either. Even at my best sprint, I wouldn't be able to make it a half of a block before the figure in front of me crushed me like a bug.

I was only broken from my terrified reverie by a short shushing sound by my ankles. Looking down, I saw a grated storm drain in the curb—I would have looked away if I hadn't seen the glint of eyes underneath it. I jumped back but saw that it was the face of the young child I'd seen in my dream before—green skin, hazel eyes, and a mop of messy hair. They caught my eyes and raised a single finger to their lips. Before I could even begin to interpret their meaning, a crunch told me the giant was stepping closer. But the kid in the sewer just shook their head, taking a deep breath and putting a hand out like they expected me to join them in a morning meditation.

Despite everything, I began to take a rough breath in, but the crunching of the Manhattan skyline drew my focus.

The giant had gone full kaiju, flipping cars and smashing street lights. With each power line he brought down, transformers burst into sparks, crackling along the pavement. My feet began to move before my conscious brain could catch up, and I was tearing down the street away from the chaos. I had no plan, no clue where to go—eventually I'd hit Battery Park, and I'd swim away from the giant through the Hudson if I had to.

A giant, hairy foot—now ruddy flesh and blood instead of shadow—crashed into the street next to me, sending cracks racing through the asphalt. I staggered away from it, nearly falling to the now uneven ground. Already the giant was nearly on top of me, stretching into the air and blocking the sky behind him. Even this close, no features were discernible in his face and body. He was merely a dark outline of things to come, unknowable and unstoppable.

The giant stretched his arms wide, encircling both the buildings on either side of the street. Flexing with effort, he began to push them down, and the towers, with all their office space and corporate coffee shops, folded like cheap cardboard, nothing holding them to the earth except a few pipes and wires.

There was nowhere I could go, nothing I could do to stop the calamity coming for my head. Fire ballooned up from the base of one of the skyscrapers, a ruptured gas line giving it the strength of a dragon's breath. The rush of heat and light tore through the surrounding smoke, and I shut my eyes, hoping whatever nightmare vision the candle ritual had summoned would just go away.

When I opened them, the chaotic explosions of Lower Manhattan had been replaced by the single flame of the ritual candle in front of me, the violet runes glowing softly along its length. The smoky void around me was dark, but it seemed like small, flickering lights were coming into focus from far away.

Looking to my left and right, I saw Alice, Jacqui, and Linden, still in their pajamas. Alice waved to me and said something, although in this weird, smoky realm her voice didn't carry. When we all realized this, we shared a smile and a silent laugh, and turned back to the magic unfolding in front of us.

The light from the candle intensified, or maybe the smoke cleared, and what started as a neon purple glow softened, turning the reddish-violet of a sunset. Through the filtering light, figures started to emerge. I tensed, imagining the smoke giant appearing before I saw that the silhouettes were other people of the Apple, sitting around identical candles.

Cade floated silently into view, saluting me with a beer from a barstool between his Red Hood squad mates. Before I could do more than wave, they drifted back into the smoke, replaced by Isaak and Miranda, who had apparently reconnected if the state of their rumpled clothes was any indication. As the next cloud came into view, it took me a second to recognize Josefina Campbell without her wig, looking prim in a nightgown and a satin cap. It was the largest gathering of people I'd seen since the day Castle Fortnight disappeared, and I found myself tearing up just seeing *people* again.

Whatever spell was connecting us, the haze kept filtering in and out, showing us the hundreds of people who had gathered. Some smiled and waved, others held hands with the people beside them, and two witches had a tearful reunion in sign language. Even without sound, I could see people's shoulders drop, their bodies filling with breath for the first time in weeks, if not months.

It was hard to tell how long we sat there, smiling and connecting with everyone who had stuck it out in the Poisoned Apple. Every so often, a series of magic symbols floated by, stitching together the various living rooms and taverns of the Apple into one magical gathering place. As I looked closer at the runes, the feeling of recognition from before hit me: these were Ravenna's spells. I'd seen enough of her magic to recognize the purple glow and delicate calligraphy. Somehow, with the limited magic still dribbling through the Apple, she'd concocted this entire plan to connect everyone still hanging on.

Soon, the flame of the candle began to sputter, and everyone waved goodbye as the image before us flickered and died out, replaced by the darkness behind my eyelids. But somehow, after what I'd just seen, the darkness was anything but lonely.

I'd really needed this.

Now that sound had returned to the world, I heard my roommates moving around in their rooms, also released from the spell. I kicked my covers off and got up, opening the door to the hallway just as Jacqui and Alice opened their door. Linden emerged from Cade's old room, a smile on his face.

"For once, it was nice to share that dream," he said quietly.

"Did you have something to do with that?" I asked.

"Guilty," he said. "Ravenna actually used a bit of my hair in the candlewick to bring everyone together in the Dream Slip."

"Gross," I said warmly.

"It was beautiful," Alice said, giving Linden an affectionate squeeze on the shoulder. Before he could react, we all heard a knock on the door and froze.

Linden gave a coy grin. "I think it's for you, Bri." I raised my eyebrows but went downstairs anyways. It was after midnight, so I grabbed a mace from our umbrella stand before looking through the peephole.

It was Ravenna herself, in a sleek black trench coat. Her hair was pulled up in a bun, as opposed to its usual flowing waves, but she gave me a quick hug as I opened the door.

"Rav, that was amazing," I said as she squeezed me a little

tighter than usual.

"Thanks, I—" she shook her head, clearly a little overwhelmed. "I needed to do something to give back, after what the Royals did with my research. I know it wasn't much—"

"It was a lot," I said, grabbing her shoulders and looking her in the eye, trying to make sure she heard what I said next. "Bringing us all together like that—giving people that escape, that connection—gave us all hope."

The wizard raised her head and looked at me through her thick eyelashes. Despite everything she smirked a little. "You're not going to say something cheesy like 'and hope is the greatest magic of all,' are you?"

I snorted. "Please. Hope isn't magic. If I've learned anything the past six months, it's that hope is hard Grimmsdamn work. Just like in the ritual, everything was pretty dark before people started lighting their candles."

"What do you mean?" she said. "The ritual began with everyone seeing the candle before your dreams were connected."

"Wait, really? Then what was the whole drama I saw with a smoke giant? Just my own subconscious?"

"Most likely. Unless someone else got to your dream before the ritual kicked in."

I didn't like that idea. I didn't like it one bit. But I didn't let that show.

Ravenna finally began to relax, and as she exhaled I swear I could smell the tension and guilt that had hovered over her for weeks drain away in that one forceful breath. "Thanks," she said with a smile. "Now I have one more surprise for you, waiting in your back garden."

My blood turned to ice, and I wondered if the hope igniting in my chest could be true, or if it would just be another disappointment. "Is it—should I bring my mace?" I said, hefting the spiked weapon in my hand.

"I don't think you'll need it, but I'll leave that up to you." She smiled. "Now go!" Ravenna gave my shoulder one final squeeze before turning back into the night.

I dropped the mace and ran to the French doors leading to our backyard. I heard Jacqui call from the other room, but I couldn't wait. The flickering candlelight from our kitchen caught the silhouette of a figure I would know in the darkest night.

Antoine DuCarr smiled as I burst through the doors and ran into his arms.

I LET MYSELF SOAK in the feeling of Antoine's arms around me—his real arms, not a pale reflection through a magic mirror—for about thirty seconds before I punched him lightly in the arm. "How long have you been back?!"

"Only about an hour," Antoine said. "I've been living in a timeless ether for over six months, and I wanted to take a shower before I saw you."

My irritation melted like butter on a dragon's belly. "Still, how long have you known you were coming back? And not told me?"

"Ravenna and I didn't want to get your hopes up—she's been working around the clock for weeks, trying everything while still working on her candle spell. We had no idea if her final idea would work, but with the Worldpool water she'd gotten from the Royals she was able to recreate the portal that trapped me."

My brain struggled to believe he was actually here, that I could touch him, feel the breath of his words on my face as I nestled into his chest. The garden around me felt unreal, the budding roses like ghosts lit with pale candlelight from within our house. The darkness almost made me feel like I'd joined him in the Mirror Mainframe, floating in nothingness. But I was glad for the shadows when my eyes unexpectedly filled with tears.

"And you're—" I swallowed, trying to keep my words from damming up in my throat. "—you're here for good?"

Antoine heard the fear in my voice, the vulnerability that I normally covered up, and immediately pressed me tightly against him. "I'm here, Bri. I'm here forev—for as long as you'll have me." I felt the weight of him, the solidity of his body as he calmed my fears.

The roses around me weren't just glowing from the candlelight anymore.

We both kept a hushed silence as my magic infused the garden with light, prismatic purples and cyans, glowing with possibilities, with my feelings as I looked forward to a future I hadn't thought would come.

Indigo and teal traced the lines of Antoine's face, limning his cheekbones and catching in his brown eyes. "It's no Paris nightclub," I murmured as I entwined my hands behind his head and brought his forehead down to press against mine, "but are you happy to be back?"

"Honestly, the lighting is better," he whispered, before he kissed me and the garden lit up like a firework display.

Jacqui and Alice had kindly made themselves scarce, so there was no one to witness Antoine and me sneaking in like teenagers, laughing, holding hands, and pausing to make out against every available surface as we made our way up to my bedroom.

Finally, things started to feel real again.

After, cocooned in bedsheets, I still couldn't get over the feel of him, the weight of his chest pressed against my back, warm breath on my neck. His minty scent, the gentle scratch of his beard against my cheek—there were so many physical sensations that made up Antoine DuCarr that I had never fully appreciated until I was cut off from them.

"So the entire six months you were gone you were just…thought, right? Some sort of mind-data construct without a body?" I squirmed around in Antoine's arms so I could get the unmitigated pleasure of watching his brown eyes blink blearily awake from a doze. Early morning light from my bay window streamed across his face, sprinkling his chestnut hair with leopard spots of gold.

"Mmmm, yeah, I guess?" he said groggily.

"So it's been a whole half of a year since you farted?"

"We were having such a nice moment." He rolled his eyes but I could see him fighting to suppress a smile. "Besides, I never pass gas around a lady."

"As your partner, I can say categorically that is a Grimmsdamn lie." I ran my hands up the curves of his chest mischievously.

His fingers caught in my hair and gently tilted my head, the better to see the heat in his eyes. "There's a lot of things I haven't done for six months."

Before I could ask about the mirror-world pooping situation, he brought me in for a slow, brain-melting kiss. It was so good that by the time we'd separated, I'd forgotten all about teasing him.

It was wrapped up in his arms, feeling momentarily safe for the first time in a long time, that I felt like I could finally ask, "Do you think we're going to make it?"

I felt his muscles tense behind me as I stared up at the water damage on my bedroom ceiling. When he answered, his words tripped over each other like he was simultaneously trying to be as polite as possible and figure out what I wanted to hear. "I guess—I hope so, I think we should, now, after all this time of me being away, give it a try to be, you know, as they say, *together*, if you would like—"

He was just too cute sometimes. "No, no, not are *we* going to make it like you and me," I said, pressing a kiss into the back of his hand where it wrapped around my shoulder. "Of course we're going to make it."

"Oh. Uh, good," he said, and I could feel his cheek form a smile from where it was pressed against my head.

"But are we going to make it? The Poisoned Apple?" I asked quietly. I wondered if Antoine could hear my heart hammering within my chest, the way it always did when I cast my mind forward to the future. Or whatever awaited the Poisoned Apple instead of a future.

Antoine went quiet for a moment, letting his long-fingered hands trace slow, soothing patterns along my arms while he tried to think of what words might relax my mind. "I wish I could say for sure," he said after a moment. "But I do think there's something I learned while I was trapped over there, in the mirror realm—"

"Not farting?"

"Not farting, yes, but also trying desperately to hold onto hope that what I was experiencing in the present wasn't going to be forever." His voice took on a hollow quality, and I gave his hand a squeeze, letting him know he could go on if he wanted to. "I just didn't know," he said, voice almost down to a whisper now. "I didn't know if I would ever get back, if I would ever see the world again." I felt a hot tear slide down his cheek and into my hair, and all I wanted to do was hold this beautiful knight forever, wishing there was a way to get back the time we lost. "I didn't know if things would still be the same when I got back, *if* I got back but—" His voice hitched, and his next words were incomprehensible as he rasped them into my hair before taking a ragged breath and repeating.

"You were my hope, Briar."

I gave an epically loud sniffle as my eyes started streaming to match his. "But—*why?* All I ever did was call you to give you recaps of the latest *Real Housewraiths*, or complain about my day, or—I was so selfish."

"You weren't," he said. "You gave me what I needed to keep going—someone to laugh with, someone to tease me and get me out of my head. You were exactly what I needed," he said, the heat of a few moments before returning to his voice. "So do I think we can save the world? Maybe. I hope so. But I know without a doubt you already saved my world, so my money is always going to be on you, Briar Pryce."

Some fairy tales are made of ballgowns and glass slippers, costume balls and golden crowns. They're played out on the world stage, for all to see and envy. But there, in a messy rental cottage, wrapped in sheets that most definitely needed to be washed, I finally started to dare to believe in happily ever after.

"I'm so glad you're back," I said, twisting to press as closely into Antoine as I could, giving myself this one moment to imagine a happy ending I had no idea if the world would allow.

"Me too," he said happily. Something in his tone finally made my heart start to beat slowly, steadily. The iron grip of uncertainty that had made its home in my chest eased for once, and I welcomed the relief.

"So even after being trapped in a mirror for months, you're still holding out hope for the Apple? You're not going to run away?" I asked lazily, my mind already drifting towards sleep.

"That's the thing I learned about hope," he said as I closed my eyes. "You have to feel it first, when you don't know how things will play out." His hand traced calming circles into my back as his words eased my mind. "But if you can hold onto the feeling, despite what the world throws at you, soon your mind will follow, and you can think of how to make that hope a reality."

I WISH I COULD SAY the perfect plan came to me in a dream, nourished by my unconquerable sense of hope. But I must have gone to bed a little hungry, because all I could dream about was the silly image Alice had put in my mind weeks earlier on a rooftop in Olympus: all my friends gathered around a table, having brunch together. Except it was a dream, so I think instead of pancakes we were eating flower petals and pages from my middle-school diary. *You do you, subconscious.*

But I did awake with a feeling. And that feeling pushed me to start on a plan.

Two days later, I gathered my friends together at the Second Breakfast. Flora, the proprietor, was running a free breakfast in the mornings and a food pantry in the evenings, but she lent us the big backroom for the afternoon. It was a little upsetting to see the bright, two-story windows of the cafe boarded up against monster attacks, but even with the clouds covering the sky, the grey light still filtered through the cracks.

Antoine rubbed my back to calm me down as everyone began to arrive: Rick and Tarris brought a mountain of Danishes; Linden and Ravenna helped Tamsin serve her favorite loose-leaf tea; and Jacqui, Alice, and Cade pushed tables together until we could all gather around one huge spread. For a moment, I worried that Miranda wouldn't show, but she came slinking in like an alley cat about ten minutes after we started.

After everyone had food in their stomach and a second helping of tea in their mug, they turned to me, eyes expectant. For once, the trust in my friends' eyes didn't make me panic—it was solid ground from which I could take a leap of faith.

I cleared my throat. "Thank you all, truly, for coming here. I know you've all been helping out in your own ways, so I will try to keep things brief. Antoine, please give everyone a copy of the handout."

My friends all looked at the sheets provided to them, complete with bullet points and diagrams, with mounting horror. Ravenna took out her magical opera glasses. "She's not a doppelgänger, or under the effects of a compulsion…"

I smirked. "Thank you. If we needed any more proof that the end times are upon us, yes, I did prepare a spreadsheet.

"As I've been trying to come up with a plan, I kept hitting a wall where it felt like nothing could work. I couldn't think of any way for me to get inside Castle Fortnight, past the array of monsters and defenses Caesura has patrolling all hours of the day, defeat her, and stop the Shudders. It was impossible. Then I realized…I was right. It was impossible for me to do all of those things. But maybe, just maybe, it won't be impossible for *us* to do all those things."

So I told them my plan. And to my complete surprise, they didn't laugh me out of the Second Breakfast.

They agreed, realizing they'd all be putting their lives on the line for one last-ditch, hail-fairy attempt to save the Apple.

After I'd finished thanking them a million times, everyone left to get to work. Antoine and I had just finished putting the room back in order when I felt him come up behind me and wrap me in a big hug.

"Did I mention you were incredible this afternoon?" he purred in my ear.

"Incredible, like hard to believe? Lacking the credit to be trusted?"

"Nope. Like amazing. Like astonishing," he said, with a kiss to my temple after each adjective.

"Well, thank you, sir," I said, planting my own kiss on his hand as it kneaded my shoulder. "I have you to thank for my inspiration. I just followed your instructions. First, feel hope.

Then, make a plan."

"I gave that advice thinking you might clean your closet. Not create a brilliant plan to save our world."

I turned in his arms, basking in the warmth of his smile. "On the upside, if the Apple is destroyed, that closet can't get much messier."

IT TOOK ANOTHER WEEK to get everything in place—Jacqui began to rally the people living around Castle Fortnight, letting everyone know enough to be prepared without tipping our hand to Caesura completely. Alice gathered intel from all of her friends among the Nobles' servants—or former servants, as their masters had all run away with their tails between their legs. And Cade liaised with the Red Hoods, who readied their haggard forces to surround Castle Fortnight when the time called.

Tamsin and Ravenna worked with an enchanter to perfect my other request: an ensorcelled pouch that could both contain the world-altering magic of the Gaia seed and keep any divining magic from seeing what was inside. They were able to finish it right to my specifications, although…

The thing looked like the unholy offspring of a wallet and an unfortunate fanny pack. Apparently the powerful spells were best contained in braided leather tassels.

I adjusted the chunky monstrosity on my belt as I followed behind Antoine and Miranda, keeping my head low to avoid the moss hanging down from the curved ceiling of the access tunnel we'd been trekking through for the last hour. Our torchstones glowed dimly in the damp, humid air, highlighting the lichen and vines caking the stone walls. Clawed feet pawed on the ground above our heads, indicating we must be getting close to the monster-infested heart of Castle Fortnight.

Between Jacqui, Alice, and me, our council of troublemakers had decades of experience breaking in and out of the castle, and it only took us a few tries to find a tunnel entrance that was unguarded and unwarded—that is, unguarded to anyone with Miranda's ability to reshape stone around the security grates and push them out of her way.

Sunlight filtered around the next corner, which was either a sign we'd reached our destination or that we'd gotten completely turned around in the subterranean labyrinth. I traded a look with Antoine.

"Do you think that's the exit to the castle?" I said, my voice wavering more than I would have liked.

"If it's not, we'll retrace our steps until we figure out the right way," Antoine said resolutely, his hand flitting over to give my neck a quick rub. "Either way, let's check in with the others to make sure we're ready to go."

I nodded, pulled out my mirror, and waited for the reflective surface to resolve into an image of Alice's face. "What's Linden's status, Al?" I said.

"Let me check," she said, the perspective from her mirror swinging wildly as she walked into our spare room.

"I kind of miss you being my handler," I murmured to Antoine while we waited.

"Is it because of your unhealthy obsession with *Alias*?"

"No!" I said, elbowing him in the ribs. "Actually, maybe. Jennifer Garner really deserved an Emmy—"

"Bri?" Alice said from my mirror. "Someone here wants to say goodnight." She tilted her mirror to where Linden lounged on Cade's old bed, morning sunlight playing on his ratty DJ DREEM EATR t-shirt from his former life as a nightclub headliner.

"You ready, cuz?" I asked him, smiling despite the pressure

of it all.

"Just popped a melatonin," he said, grinning. "I'll see you all on the other side."

"Sweet dreams. Or at least, as sweet as you can make them," I said with a wink. We were lucky Caesura seemed to have taken the bait. Through Alice's network of former Castle Fortnight workers, we'd "let slip" the rumor that there was a Free Spell willing to join forces with Caesura and help her usher in her new world order. Pretty soon after, Linden had received a scroll, in the same acid green handwriting that our evil great-great-aunt seemed to favor. She'd been the one to suggest a dream meeting, perhaps to suss out Linden's powers to see if he was worthy of her attention. Our hope was that he'd be able to distract her long enough that she wouldn't see our incursion coming until it was too late.

Say what you will about his taste in music, but Linden could be very distracting.

We waited a few more minutes for Linden to join Caesura in whatever dream connection that we Fata shared, then we crept around the corner. Antoine had the grace to not be smug as the unmistakable outlines of the castle grounds were visible beyond a large iron grate. Miranda spread a bit of her ground stone on the rock surrounding the immovable metal, and the stonework flowed like water until Antoine could pop it out of the foundation. As we moved into the shade of a small pedestrian bridge on the castle grounds, Antoine popped the grate back into place.

The translucent shadows of banshees floated across the cobblestones as we edged closer to the side of the bridge. The once-bustling castle grounds were jagged and barren, like a pile of broken pots where flowers used to bloom. From our hiding spot, we could see the main entrance to Castle Fortnight, the embattled portcullis that we had fled through on the day the Royals disappeared.

"Tarris, it's time," I said into the mirror.

Some of Alice's commoner friends were able to smuggle Rick and Tarris into the main guard tower, which had been left behind when the rest of the Castle disappeared. If they took even a step further into the main castle grounds, they'd immediately be surrounded by Caesura's monstrous forces.

But all Tarris needed to do was touch the stone.

The two wide, crenellated walls reaching out from the tower began to writhe, raising off their foundations like snakes. The stone arced, becoming two massive arms each the size of a train. One reached up, swatting a trio of bats out of the air like they were fruit flies. The other slammed down, blocking a squadron of orcs from rushing the guardhouse where Tarris and Rick were huddled. Soon, the banshees floating over our heads flooded towards the main gates like spooky laundry caught in the wind.

Just as we'd hoped.

Before Caesura's forces could mount a full attack on Tarris, scorching purple runes appeared on all sides of the grounds, covering the former center of the Apple in a dome of magic. As I leaned out from the protection of the bridge, I could just see Ravenna and Tamsin on a pair of borrowed broomsticks, warding the monsters of the Apple into one place so they couldn't swarm out and overwhelm the unprotected city.

The two wizards couldn't sustain the containment spell for long, but until it fell, we were all trapped in here together: the monsters, Caesura, and the three of us.

Antoine, Miranda, and I shared a wordless look as the reality of what we'd done sank in. There was no turning back now. But if we couldn't finish what we came here to do, there'd be no Apple to return to when the spells fell down.

CHAOS BROKE OUT over the castle, as the monsters that had been kept in check by Caesura's influence were caught between Tarris's attack and the magical containment field.

That's the thing about building an army out of fear: without the threat of Caesura's immediate reprisal, there was nothing keeping all the predators from immediately turning on each other.

A pair of gargoyles lifted a draugar in the air, the murderous corpse's knife hacking uselessly at their stone skin. Dozens of wyverns threw themselves against the purple barrier blocking them from the Afterwoods; when the barrier proved immune to their attacks, they turned their claws on each other.

And in all the panic and confusion, no one seemed to notice the three of us slip out from under the bridge and sneak towards the former site of the Black Duchy. The gardens around us looked post-apocalyptic, the formerly manicured lawns scattered with stone debris, piles of broken furniture, and fire pits containing the roasted remains of something with way too many legs. After the occupation by a hoard of monsters and the disappearance of the waitstaff, it was no surprise.

Hugging the low stone walls and keeping low, I really thought we were going to make it to our destination without incident.

The throwing knife that nearly pierced my septum disabused me of that notion.

Five redcaps scampered over some nearby crates, knifelike teeth glinting as they surrounded us, confident in their advantage of numbers even though they were each half our size. The brittle, clicking laughs leaking through their metallic smiles sounded almost insectile as they circled us, penning us against the wall.

The first one sprung up, more quickly than I expected, jumping like a cricket towards Miranda. Her feet stuttered on the grass beneath our feet, and she collapsed heavily against the crumbled stonework behind us.

I was close enough to see her smile as the creature fell for her feint. A stone turret sprung out from the wall just in time to knock the redcap off course, his spindly body skidding across the uneven ground before he sprang up snarling.

"Watch out!" Antoine yelled, just as another pair of the things ran at my legs, their knives whirling in unpredictable arcs that made them a danger to themselves and others. I danced out of the way, pulling a rose into my hand with pure will. I splashed a redcap-sized dose of fear into the petals, but as I sent the blossom at my attackers, they rolled in opposite directions, their frantic movements like squirrels on Red Bull.

Before I could track their movements, I saw another redcap dive mouth-first at Antoine, trying to gnaw his face off. For a heart-stopping moment, I saw Antoine turn to face his attacker, the moment spreading out in time as the beast's grey teeth glinted in the afternoon sun.

Then I realized that time wasn't slowing down, Antoine was just moving backwards to keep his nose from becoming a snack.

Antoine landed lightly on his back as the redcap soared through the space where his head had been. In a moment, the knight had kipped up and stabbed his rapier down into the earth, spearing one of the petals I'd thrown at my own pair of pint-sized cannibals. With a flicking motion, he sent the fear-filled flower into the back of the redcap's head as it landed, just in time for it to shriek and run away.

It was, admittedly, a very cool combo.

Two more redcaps had cornered Miranda, realizing she couldn't move from the wall without giving up her connection to the stone. One of them quickly slashed at her leg, drawing a line of red on her thigh before dancing out of the reach of the stone fists that defended her.

Miranda stumbled, losing her connection to the wall, and the redcaps took that as their cue to attack.

I ran forward, drawing Prick, but there was no way I was going to make it there before the redcaps got within striking distance.

I really shouldn't have worried.

Miranda had used her faux stumble to palm a broken chair leg, which shot out to dislodge the closer redcap's jaw. The second redcap turned to watch his friend tumble ass over teakettle, meaning he didn't see Miranda plant her foot and punt him like a football.

I staggered to a stop ineffectually just as Miranda shook her head. "They fell for the injured princess move literally twice in one fight. Grimmsdamn idiots." She cracked her neck, and the remaining redcaps scurried into the shadows. "Let's keep moving," Miranda said. If her injured leg bothered her, she didn't let it show.

More shapes began to emerge from corners and alleys, drawn by the sound of violence. A slavering wolf in a blood-red waistcoat jumped from behind a fallen column, but Miranda threw her makeshift cudgel like a javelin and beaned him right in the snout. As we passed his crumpled, whining form, I tossed another rose behind us, forming a line of petals that would emit enough aversion to stop all but the most determined predators from running us down.

Antoine watched our backs while we hurried down a set of stone steps towards the remnants of the Black Duchy. The crashes of Tarris's assault were slightly more muted in this area of the castle, but it felt exposed to the attention of the monsters who weren't bothering to head to the front gates.

Miranda and Antoine watched nervously as I strode up to the buttresses, my throat dry. This was where my first gamble would either pay off or doom our plan just as it was getting started.

The spider-like buttresses spread out like a megalithic circle, surrounding the flat foundation left behind when the Duchy had been transported to Olympus. I ran my hand across the ground, which on closer inspection was some sort of black, obsidian-like crystal.

Miranda sprinkled a little of her ground-up stone from Grimmour Tower onto the foundation but shook her head. "Whatever this material is, my magic loophole won't work on it. Looks like it's up to you, Bri."

I examined the seam where the new construction of the buttresses had been slapped onto the older structure. This close, it was easier to see that the modern exterior of the buttresses surrounded something older and stranger. They'd covered it up, but nothing could completely hide the uncanny essence of the structure.

Last year, when my friends and I had ventured into the Afterwoods to try to break the princesses' sleeping curse, we'd come across a giant, inverted tree where the Fata monitored the many worlds they'd created. The massive, incomprehensible structure had been equally inaccessible, until I'd tried my magic on it.

I was gambling the fate of the Apple that I'd be able to jimmy one of the Fatas' magical locks again. And even if I could, I was also gambling that the Black Duchy itself wasn't the key to the giant's heart. If I was right, the foundation underneath was the true entrance.

I closed my eyes and reached out with my magic, trying to ignore the sounds of chaos echoing across the castle grounds. I cleared my mind and—*there*.

The last Fata ward I'd encountered was structured like a call and response. It emitted an emotion like a beacon and could only be opened when it received a complementary feeling. But that giant tree had a signal like a lighthouse, while the faint feeling coming out of the Black Duchy's base was more like a hidden message. Maybe whoever had built it wanted to make sure the magic was subtle enough that no one would find it without knowing what to look for.

As I concentrated, the feeling began to unspool in my mind. It had the dusty smell of finality, the loamy scent of closure with a hint of satisfaction. The feeling of dropping your burdens after a job well done.

"Briar?" Antoine's voice broke through my reverie. "What's it looking like?"

My eyes fluttered open only to see more advancing redcaps. Miranda had grown a small wall in front of us, but there was only so much stone to manipulate, and claws were scrabbling up the other side of the barrier. In a few more moments, they'd be upon us.

"I found the feeling," I huffed, putting my hand back on the stone. "But it feels…done. What feeling goes with being finished?"

"If I enjoyed answering questions like that, I wouldn't have made my prison therapist cry so much," Miranda growled as she drew a dagger from her waistband. "Can you get us in or not?"

I ignored her and turned back to the crystal at our feet. I searched about hopelessly for a clue—the Fata must have built the Duchy in the early days of the Apple, making it appear like a human-built structure as best they could. At some point, the Royals had added the buttresses, whether to hide the building's origins or merely for aesthetics, I couldn't tell. But I tried to put myself in the alien mind of those first Fata. They'd put a giant to sleep and built a world on top of him, with this slab of crystal as the only access point to his sleeping heart. It must have been their true feelings etched into the stone, the long-awaited exhale after an exertion.

So what came next?

"Briar!" The warning in Antoine's voice told me I didn't have much time.

For a moment, I hesitated. I had gotten the answer to the last Fata lock right in one guess. What if there was some security system that engaged if I got it wrong?

And would it be worse than a horde of ravenous redcaps?

What came next?

I concentrated, and a rose appeared in my hand. If I was anything like the Fata who built this place, if there were echoes of them in my blood or in my heart, I just hoped we had the same feeling, coming home after a long day. I pictured throwing my messenger bag down by the door, hanging my coat up, and kicking off my shoes.

The first breath I let fall into the rose was rest, the releasing of tension when a task came to an end. But I knew it wasn't enough. With an inhale, I breathed a spark into the flower, golden light filtering through my closed eyelids as I painted each petal with the shining promise of a new start.

I forget which bard said it, but every new beginning comes from some other beginning's end, right?

Opening my eyes, I planted the golden rose into the rock, turned it like a key, and watched as a spiral staircase opened below us.

KNOWING MY FATA FOREBEARS, there was no way to tell if the stairway was the reward for a correct answer or a one-way trip to a grisly death. But we'd come this far, so what was one more leap into the unknown?

"C'mon," I said, moving onto the first step and turning to

my friends.

Miranda laid one more hand on the barrier she'd built and coaxed it as high as she could. It wasn't a foolproof defense, but it would slow down the monsters behind us.

"Took you long enough," she muttered as she walked past me into the darkness, but I thought I caught the hint of her smile reflecting in the gloom.

Antoine looked between the wall and the stairway into the blackness, a pained expression on his face. "Bri," he said quietly, "I think this is where I leave you."

"What?" I said, my boot poised to take the next step.

"This wall is only going to slow our pursuers, not stop them. We need someone to stay behind and cover our rear." A tightness grew in my chest, stopping me from even making fun of his phrasing.

Antoine noticed my hesitation and placed his hand briefly on my cheek. "I don't want any monsters sneaking up behind you. It's the right tactical decision," he said, leaning in to give me a kiss. "Now go. You've got a world to save."

I swallowed the thick lump in my throat and turned to the stairwell where Miranda waited impatiently. It felt like the solid rock on which I'd been planted since his return was crumbling beneath me.

"You better stay safe," I grumbled, lingering for just a moment longer in the warmth of Antoine's presence.

A scrambling noise outside the haphazard wall heralded the arrival of more of Caesura's forces. "I will," Antoine said with all the formality of an oath. "I didn't cross dimensions to be with you only to get taken out by a few dozen redcaps."

With the stubborn courage it takes to rip off a bandaid, I hurried down into the depths beneath the Black Duchy.

After a few rotations of the spiral staircase, the noise from above us faded away, leaving us in still, stagnant air. The cloudy black crystal walls reflected our torchstones wanly, the light catching each facet and groove. I couldn't tell what material it was, only that it was hard and smooth.

"Do you want to give your loophole one more try on this stuff, now that we're below ground?"

Miranda shrugged. "Worth a shot." She sprinkled a tiny bit of grey powder onto the floor and placed her palm on it, frowning. "Nothing."

I grimaced. That would've been a nice failsafe to help us deal with whatever waited at the end of this stairwell. But her stone shaping wasn't the reason I'd brought Miranda along.

However the Fata had carved out this stairway, the construction had stood the test of time, the edges of each stair still knife-sharp and glinting. As we descended, little sconces appeared, but instead of holding any light source, each framed a prehistoric-looking cave plant. The succulents' serrated leaves were equal parts stunning and threatening.

I ran my hand along one of these sconces, a film of dark moss blunting the edge and making me remember my trip to Gaia's gallery. "I think this is one of those…" I scrunched up my face, trying to remember the phrase Ravenna had used. "End-of-the-trip Galways."

Even in the dim light, I could see Miranda's eyes roll. "Entropic causeways."

"Yeah, the ones that take you into a World Slip."

"I think you're right," she said begrudgingly. "Which doesn't make any sense, because we know the giant's heart is located at the nexus of the ley lines underneath the Apple."

"Maybe the ley lines get their power through the causeway because…magic?" I said with a shrug. I checked my mirror—no service to the outside world, which meant no way to ask Ravenna or Tamsin what the elf was going on. "Whatever the reason, we're stuck in here on our own."

That declaration silenced us until we came to the end of the stairwell. With bated breath, we scanned the cavernous room we entered for any signs of life, but it seemed empty. Expanding the spiral from the staircase, this enormous atrium's walkway continued deeper, hugging the walls around a large empty space in the center. Ringing the walls were dozens of stained-glass windows, their prismatic light painting the entire room in greens and blues. By my estimation, we'd walked at least six stories underground, but something on the other side of these windows lit them with flickering sunlight.

World-saving mission or no, Miranda and I still paused to inspect the first window. My breath caught for a moment at what seemed like movement; in actuality, the glimmering not-sunlight caught the expertly crafted glass panels at such an angle that it looked like the leaves in the glass trees were rustling. The main figure of the panel, a blond knight holding a glowing sword aloft, had a billowing cape that seemed to twist as his blade pulsed with magic. Around him was an assortment of peasants, forest creatures, and farm animals, all with blandly beatific faces of wonder as they kneeled and bowed.

I'm not sure what face I would make at a guy with Farrah Fawcett hair brandishing a sword at me, but I know it would not be one of subservient reverence.

"My father has a tapestry quite similar to this," Miranda said. Her voice was distant, as if she weren't really talking to me at all. "Supposedly it depicted the first Grimmour, drawing the staff from a tree in the middle of the Black Forest that displayed his fitness to rule."

"It's easy to claim a divine right to dominate when you've got a big stick."

Miranda snorted a laugh, but there wasn't much humor in it.

The subsequent windows told similar stories, all familiar but nondescript: princesses with small waists and blank expressions, lined up awaiting their equally blond princes; wolves with fiery eyes and biologically inaccurate hungers, called monster before they learned their own names; and witches with craggy faces and cauldrons full of undiluted malice, the first in line for the pyre when their potions stopped being useful and the village needed a scapegoat. The more we saw, the cruder the depictions became, until the peasants often ringing the background of each scene were just faceless grey blobs, as inconsequential as a baseboard.

It all felt…hollow. Variations on a theme until the original tune was lost and unrecognizable. To someone like me who had grown up in the Poisoned Apple, these stories were like oxygen: ubiquitous and rarely examined. But seeing them here, laid bare to their most basic building blocks, something felt…off. These pictures told clear stories of who was important, who was magic, and who was just lucky to be a background player.

The last few windows before we reached the end of the stairs were bare sketches at best, blocks of color that nonetheless communicated the purity of nobility and the violence of swords. I was happy to leave the stained glass behind as we came to the floor of the chamber.

Only most of the floor…wasn't. The bottom of the entire room was a large, circular hole, nearly thirty feet across, with a small stone walkway surrounding it. Tendrils of gold and green light drifted up from the hole like tall grass, swaying in an unfelt breeze. A chain had been run around the circumference of the well, a little barrier to allow onlookers to view it without falling in.

I grasped the chain and tried to shield my eyes against the pulsating crystal light flowing up from beneath. After only a few moments I had to scrunch my eyes shut, afterimages of energy swirling across the inside of my eyelids. But I was pretty sure I saw something impossibly large underneath the aurora, something heavy and organic and slowly, inexorably beating.

"The giant's heart," I murmured, opening my eyes and giving Miranda a significant look. "The core of the Poisoned Apple."

"This is it," she said simply. "Where it all ends."

"I couldn't agree more," said Caesura, stepping out from the shadows behind us.

THE FATA-HUMAN WOMAN STOOD TALL, blocking off our exit. She wore a flowing lilac dress with a high collar that contrasted with her grey-brown skin. Her long skirts concealed a crumpled shape behind her back.

"I've had quite the morning," she sighed, like an office worker who'd had to wait in a particularly long Starbucks line. "My first meeting looked very promising, but it turned out to be a bust." She reached behind her and grabbed the motionless form of Linden by the shirt, tossing him forward as if he were a sack of cotton balls. "Really, Briar. I've been alive for centuries—you can't expect to me fall for such sophomoric ploys."

My heart trembled as I looked for evidence that Linden's still beat. The shifting light of the Apple Core made it hard to tell, but I had to believe that his chest was rising weakly, shallowly.

Caesura remained where she was, but Miranda and I instinctively backed up, closing ranks with each other before we could see what she did next.

"How did you get ahead of us?" I asked, if for no other reason than to buy us some time.

"You and your cousin here have only begun to scratch the surface of what we can do," she drawled. I'd apparently gambled correctly that she could be provoked into exposition. "Entering a dream is simple. Traveling through the dream realm to another destination takes much more practice."

"Then why let us get this far? Just being sporting?"

Caesura's laugh sounded like dry logs rubbing together. "Not exactly. Calm down, youngling. I'm not going to kill you yet. Not without telling you a story first."

My eyes darted to Linden's body on the crystal floor. Even if he was still breathing, it was hard to say how many breaths he had left.

"Make it quick," I grunted.

Caesura fixed me with a dark glare, but continued as if I hadn't said anything. "Once upon a time, there lived a people whose very language was magic. They told stories, and the world changed. They traveled through the world of dreams and began to craft their own—cities spun of starlight, trees that grew from one world to the next, pools of water that reflected the million possibilities of the universe.

"But as so often happens, these dreamers lost sight of what was occurring underneath their very feet. With every new creation they drew from the chaotic stream of their dreams, more things were growing in their wake. Possibilities festered in the deep—great, looming creatures that answered to no rules of logic or narrative.

"These great beasts slumbered, their own dreams surging with magic unparalleled. The ones who had accidentally created them knew that if even one of these chthonic sleepers woke, their entire world could change. Their entire world could end.

"So the dreamspeakers looked for some source of magic, some weapon they could use against these slumbering titans. They searched through many worlds, many dreams, until they came here."

"To Manhattan?" I said blankly, my mind still processing.

"To *Earth*," Caesura growled. "Here they found creatures who not only told stories, but could become so captivated by them that they generated their own magic. Humans were the perfect system, able to both spread dreams and take inspiration from them.

"So they harnessed this captive audience. The beings listened to human myths and legends and crafted them into entire worlds, each one an endless cycle of story. And every time the stories were told, they powered magnificent curses, gilded cages keeping the monsters underneath each world sleeping for another age."

Silence fell as Miranda and I each quietly swept up the metaphorical pieces of our shattered worldviews. "So the entire Apple," I ventured, trying to wrap my little mind around something vaster than human history, "is one of those spells, created by the Fata? A whole world created as a trap for a sleeping giant?"

"They are called the Chthonics. Every World Slip has them, some dreaming beast who has been kept dormant for centuries. The giant under the Apple is one of the younger ones, created in the tumult and tragedy of this land's colonization. The Fata worked quickly, stitching together hundreds of disparate stories to piece together a realm powerful enough to keep him sleeping."

A migraine bloomed behind my eyes, but I shook my head in a futile attempt to clear it. "So why would you wake this…Chthonic? Why risk whatever horrors he could unleash?"

"Because the Fata were wrong," Caesura said, her voice picking up in speed as she began to move forward towards us. "The Fata were weak. They saw the Chthonics as a threat, as opposed to an opportunity. They created so much power but were terrified to *use it*."

She looked between Miranda and me, frowning. "Come

now, both of you, in your own ways, have known this world is a trap for a while now, haven't you? A carousel of pageantry and oppression, played on repeat." Caesura drew closer, and I stole a look at Miranda. Her face was unreadable, and in the back of my mind, I wondered if the unpredictable princess would take Caesura's bait.

I began to shift my position so my back was less exposed to either of the women in front of me.

"So why not make this next part easy on yourselves?" Caesura drawled. "Just give me what I want, and you get to walk away from this. Enjoy the new world I create, finally tapping into all the dormant power of the giant beneath our feet. Just stop this pointless fighting, especially when you've already helped me so much."

My eyebrow twitched on my otherwise neutral face, and Caesura immediately pounced on the signal. "What, you hadn't guessed? You, Briar, were the final piece of my plan. Your wizard friend already recognized that the only way to affect the Chthonics is with a piece of raw Fata magic. So that little seed at your side there is the only way I'll be able to put the giant under my control."

Caesura had drawn close enough that I could tell our conversation was about to end. "So you used me as your personal Uber Eats for magical artifacts?"

"There was no way Gaia would have given me her seed," Caesura replied with a smile. "It was much better to have you bring it here for me."

Her posture shifted, a predator ready to pounce, and in a moment I sank into a defensive stance with a rose instantly in my hand. "Miranda," I said with deadly calm, "get Linden."

Caesura surged forward, her bare feet lifting off the ground and her hands extending on either side, fingertips pointed in claws of pure shadow. I stutter-stepped away from her first strike, throwing the first emotion I could find into my rose, the peach-colored petals turning electric green.

I just hoped my fear could keep me safe.

The neon blossoms floated off the stem and drifted in a whirlwind around me, pulsing with magic that seemed to drive Caesura back a step. Out of the corner of my eye, I could see Miranda get her arms beneath Linden's shoulders and drag him away from Caesura and me, towards the ramp leading back to the surface.

With a thought, I summoned two more roses into my hands, each one glowing with lightning-blue sparks of pure adrenaline. Draining my emotions into the blossoms left me supernaturally calm and focused on the fight in front of me.

Even as Caesura rushed forward, quicker than the eye could see, the fear petals circling me flashed in warning, giving me a half-second to roll out of the way. As I came up on my feet, I swung back with my right hand, scoring a hit on Caesura's powerful thigh. The other woman jumped back, some of the emotion getting through to her.

We squared up again, and I saw her breathe out heavily, a lime-green mist of emotion trailing from her nostrils. As quickly as I was able to hit her with feelings, Caesura could use her centuries' worth of practice to simply exhale the emotion with a thought.

She smiled and dragged a translucent claw across her lips. "Not bad," she said. "For that impressive hit alone, I'm willing to spare you. Let you flee this city and its pathetic, doomed denizens."

"Fat chance," I grumbled. "I'm a New Yorker with rent control; no force in the universe will make me move."

Caesura grinned at my defiance, clearly eager to continue our fight. She darted forward, sweeping her claws in wide horizontal arcs. I was able to whirl out of her way, but with the gaping pit of the giant's heart at my back, I didn't have much ground to work with. "Why keep fighting, Briar?" she asked, her words punctuating her strikes. "Give up. Move on. Why give your life for these stupid little stories?"

Leaping forward, Caesura brought her hand down, claws aimed right for my eyes. With no room to retreat, I raised my rose to meet her dark talons. In a brilliant flash of fireworks and flower petals, her hand bounced away, stripped of its claws momentarily. Unfortunately, my rose also flew free in the small explosion, arcing over my shoulder and into the glowing pit behind me.

"Stupid girl," Caesura said fiercely. In an instant she flashed forward, under my guard, and grabbed my wrist. With a jerk, she lifted my arm to the sky and sank her dark, cold claws deep into my side. "What use are your fairy tales when there are things in this world that can shred your soul?"

My body began to spasm as she withdrew her claws from my torso and kicked me into the gaping maw of the Apple Core.

MY VISION WAS a wash of light and green and yellow and pain. I fell for an indeterminate amount of time, or maybe I blacked out, but when my eyes and my brain both decided to start working, the waving lines of jade and sepia above me resolved into shifting leaves in front of a clear blue sky. I felt the tickle of grass along my neck and the support of earth beneath me. At some point during my fall, the ground must have sneaked up behind me.

Instantly my sore arms wrapped around my torso, but my questing fingers couldn't find any wound where Caesura had sunk her claws into me. In a weird way, that absence was more concerning than a sucking chest wound.

Slowly, I pushed my way up into a sitting position, my eyes adjusting to the light of a sunny day in an idyllic field. Tall, unkempt grass stretched in all directions, becoming rolling hills with not a speck of civilization anywhere to be seen. Everything around me was lush and verdant, stalks of wheat and ragweed hanging heavy with seeds and pollen.

If I was dead, I could already tell that heaven was going to be hell on my allergies.

I swore in frustration as the cacophony of questions and uncertainties reached a fever pitch in my mind. I felt like the final battle for the future of the Apple was happening, somewhere, and I was stuck in a Grimmsdamn desktop background. I had to escape, had to claw my way back into the real world to protect my friends.

Around me, the grass waved lazily in the wind, immune to my concerns. And despite my best efforts to cling to the chaos in my mind, I found myself taking a deep breath of crisp, country air, letting the silence around me fill me up. As I sat back and watched, the hills in the distance undulated, slopes lowering down into the earth while others took their place, like an ocean of ground billowing in slow motion. The land itself shifted, peaks and valleys taking shape and then eroding away.

Wherever I was, there didn't seem to be much chance of me learning the landmarks. So I chose a direction and started walking.

There weren't any paths to speak of, so I meandered along hills, skirting trees and a thin, waving brook of crystal-clear water. No matter how far I walked, the landscape varied but remained peaceful and idyllic, and after what felt like an hour, the sun hadn't moved from its position in the sky, casting late-afternoon light that might go on forever.

Not long after I realized that the sun was still, I began to feel like I was being watched.

There weren't any other creatures here that I could see—no birds spinning circles in the sky or squirrels scampering up trees. But whenever I moved my head particularly fast, I could swear there was a shifting of foliage, a slight disturbance in the grass as if someone or something had just ducked out of sight. Once, when I said a particularly foul word after stepping in a hidden pocket of mud, I could have sworn I heard a giggle.

The eyes on me didn't feel particularly malevolent—the snicker had felt mischievous at best. But given that I had been teleported to an unknown otherworld, it still didn't feel great. So the next time I passed by a large tree trunk, I made a big show of stopping to retie my boot. Halfway through, I spun around to look behind the tree.

My observer wasn't expecting it, and I saw a cloud of brownish-grey hair duck into a stand of cattails.

"I saw you," I called out, because that felt like an important point to make in whatever game we were playing.

"No, you didn't!" a childish voice called back, affronted.

"I saw your hair."

"Doesn't count!"

"Well," I said, still unclear what I was dealing with, "I know you're there now, so maybe we call it a draw and you come out from hiding?"

There was an indecisive shifting amidst the cattails, and the figure appeared to make a decision and stepped out from between the stalks.

A child with fluffy hair and light-green skin gaped at me, their hands stuffed into the pockets of cream-colored linen overalls. I knew them, the strange presence that had been tracking me through my dreams the past few months.

"What are you doing here?" the child said, their musical voice filled with suspicion.

I figured the simplest answer was probably the easiest. "Walking. What are you doing here?"

"I live here."

"And here is…" I gestured to the verdant vista around us, "…where exactly?"

"You shouldn't be able to be here," they muttered. "Something must have gone wrong with the barrier." Their hands strayed to a blossom tucked into their pocket.

"Is that my rose?" I asked, recognizing the rose that Caesura had knocked from my hand.

"This is yours?" I nodded. "Are you Fata?"

"Sort of," I said, squinting at the form of the creature in front of me. Something in their smile held a bit of familiar mischief. "You were in my dreams a few times, weren't you?"

The kid nodded. "I get bored down here. Lately I've been restless."

Their words were simple, in the way that children believe their own emotions explain everything. But something about the way this being spoke belied a greater power. "Are you the giant?"

The child shrugged in what I thought was an affirmative. "Call me Pip. Want to see some baby birds?"

My mind whirred, but I couldn't choose which of the million questions I had to ask first, so I just said, "Sure."

Pip flashed a grin and began to dart up the tree I'd stopped by. In an instant, they were close to the top, waving me upwards and somehow making me feel very old at twenty three. It took me roughly thrice the time to get up to the same level, and even then, I was a few branches down to be eye-level with Pip.

They pointed to a nearby evergreen, where a prismatic blue bird I'd never seen before guarded a nest. After a moment, three little hatchlings became visible, their pink skin sharing the oily sheen of their mother. Somehow, close to Pip, the world was inhabited with birds and bugs and crawling things.

"So this is its own little World Slip," I said, watching the mother begin feeding her young.

"S'pose so," Pip murmured, rapt with attention. "The Fata thought they could keep me here forever and ever."

"But they couldn't?" I said with surprise. Pip glared at me and pushed a finger to their lips. "Sorry," I whispered, so as not to disturb the birds. "You can leave?"

"Course I can. Their magic keeps my body sleeping, but it's easy to dream my way up to the Poisoned Apple and live up there for a while. When I get bored down here, I watch what is going on up there. Look, there's the other one!"

A second bird came in with a worm to feed the babies, and I couldn't really appreciate the birdwatching knowing that all of this was still some sort of Fata-made nesting doll of World Slips within World Slips.

Just as easily as they had been fascinated, Pip lost interest and skipped their way down to the ground, picking a reed and using it to whistle a tuneful melody. By the time I'd made it down the tree without face planting, they'd crossed the field we were in.

"So do you even want to wake up?" I asked, slightly winded as I caught up to the child. I swear their tune changed into a lyrical variation of "Row, Row, Row Your Boat."

"If I wanted to wake up, I would," they said after a moment. "It's the last few months that things have been getting weird. I can't sleep, I can't dream and…I know if I wake up, it means the Apple goes away," they said sadly. "Just when it feels like things are getting good.

"We've met, you know," Pip said suddenly, turning to face me with their glittering amber eyes. "In one of the lives that I live up there. So I know that you and I both love the stories of the Apple. But just because you love something doesn't mean you can force it to stay the same."

"What do you mean?"

"The Apple is changing…The Royals wanted to keep everything the way it's always been, Caesura wants to wipe everything away, but you…you seem like you can help it grow into the next chapter."

A breeze blew by us, tousling the hair of the strange, semi-immortal child next to me. For a moment I just stood in the field, watching the horizon shift into new curves and configurations.

"You better get up back up there. The story isn't done yet," Pip said, scanning the sky for something that my eyes couldn't see. "And I can't wait to see what happens next."

And then the little jerk swept my legs out from under me, pushing me backwards into the grass. Only the ground had become insubstantial and gave way beneath me until I was falling through green light once again.

I COULD TELL THE MOMENT I popped back into the real world, because four nasty stab wounds from Caesura's demon claws reappeared on my side. Nothing says reality like blood loss.

Not long after, the verdant auroras of light around me began to dim, and I was floating up into the massive round chamber I'd left, the shine of the stained-glass windows coming into view above me. Whatever transdimensional trickery Pip had played on me, it was starting to wear off, and my levitation petered out as I arced onto the stone ring surrounding the Apple Core.

Leaving me face-to-face with Caesura, who, for the first time since I'd met her, actually looked surprised.

"That would explain why none of my attempts to access the giant's heart were working," she said, quickly assuming a nonchalant expression. "You've still got the seed I need." Her obsidian eyes flicked down to the pouch at my waist.

"Caesura, wait, can we—" My words were cut off by her talons nearly cutting off my nose. I dodged out of the way, but I was injured and unbalanced, and she was blocking the only exit from the small ringed walkway surrounding the vastness of the Apple Core.

The gashes in my side throbbed as I sidled along the chains ringing the hole, trying to keep Caesura from getting a clean shot at me. She circled me like a wolf with a wounded deer, tiring me out before she could deliver the final blow. Out of the corner of my eye, I saw Miranda's blond mane peek out from behind a column, a few levels up from where we were. At least she'd gotten out. Maybe Miranda and the rest of my friends would get as many people out of the Apple as they could before it imploded. They could all live long, happy lives in Olympus. We fought, and we lost. But at least they wouldn't have to die for my epic gamble.

My fingers tightened on the chain as I gritted my teeth. *No.*

I wasn't going to settle for that same, defeatist story anymore. If Miranda got to dig her way out of this to go home to *Isaak friggin' Krakelev,* then I was going to do my Grimmsdamndest to get back to Antoine and kiss him on his stupid mouth.

A bright blue light flowed out from my fingertips, accompanied by a swirl of rose petals, each glowing with sapphire light. I hadn't even remembered a rose floating into my hand, and part of me was pretty certain that the petals were just coming from…me. No rose required. And the emotion I'd put in them—it wasn't hope in the traditional sense. Not the idle, wishful daydreams I usually associated with that word. It was weighty and jagged, a cross between a dream and my survival instinct. It smelled like fresh soil after a rain and a shot of espresso after a long night, and it left some grit in the back of my mouth.

Happily ever after or not, this was ending here.

Caesura recovered from her surprise a fraction of a second sooner than I did and lunged towards me. I leapt over the chain into the open air and hoped my hope was enough for this next part.

As my boots landed on the petals, there was give, but they supported me, dangling up hundreds of feet over the giant's heart. Another cloud of teal petals flew up to meet my other foot, and soon I was floating on rose blossoms and a prayer. The only thing I could do was keep taking steps into the unknown, hoping my flowery feet didn't fail me.

I made sure not to look down.

I'd floated about three-quarters of the way across, probably fifteen feet from the solid ground of the stairs, when a deep, melodious laugh filled the room—just grade-A villain stuff, a real quality cackle. What concerned me most, however, was that the laughter was coming closer.

I managed to turn around mid-air without face planting out of the sky, only to see Caesura was eye-level with me across the room. She'd levitated into the air, a trail of dark, spiky shadows projecting from the bottom of her dress so she looked like the terrifying angel on top of a demonic Christmas tree.

"You are full of surprises, child, I'll give you that," she called out from across the chamber. "I knew I'd chosen well, all those years ago, when I decided you'd be my project. Power has never been your problem. It's your attachment to the way things are that prevents you from achieving my level of greatness."

"I'm not your child," I growled. "And if all you wanted was to create a lesser copy of yourself, you're not a parent; you're a narcissist."

I stood my ground—er, air—and drew Prick.

"I gave you that blade, girl," she said, her voice as sharp as a slap across the face. "And I made sure that, for all its power, it wouldn't work against Fata magic, remember?"

"Still has a sharp point," I muttered, before throwing myself across the open air at Caesura. The audacity of the move surprised her, but she got her forearm up to stop my blow to her heart. Instead, I grazed her arm, opening a surprisingly normal-looking scratch on her brown skin.

If she really was a goddess, she still bled like the rest of us.

My momentum carried me up against one of the stone columns running along the circumference of the room, and I spun to face Caesura. She'd floated further above me, centering herself in the round room. "Give up, Briar. How do you expect to win? Because your beloved fairy tales told you that you were special? That good beats evil and everyone gets what they deserve?"

I pressed my feet into the side of the wall and pushed up towards her, hoping my petals would continue to support me—it wasn't ideal, learning to fly during a dogfight. Before I could sink Prick into Caesura's leg, a blade reached out to parry mine.

The knight's sword was glass, but the Fata magic Caesura had pumped into it made it strong enough to deflect my strike. One of the holy conquerors from the stained-glass windows was extending out from his frame, twisted glass stretching out behind him like a shadow. The other, less-important figures from the scene were visible in the molten trail behind him, peasants and damsels condensed together in a multicolored arc to hold him up.

I drew back my dagger for another strike, but a cold hand around my ankle threw me off balance. Looking down, I saw a dead-eyed queen wrap her bony fingers on my leg. Before I could stab downward and free myself, the knight by my side struck out with his sword, knocking Prick clean from my hand and onto the stones far below us.

"I know the stories, too," Caesura rasped as a glass dragon wrapped its tail around my other hand, suspending me in mid-air. "For every Cinderella, there are a thousand maids who live and die, thinking that one day their prince will come. That's why the Fata thought these stories made the perfect trap: the dream that one day a person will get their escape keeps everyone else content, waiting for their turn for a happily ever after."

I struggled in the air as the stained-glass knight grabbed my free arm and wrenched it behind my back. I roared in frustration, but Caesura's flunkies had me trapped in their iron-tight grips. One by one, I felt the hopeful petals stuck on my boots fall away.

"Now stop struggling and give me what I need," Caesura said, floating to where I was pinned by stained glass. I twisted as much as I could, but her hands found their way to the pouch on my waist, peeling it open like a birthday present.

At least I was close enough to see her face when she saw that it was empty.

Despite the situation, I grinned at her stunned expression. "You think we were going to walk in here with the key to accessing the source of all magic in the Apple? The seed is safe inside a vault at the Academy of the Iron Wand."

Caesura ripped the ugly pouch off my belt, a favor for which I couldn't thank her enough. "But it's…these anti-scrying runes…"

"I figured you'd notice how far we'd gone to hide the pouch from your spells and assume the seed was in there," I said, trying to keep a shit-eating grin off my face and failing. "I knew you'd underestimate me, but I was pretty sure I was reading you exactly right."

Her fingers at her sides turned to claws, which clenched into fists of sizzling darkness. "So you got one over on me. I'll storm the Academy of the Iron Wand, get it back, and change the world. Your little ruse only delayed the inevitable."

"If I don't come back, my friends are going on the run. They've got a portal prepped to go on a worldwide World Slip Road Trip," I said. "Do you like the name? Came up with it myself."

For a moment, it looked like Caesura was going to drag her talons across my throat, but she kept herself in check. Instead, I could feel what she did next not with my physical senses, but my magical ones—our powers were similar enough. There was a strange sense of familiarity as I saw Caesura clench her fist and drain all of her hatred and frustration into a glittering thorn so dark it absorbed the light in the room like a black hole. The air around us smelled of charred earth and death.

"Unfortunately, you have to be alive for this next part," Caesura growled. Her eyes had narrowed to triangles of jet-black fury. "But I'll take pleasure in knowing that when I see you next, you'll beg me to put you out of your misery."

And she stabbed her thorn of hatred into my heart.

IT FELT LIKE my blood was on fire as my heart raced to try to push the poison out of me. The thorn was something altogether new—condensed magic with just enough physical form to make it hurt like a mothergooser.

My vision began tunneling, but I could faintly see the other end of the thorn leak some kind of dark smoke, which Caesura wafted towards her nose. With a deep inhale, she consumed my…essence, or whatever she was draining out of me, and I watched as her features melted like wax to become the perfect mirror to my own.

"It takes pain to really distill the truth of who someone is," Caesura said to me with my own voice, her haughty inflection sounding foreign in my ears. Whatever magic she'd used to steal my form had also reflected my clothes, so I had the distinct pleasure of seeing I had a stain on my jeans before my death.

"Antoine will be so excited to see you emerge victorious," she continued, running a finger along my cheek to catch the cold sweat that was accumulating there. "I bet he'll be happy for us to go back to the Academy to celebrate."

My throat was dry and ragged, and no quippy response came to mind as my body spasmed with magical pain. But I kept my eyes narrowed, trying to stay focused on Caesura's face as unconsciousness beckoned.

"See you soon, Briar. Or should I say, '*Seed* you soon.'" She chuckled at her own joke. "Your essence really has a lot wrapped up in being good at puns, by the way."

And with that she turned in midair and began floating towards the ceiling, propelled by the shadowy black vines trailing from her—*my* boots.

The longer the thorn stayed lodged in my heart, the harder it was to form any complex ideas. Caesura's hate was like a hot-red poker burning away any other feelings or sensations besides the all-consuming fury of it. But as I hung there, wracked with fire, I was able to come up with one final thought:

I lost.

Before I could hang my head and let the pain scour away the rest of my consciousness, a scrape from above caught my attention. Looking up, I saw Caesura notice the noise as well.

"Ah, right," she said, floating to the source of the sound. "The rebellious royal and the half-dead half-breed. A pity they didn't make it through the final battle. I'm sure Antoine and the others will understand."

Through the tears in my eyes, I could see Caesura swoop in and grab Miranda by the hair.

I struggled, but the stained-glass stories held tightly around me, as inevitable as death. They'd become the literal trap that Caesura had described, holding me in place with pretty colors and empty promises.

Miranda writhed like a wildcat, but her strikes kept coming up short as Caesura utilized my long arms to hold my friend at a distance. With a flourish of her wrist, Caesura's magic summoned Linden to her other hand, fingers digging into his shirtfront as his head lolled to the side.

I looked down at my bonds, willing them to come undone with whatever magic I had left. But the characters encasing me had become stock-still outside of Caesura's influence, frozen in their shallow beauty.

Caesura pulled my two friends into the open air with her, looking into Miranda's eyes with her copy of my own. "I guess this is the end," she muttered in the absolute stillness of the room.

And she let my friends drop.

A flicker of light from below refracted in the stained glass and, through my terror and adrenaline, I felt myself leaving my body, my magic flowing out into the room to encompass everything. Time seemed to slow as my power traced the outlines of the figures holding me captive—the firm lines, the stoic faces. Caesura's control over them was complete; she'd told them who they were and what they meant. There was no way I was going to overpower her commands and bend them to my will.

But maybe, just maybe, I could help them slip free of their shackles and become something new entirely.

I pictured the dragon soaring through clear blue skies, free of its hoard and the dragon slayers that came with it. I saw a queen valued for her clear judgment and leadership, not her lips as red as blood and her skin as white as snow. And the knight…I pictured Antoine, using his sword not for the glory of a noble house but for the vulnerable—righting the wrongs of the world on his own terms.

They were each beautiful fragments, but it was time for them to find new wholes.

The glass around me began to crack and reshape, as if eager to reform itself into new possibilities. With my hand free, I grabbed the thorn lodged in my chest, feeling the darkness leaking out of it hit me all at once—pain, rage, and fury so intense it brought tears to my eyes. Gritting my teeth, I pulled and pulled, the pain throbbing with each tug. I realized that while the most recent wound was from Caesura, there were thorns growing around my heart from long before—briars and spikes I'd let take root there, hoping they'd protect me. But for every thorn I'd left facing out to the world, a dozen more caged my own heart, piercing it and stopping anything else from growing.

I nearly stopped entirely, my palms slick with sweat and my head throbbing with the enormity of it. But, somehow, I could tell this was a good kind of pain, the kind you have to feel before you can heal.

With one final wrench, I pulled the dark thorn from my chest and tossed it aside.

In an instant I was swooping down, following Miranda and Linden's forms. My hope-filled petals were long gone, but I could feel the glassy green wings of the dragon stretching out from my shoulders, eager to feel the open sky and chase the wind. Just before my friends hit the stone walkway at the bottom of the room, I had one of them in each arm, a supernatural strength in my muscles as the knight's shining armor twisted around my limbs. I felt an echo of the knight's pride, the power to protect flowing through each gauntlet.

Miranda's eyes were wide as I set her down, the shock just setting in—Linden was mercifully still unconscious. I turned away from them to face Caesura where she floated above us. Cool glass slid against my forehead, as the liquid gold from the stained-glass queen pushed back my thick hair, forming a crown that was half helm, half tiara. I wasn't sure where Prick had skittered to when it fell, so with a thought I pressed molten glass into a shining sword, razor sharp and glittering with light.

Wings of a dragon, sword of a knight, and the crown of a warrior queen. Even the Poisoned Apple had never seen anything like me before.

Flapping my wings, I took off from the ground and met Caesura in the air. Taking the thorn out of my heart must have somehow forced her back into her true form. Which was good, because I was done beating myself up.

"You don't look so good," I said, enjoying the confusion and anger fighting for dominance on Caesura's face. The powerful beats of my wings kept me suspended in the center of the chamber as Caesura shied back to the walls.

"Briar," she hedged, "think this through. We could create a brand new world, one without Royals and wizards, where we get to decide—"

"We have a new world," I said. "Every single day. If you're not imaginative enough to see that, I don't see any place for you in the Apple." I lowered my sword. "If you leave and vow to never come back, I'll let you go." If the stories weaving about my body could find new forms, I thought maybe Caesura could too. I had to give her that choice.

Caesura's hands dropped to her sides, and her brow furrowed as she considered my words. But her thoughtful expression never reached her eyes, and I caught the tart whiff of condescension just before she struck.

The thorn she'd palmed flew directly at my face, but I got

my sword up in time to swat it out of the air. While I was still off balance, Caesura threw herself toward me, the shadowy briars behind her thrashing as she clawed at my eyes. With the extra weight, my glass wings couldn't keep us airborne, and I began to plummet. Every time I tried to extricate myself, her claws gripped me with wildcat strength, cracking through the silver glass of my armor.

The finality in her glare told me she wasn't trying to defeat me anymore; she was resigned to taking me down with her.

With a final push from my dragon wings, I was able to slow our descent, but I clipped one of the crystal columns holding up the entire chamber, and shards of emerald sprayed where the wing snapped off at my shoulder blade. The other wing wrapped itself around us, cushioning most of the blow as we hit the stone, not far from where I'd deposited Miranda and Linden moments before.

Entangled with Caesura, I managed to get my feet up between us as we tumbled, and I kneed her in the stomach, finally separating us. Her thorny mess of shadow vines writhed, leaving scratches across the floor as she brought herself to a stop.

I was on my feet first, blade extended to keep her from getting close to me again. Caesura let out a heaving, bitter laugh while lying on her back. "You're fighting for a prison," she said, slowly getting to her feet with a weariness that shocked me. "We can't even contact the Apple Core. Only Fata magic can get us in. We're like children locked out of the basement, where all the power tools are."

I quirked an eyebrow at her. "I'm not kept out. I just spoke to the giant when I fell down there. It was chill."

The other woman stared at me. "But how—"

"My rose." I thought back to just before Caesura had stabbed me. "It fell down there, and it must have opened up the giant's defenses."

I could tell I'd made a mistake when I saw Caesura smile. All this time she'd been trying to get into the Apple Core, and by thinking out loud, I'd just told her that I'd left the door open.

Caesura's eyes flashed, and she raised her hands into the sky. Instantly, the threads of orange and green magic drifting up from the giant's heart began surging towards her, darkening to a stormy crimson. The power began to curl into her nostrils, and she lifted off the floor. Her head lolled back in ecstasy as the magic filled her. "This is it," she said, rolling the power through her fingers. I could feel her beginning to break the giant's sleeping curse once and for all, forcing Pip awake and bringing about the end of the Apple.

I wasn't sure how exactly to counter her spell, but it turned out six inches of glass sword to the gut will disrupt most magic.

Caesura's eyes widened as I withdrew my blade, and she stumbled backwards. The Apple Core's magic still roiled above us as she dropped to the ground, holding her side and coughing up dark blood. "Guess you had more Fata in you than I thought," she said, her breath ragged, but when she looked at me, I could almost see pride in her black eyes. "Checkmate."

Then she crumpled over the side and fell into the Apple Core. I just hoped the giant would know what to do with her.

The storm of magic that she'd leeched from below us didn't follow her back, however, and before I could react, it darted down at me and deep into my lungs. Power filled me, blowing through my paltry defenses like a tornado through a Walmart.

Echoes of Caesura's words came back to me, and suddenly I could see exactly where she'd gone wrong. She wanted to build a new world in her image, but with the power coursing through me, I could simply set things right in the current one. My roses could finally fix the flaws in the Apple, push people exactly where I wanted them to go. Snuff out the conflict and violence that bubbled up, and finally write the story that I wanted.

Plenty of people wanted to live in a fairy tale, but I could make it happen. I didn't have to be a pawn, pushed around by fate. I could be the storyteller—the only voice that mattered.

I inhaled deeply, reveling in the power around me, and the ground at my feet blossomed. Grass and greenery sprang from the earth. A throne made of branches and thorns grew behind me, and I settled into place, finally ready to rule.

I only saw a flash of silver as Miranda sank my own dagger into my flesh.

ONCE UPON A NEW DAY, I was milling through the streets of Tuffet Town in the sunshine of a late summer morning, breathing in the sights and smells of a world come back to life— specifically, the scent of a bag of cinnamon rolls I'd picked up from a little hole-in-the-wall bakery in the Gingerbread Tenements. If anyone on the street noticed me stopping every block to huff the gooey scent of frosting and barely cooked dough like a carb-filled oxygen mask, they were polite enough not to mention it.

The boarded-up windows and cracked cobblestones from the Shudders had all but disappeared as the people of the Apple returned to the city and began to fix what was broken. Tuffet Town, once full of glitzy shops catering to the Royals, had changed its boarded-up storefronts to community pantries and after-school programs. Chin deep in my bag of pastries, I almost ran into a gaggle of kids—some human, some goblin, and some dwarven—as they ran by, skipping easily through the crowded street. The joy in their laughter had a surprising weight to it, a resilience that I thought the Shudders had drained out of the Apple by force. But it sounded like, magical cataclysm or not, the kids were alright.

I rubbed the small scar on the meat of my left thumb, a habit I'd picked up in the past few months whenever I had to ground myself, to remind myself of the new chapter that had cracked open for the Apple. It was the point on my skin where Miranda had poked me shallowly with Prick, draining the excess magic I'd accidentally inhaled from the Apple Core before it made me go full Fata queen of darkness.

It was the tiny cut through which my magic drained away, leaving me just another twenty-three-year-old in a weird, beautiful World Slip with no idea what comes next. Rubbing the scar was a bittersweet reminder that I was no longer the girl I'd been, for better or for worse. I may have lost my Free Spell powers, but I was far from powerless.

And neither was the Apple. I rounded the corner of Oncegate—an entrance to the former grounds of Castle Fortnight. The walls and guard towers that had separated the city for decades had been repurposed, plant boxes and hanging baskets of herbs replacing the arrow slits and murder holes. I watched the kids I'd nearly run into earlier race up and lean between two of the parapets, grabbing bright red apples from a nearby tree. A woman, stooped with age and wearing a dark cloak and pointed hat, stopped the nearest dwarven girl and beckoned her closer. For a moment, I paused and held my breath. Then the witch winked and gave the girl a basket of blueberries and sent her on her way.

I wove through the plots of community gardens to the outline of a wide structure a single stone high. As I watched, Tarris and Miranda Grimmour placed their hands on two of the corners, facing each other as a building grew between them, columns and archways growing out of the earth into a delicate, open-air edifice, like something between a farmhouse and a mausoleum. The twins spent a few more moments making adjustments before stepping back and wiping their hands on their respective jumpsuits.

"C'mon, you two," Rick said disapprovingly, coming up behind me with a large architectural blueprint unfurled in front of him. "That is *not* what we discussed for the entablature. And I said a lunette for the main entrance, not an archway!"

"Apparently the fall of the Multiarchy left a power vacuum," Tarris drawled as he came over to join me, "allowing my boyfriend to step in as dictator. Please tell me you brought snacks."

"As promised," I said, handing him the bag of cinnamon rolls.

"Oh, please," Miranda said, coming up behind her brother and bumping his shoulder. "You know you love it when Rick gets bossy."

"I wouldn't call it bossy," Rick said, eyes still darting between his plans and the building the Grimmours had raised from the ground. "I call it being right." He rolled up the blueprint and gave me a quick hug. "You're a lifesaver, Bri. How are you doing?"

I shrugged. I had kept so busy the past few months, keeping my head down, trying to help where I could, that I hadn't given much thought to myself. No longer was I endlessly spinning, questioning my own happiness and place in the world. Some days were good, really good, but some nights I woke up in a cold sweat thinking of Caesura trying to encase me in stained glass.

But I was taking each day as it came, and, somehow, remembering how to have hope again.

"Today?" I answered, taking back the bag, now three cinnamon rolls lighter. "Excellent." I gestured to the building they'd created together. "What's this supposed to be?"

"New program the city council voted on last week, spon-

sored by our fave princess turned local politician. They're starting a breeding program to help the endangered talking animal
species."

"And this is…?"

"Speed dating pavilion," Rick said. "Which is why we
wanted the romantic atmosphere of lunettes above the entrances,
not *simple archways*. It's like you don't even believe in love,"
he said, gently elbowing his boyfriend.

"Oh, I know love exists. It's all that's stopping me from
smashing this cinnamon roll in your face right now."

The boys continued to banter, their insults as sweet as the
frosting caking their lips. Miranda looked on, her smile open to
the world for once.

"You want to stay and help, Bri?" Rick said, after wiping
the icing off of Tarris's chin with a laugh. "We still need to
make a talking animal marriage counseling center."

I smiled and shook my head. "Still one more delivery to
make, I'm afraid."

Tarris pouted and wrapped an arm around Rick's waist.
"Please stay. As soon as you leave, my hard-ass boss is gonna
put me back to work."

I chuckled. "You'll be fine. I will see you three tomorrow
though, yeah?"

Rick and Tarris nodded, but Miranda hid behind her hair
and made noncommittal noises. "Nope," I said before she could
fully retreat, "you too, lady twin. You are invited. People want
you there."

She crossed her arms and gave me a death stare, but I could
see her mouth struggling not to smile. "Sometimes I regret stabbing you. You were less obnoxious when you were about to
become a dark goddess."

"Well, you did stab me, and regrets or not, we're apotheo-
sisters now. Which means you're coming tomorrow."

We said our goodbyes (although Miranda used a less polite phrase) and I walked back to the edge of the forest, where the castle grounds were still being reclaimed and turned to new purposes. A lone figure was jumping on a shovel, trying to uproot some prickly bushes at the end of a new flower bed.

"Need a little extra leverage?" I asked, taking the shovel from my dad and using my superior height to unearth the root ball.

"Hey, thanks, honey," my father said, taking a long swig from his water bottle. Hank Pryce had a freckled tan from putting in countless days trying to tame the castle grounds where he'd worked as a gardener for so many years. I'd gotten him to start wearing sunscreen and a ridiculous hat, and at least his ruddy skin contrasted with his wide smile.

"You know," he said, "when I asked for a project, I wasn't really expecting a full-time gig rehabilitating a castle's worth of land."

"What can I say, I overdeliver," I grinned. Pops and I had finally brought my own garden back to life a few months before—given that I didn't need to use roses as magical ammunition anymore, we'd expanded it to a wider spectrum of flowers and herbs. It didn't feel exactly like it had before, but I was growing to like the new buffet of blooms and blossoms.

He and I took the last two cinnamon buns from the bag and pretended to clink them together. Almost immediately, molten cinnamon spilled onto my shirt collar. "Careful," my dad said automatically, "or you'll end up looking like me." He looked down at his dirt-caked jeans.

"There are worse fates, I'm sure," I said, waggling my eyebrows at him. "If I've got to change before meeting Antoine anyways—want me to give you a hand?"

"I'd love that," my dad said, beaming. He tossed me a trowel and some work gloves. "As long as you have time?"

"Sure thing," I said, smiling. "I keep telling you, there's good dirt under all this rubble. I can feel it."

"ALRIGHT, FINAL CHOICE OF THE NIGHT," Antoine said, standing next to the wall-mounted magic mirror. I'd followed up my cinnamon roll with way too much thin-crust smoked-wyvern pizza and was currently in the fetal position on our couch.

(*Our* couch meaning the couch Jacqui, Alice, and I owned together. Not Antoine and I. It had only been a few months, relax.)

"*Notting Hill* or *Princess Bride*?" Antoine asked. After a night out at the Woodsman's Log a few weeks prior, we'd made a pact to watch all the movies on some top ten list of the sappiest films of all time—Antoine said it was aversion therapy for me to learn to sob at goofy rom-coms, but he always made popcorn, so I went along with it.

Together we were learning each other's tear triggers. Antoine's included dogs, Christmas, and courtly romance. Mine so far were limited to Meryl Streep and confessions of love at airports. The search continued.

"I really think *Princess Bride* is gonna get you this time," Antoine said.

"Wow, I lose my powers and suddenly you become the emotional manipulator in the relationship."

Antoine grinned and rakishly popped some popcorn in his mouth. "C'mon, two lovers forced apart by circumstance, finally reunited? It's basically our story."

"Why does the girl always have to be a princess? That's some pro-monarchy propaganda. And as someone who unintentionally caused the abdication of an entire class of nobility, I object."

Antoine shook his head and started the movie, realizing I was going to keep snarking at him no matter what he chose.

"I wonder what people would say if they knew the Rose was still around, watching rom-coms in Havmercy," Antoine said, settling down next to me and giving me a kiss on the top of my head.

"Nothing good, I imagine. Can you picture the articles they'd publish about me? *Millennial single-handedly destroys the coronation industry.*"

"Hey, I helped!"

"Sadly, your role would be lost in the name of journalistic simplicity."

As Antoine sputtered his protest, he brought me in closer with his warm arms while the opening credits rolled.

Later that night, while Antoine washed dishes and I went in for another unadvised piece of pizza, my sleepy brain decided to ask a question that had been percolating in my mind since the film had ended.

"So do you really see that as our story?" I asked groggily around a piece of crust dipped in garlic sauce. Underneath my food coma, I was genuinely curious.

Antoine finished scrubbing the last plate and put it on the rack to dry, moving with methodical slowness as he considered my words.

"I mean, it's not an exact match, obviously. But I see some parallels. What about you?"

"I did get into an argument with Mandy Patinkin at a Sbarro once, but sadly it didn't escalate into swordplay," I said. "But I guess…I dunno, something Rick said to me during the Shudders stuck with me. Something about…happily ever after isn't set in stone. We don't ride off into the sunset and everything is perfect forever after. Sometimes we have to keep fighting for each other, again and again."

Antoine nodded solemnly. "Briar, I'm sorry if…when I disappeared, you had to do a lot of fighting."

"Not your fault," I said for maybe the hundredth time. I kept hoping eventually he would believe that himself. "And I was never fighting alone. But regardless, I guess…we're young and we've still got plenty of adventures in front of us. But even if there's no magical guarantee, I still want to keep fighting for you. Keep choosing you."

I reached across the table and grabbed his hand.

"Me too," he said thickly, looking into my eyes.

We both noticed at the same time.

"I guess that's another tear trigger for both of our lists," Antoine said, laughing.

"Confessions of love in a slightly dirty kitchen," I said, pulling him forward so we met halfway across the messy, crumb-filled kitchen table for a kiss.

In my happiness, I could barely hear him murmur, "Only slightly?" against my lips.

ANTOINE WASN'T BESIDE ME in my bed when I woke up the next morning, but I didn't spend very long fretting about it. Instead, I was more concerned with the eight-foot-tall tree person standing awkwardly by my dresser.

I jumped, which startled the intruder, and its teardrop-shaped head bumped the ceiling in surprise. Apparently, clumsiness was a Fata family trait.

"Iamb," I said, finally recognizing its threadbare sweater and general air of fuddy-dudditude. "Please don't come into my bedroom while I'm still asleep." I'd met the Fata librarian in the

World Tree, where it observed the many World Slips and recorded their stories for the other Fata. Iamb had been helpful, in its own way, but was also the one responsible for revealing my Fata heritage, so I couldn't help but feel foreboding in the creature's presence.

Good morning, little niece, Iamb said, its meaning appearing in my head without disturbing the air around us with pedestrian human notions like sound waves. *My apologies. But I am, in fact, not in your bedroom. And you are not awake.*

I looked out the bay window, where the skyline of the Apple had been replaced by my seventh-grade Elvish classroom, where I'd nearly peed my pants after Jacqui had dared me to chug a two-liter of Mountain Druid. It was honestly a much better memory than the apocalyptic hellscapes that had haunted my dreams during the Shudders.

"Ah, right you are. What are you doing in my dream?"

I read the report of your latest...exploits, Iamb said. *It's been quite the topic of discussion around the Tree*.

"So glad I could provide you with entertainment," I groused. This lucid dreaming was doing nothing to make me feel more rested. "Where were the Fata while the Apple nearly got destroyed?"

Iamb cocked its head to the side, as if the answer to my question should be obvious. *In the World Tree. Listening. And recording.*

"You didn't think that the apocalypse was maybe the time for you all to intervene? To stop your wayward descendant from becoming a dictator? To prevent the giant you'd trapped from destroying the entire World Slip?" I sat up in bed, hoping I still looked imposing in my Garfield pajamas. "What's the use of all your power if you won't lift a finger to help anyone?"

To my surprise, the Fata looked...abashed? Embarrassed? It was hard to tell, given that Iamb looked like a cross between

Groot and a face drawn on a coconut. *In recent centuries, we have pursued a path of non-intervention, no matter what the crisis. Many among the Fata blame our interactions with humanity for the creation of more Chthonics. If our power created them, what's to say what our further intervention could do?*

"So basically, rather than making things worse, you decided to do nothing?"

We listened. We recorded. Iamb knelt down by my bed and put a hubcap-sized hand on my shoulder. *But you did something. You did what we could not.*

"You're Grimmsdamn welcome," I growled, pushing its wooden hand aside. "Now what's to stop the next Caesura? How do we know another member of our merry little family isn't going to make a bid for power?"

They might, Iamb said, a frown on the crack of its lips. *Or they might become a hero like you. Or something different entirely. To be Fata is to be a force of change.*

"I…" It was hard to keep up with the demigod's thought process. "I didn't sign up for this. I didn't want to be a part of your family. I've got my own."

After centuries of watching your world, I have yet to see a connection between what a person wants and what they get.

"So what's the point of it all? The whole lot of you, holed up in a tree and writing down stories you don't even share?"

The world is a place of disorder and chaos, but the Fata, and the stories we preserve, create some order.

"So the Fata are forces for change *and* champions of order?"

Yes.

No further explanation was forthcoming.

I turned Iamb's words over in my head, unsure if they would ever make sense to my limited human mind. "So why are you here? What do the Fata want from me now?"

The Fata are unaware of my visit here, Iamb said, a speck sheepishly. ***I just felt…compelled, to tell you that what you've done to your world, the way you have reshaped the stories that the Fata wove into the very earth beneath you, has been no-ticed. I have noticed.*** The way Iamb's lips formed the word *I* made me think it was a somewhat unfamiliar pronoun to the Fa-ta. ***You have told a new story, one that might change things for centuries to come.***

"…And?"

The Fata walked over to my bedroom door and opened it, revealing the book-lined tree trunk of the World Tree. ***As I be-lieve you would say in your world, I'm a big fan.*** Iamb stooped to fit through the doorframe and stepped out of my subcon-scious.

WAKING IN THE MIDDLE of the night, I felt my beating heart slow once I realized Antoine was actually still beside me. As my body began to quiet after my strange conversation with Iamb, my eyes finally rested on the small scroll on my bedside table, the one that had rested there since my father had given it to me so many months ago. The twists of its golden tie caught the moonlight from my window, the decorative band holding the information about my parents inside. It would be so simple to undo the cord and answer the question I'd had since I was old enough to speak. But when I quieted my mind, when I really tuned into what that information might show me, the story it would tell…just felt wrong. It felt like it would bring me back into the past. Or that it would somehow define me in a way I could never undo, just when I was finally learning to define my-self.

So I took a deep breath, got up from my bed, and threw the scroll in the trash.

I paused, reconsidered, and took it out.

Then I threw the scroll in the recycling.

Dramatic gesture or not, I wasn't a monster.

AND FINALLY, THE DAY foretold by prophecy arrived.

Again.

A few weeks after we'd defeated Caesura, even while the Apple was still reeling from everything that had happened, Alice booked out the backroom at the Second Breakfast and bullied, cajoled, and pleaded with all our friends to get together for a morning where we forgot about all the chaos around us. It felt wrong, somehow, celebrating when so much had been lost. But that first time getting together, just seeing everyone in the same room, was like the first ray of sunlight after a long, storm-filled night.

And so, after the Pancake Prophecy was fulfilled, we decided to make it a monthly thing.

Flora had outdone herself yet again on the spread of not only pancakes, but also scrambled cockatrice eggs, crunchy dire-boar bacon, and waffles covered in the finest Canadian maple-treant syrup. The big wooden buffet table groaned under the weight of the food, all set beneath the tall windows looking onto the sunny streets of Havmercy. Flora was one of the few people who knew the truth about what we'd all done for the Apple, and she expressed her gratitude in her love language: delicious brunch foods.

Alice wove through the crowd, handing out a tray of mimosas as she smiled and greeted a group of people listening to

Josefina Campbell tell a raunchy story about a trio of billy goats and a certified public accountant. Alice lingered long enough for the punchline, and then spotted me by the buffet.

"Nice turnout," I said as my roommate sidled up to me, a grin on her face.

"As it was prophesied," she intoned with fake gravity. "Did you get enough to eat?"

"Have we met?" I gestured to my overflowing plate of goodies, which I'd had to put down on a nearby table when my arm started getting tired.

Alice chortled and began to social butterfly off towards the rest of our friends. "Al?" I said quickly. "Thanks for doing this. I know you started it as a joke to get me to stop being so doom and gloomy, but I think I've come to truly believe in the Pancake Prophecy. Just reminding everyone that we have something to look forward to…It means a lot."

Alice smiled and squeezed my arm. "Aw, Bri. Look at you, expressing emotions and shit. Two years ago you would've preferred to be drawn and quartered."

I stuck my tongue out at her. "Don't make a big deal out of it."

"Well, you're welcome. I'm glad I'm saving the world, one brunch at a time." She winked before leaving. "Sometimes it's the silly stuff like this that gets me through the day."

I turned to catch up with Tamsin, Ravenna, and Linden, who were deep in experimental trials of their new alternative ley line power source. I didn't understand most of the jargon they threw around, but, apparently, they were getting unprecedented amounts of power from their experiments with the Gaia Seed. Pretty soon, they were going to try to substitute that energy for the magic currently being leeched from the giant's heart in the Apple Core. It made a certain kind of sense, divvying up the magic contained in the Seed so everyone could get a little piece of it.

Linden looked better, albeit still a little peaked from his run in with Caesura. Being ripped out of the dream realm by a vengeful demigoddess had taken its toll on him, and his own ability to walk the dreams of others wasn't manifesting anymore. Usually he talked about it like a good thing, like he could finally get a good night's sleep without worrying he'd wake up in someone else's subconscious, but every so often his eyes looked a little sad, as if the sparkle behind them had been dimmed.

I knew the feeling.

After trading updates with the three of them, I joined Jacqui where she was sequestered in a corner, frantically messaging on her mirror. "Thanks," she said distractedly as I offered her a plate of fresh fruit. "Just have to finish this draft of a new broom emissions ordinance to send off to the witches' union."

"Get it," I said, placing the fruit by her side. After a few more moments, she hit send and mentally came back into the room. "How's Raye doing?" I asked.

We looked across the room to where Raye was laughing uproariously at something Rick and Tarris had said. Even Miranda looked amused, but in a smoldering sort of way. Not only had Miranda shown up, she'd brought Isaak Krakelev along. Maybe those two angsty kids were finally working things out.

"Raye is great," Jacqui said. "She's already started applying to colleges. Wants to specialize in public policy."

"Hmmm, I wonder which badass politician might be her inspiration," I teased.

My oldest friend rolled her eyes but grinned. "We could definitely use her help. There's so much to do."

"Well, we don't have to do it all today," I said. Together we enjoyed a moment of companionable silence, looking around at all the people we loved.

"This is a far cry from the four of us sitting around in our cottage eating take out," I murmured. "When did we start making so many friends?"

Jacqui scrunched her eyes at me. "You did this, Bri. You brought all these people together. For someone who claims to dislike people, you sure bring a lot of them into your life."

"I dislike people in general," I countered. "But I love these people specifically. Whether they're new allies or my oldest friend."

Jacqui smiled, and before I could ruin the moment, Cade came barging up to us, large arms laden with plates from the buffet. "What disarming technique did you use, Bri?"

"Sorry?"

"To get Jacqui away from her mirror. Some sort of arm lock?"

Jacqui chuckled and punched Cade's arm, nearly upsetting his careful stack of baked goods.

"How's it going, Cade? New job treating you well?"

After all the upheaval in the ranks of the Red Hoods, and Cade's central role in defending the Apple from Caesura and her beasties, he'd been promoted to commander, a new responsibility that he was still adjusting to.

"Eh, a lot more paperwork, a lot less time wandering the Afterwoods," he hedged. "But I'm still finding enough excuses to get my axe out."

"You finally finish decorating your new place?" I asked. The last time I'd visited, the decor had consisted of a beer pong table and some camp chairs.

"I'm, uh, working on it," he said sheepishly.

Jacqui sighed. "I've offered many times to take you to the Goblintown IKEA."

"Really, Cade. We've seen the design decisions you make unsupervised. Let us help."

Cade looked heavenward, but no help came. "Fine. But if you start using catchphrases from *Extreme Castle Makeover*, I'm out."

"Woah, that's a lot to agree to—"

Before I could finish roasting my childhood friend, Antoine came over, flanked by Cade's squad mates, Anya and Scuff. All of them looked pained.

Antoine held up his mirror. "I hate to cut brunch short, but we've got reports of a clutch of phidgeon eggs that just hatched in Bushwick."

For years, these half-pigeon, half-phoenix creatures had been a huge pain in the neck. They were endangered, sure, but also annoyingly explosive.

"The local mythological bird rescue is hoping we can help track them down," Anya said. "You in?"

Cade nodded and immediately began shoveling his plates of food into his mouth. "I'm down," he said between bites. "Anything that's not making the schedule rota for next month."

"Alright," I said, "although honestly some arson might not be bad for Bushwick. It's getting really pretentious there recently." Jacqui gave me a stare. "What? Just harmless property damage. Even I wouldn't want those hipsters to have their beards catch fire."

"They do use a lot of beard oil—they'd catch fire in an instant," Antoine said gravely. "Alright, Bri, you want to stay here while I go get our fireproof gear, and then I'll meet you there?"

"As long as it's the equipment Antoine got," said Jacqui, "and not those talismans Briar bought on Black Friday…"

"Okay, first off, the fact that *inflammable* means 'able to catch fire' is very stupid," I said, "and secondly, thank you, Antoine. That is very sweet."

"Anytime," he said with a wink as he leaned in to give me a huge bear hug.

With his arms around me, in a sunny brunch spot surrounded by all my friends, I took a deep, filling breath.

And it might have been my imagination, but deep underneath the delicious smells of our breakfast feast, I thought I smelled something fresh and loamy. Like the damp earth after a rainstorm, teeming with life and ready to grow. I swear I smelled the unmistakable scent of growing love in the air.

Maybe my powers weren't totally gone after all.

I SAID MY GOODBYES to everyone in the Second Breakfast and ran into the arms of my first love, The Poisoned Apple. The streets were bursting with life as witches streaked across the sun-soaked sky and troll construction workers steadily rebuilt the City that Always Dreams. I jumped into the flow of pedestrians on the sidewalk like a toddler into a crystal-clear pool, walking just behind a pair of centaur blacksmiths on their lunch break. I followed the flow of foot (and hoof) traffic towards the outskirts of the city, marching in the nonstop parade of wonders that I was lucky enough to call my hometown.

My path took me from the luxe shops of Looking Glass Lane to the bustling food stalls of Liars' Square, where everyone from brownie chimney sweeps in soot-covered aprons to towering ogres in sleek business suits had come out to soak in the sun. A pair of tengu women sat underneath a broad pink umbrella, perched high on one of the Square's surrounding walls, laughing so hard at something on their mirrors that feathers drifted down onto the crowd like confetti. A street performer in patchwork rainbow motley capered for a small crowd, using a giant hoop to enclose nearby children in floating prismatic bubbles. The kids laughed and screamed in delight as they drifted around the square a few feet above the cobblestones, their smiles distorted by the shimmering surface of the magic globes. I grinned back at them and threw five bucks in the busker's upturned hat.

As I climbed the hill leading out of the city to the Belvedere Door, I stopped to turn back and appreciate the view, ignoring, for once, the fact that I was pulling a total tourist move. But the vista didn't disappoint, with the sunlight glinting off the roof tiles of cottages in Commontown and the wind drifting through the verdant rooftop gardens growing up around the remains of Castle Fortnight. The skyline was nearly unrecognizable from the one I'd grown up with, but nothing, not even the Rose, could change the city's whimsical heart. The wind teased through my hair, bringing with it the scent of new beginnings, of stories just waiting to be told. There was a long time when I thought the Poisoned Apple was in its final chapter, that the amazing mosaic of magic and possibility would be irrevocably broken.

Things would never be the same as they once were, but the stories surging through the veins of the Poisoned Apple weren't going to stop any time soon.

As I crested the hill and came to the path leading to the Door and my return to the kingdom of Manhattan, I was excited to see the familiar face of Horace the Doorman back on his customary stool, reading a paperback of *The Wind-Up Bird Chronicles* and smoking out of a long, wooden pipe.

"Horace!" I said, running up to the older man. "You're back! How was your getaway?"

His eyes wrinkled into a smile as I noticed his tan. "The Caribbean is beautiful, of course, but nothing compares to being back home. The Apple always has my heart."

"I missed you," I said, patting the shoulder of his green velour blazer. "But you didn't miss much. Just another near-apocalypse."

"So I heard. And I was glad to learn that the Apple still has those who will do anything to protect it." His eyes caught mine, and in their depths I saw a flash of familiar amber, a youthfulness that belied Horace's weathered face. He grinned mischievously. "How is this brand new world treating you?"

I smiled and breathed in the air of the warm forest, a hint of maple syrup still clinging to my collar. "It's different, but I'm settling into it."

"Your next chapter will be glorious, I'm sure. The story isn't done yet," Horace said. "And I can't wait to see what happens next."

I said goodbye and made it a few more steps towards the Door before I remembered where I'd heard those words before, deep in the bowels of the Apple, from a young child who was sometimes a centuries-old giant.

I looked back at Horace, who merely grinned and tipped his hat towards me, his open face not giving away any of its secrets. Before I could investigate any further, my mirror buzzed with a message from Antoine, asking where I was. So I put that mystery in the back of my mind for a later date, adjusted my messenger bag, and stepped towards Manhattan, where I had a flock of fire birds to catch with the man I loved.

And the story continued ever, ever after.

ACKNOWLEDGEMENTS

Screaming Beauty first released at a very strange time, in April 2020. When I'd written it, the idea of a city falling into a state of emergency as a mysterious force spread through the streets seemed like an insubstantial fantasy. The ending, a tease of apocalyptic forces threatening the very fabric of Briar's world, felt like a natural step in her lighthearted hero's journey.

Unfortunately, current events stepped in and made my escapist fantasy altogether too real.

Writing *The End of the Rose* during lockdown was tough, because like many of us, I was struggling with the same questions Briar was: how do we step up to help when the world feels like it's crumbling? What do we owe to each other in times of crisis? How do we balance care for ourselves with vital care for our community? Like Briar, I don't have easy answers for these questions. But I found inspiration in the very real-life heroes who were doing their part to help the world through this horrific time—if they could live these ideals, I felt certain I could at least write about them.

Many thanks go to the people who kept me going during the writing of this book. To the Friday Night SUSpects, who provided essential laughs and a bright spot to every week. To the Dempseys and the Walters, who always feel like my next-door neighbors no matter where in the world we are. To the Cormeum Crew, who built a beautiful city together in the middle of a harsh desert. To Anna Elizabeth Johnson, whose incredible talent for graphic design is only surpassed by her ability to build community and care for others.

To the team at Owl Hollow Press, who took my books under their wings and gave them a beautiful home to roost. To the fine folks at Bleeding Ink Publishing, who provided a wonderful birthplace for Tales of the Poisoned Apple. Indie publishing is a harsh world, but I've been so lucky to find talented, creative, and dedicated people with whom to navigate it.

To my family, who made sheltering alone in my studio apartment never feel lonely. To Hercules, who came into my life not long after submitting this manuscript and made me remember that real life, too, can come with magical plot twists and happily ever afters.

And finally, to every reader who sees books like mine, takes a chance, and walks in someone else's dreams for the span of a few pages: thank you.

SCOTT MOONEY is a writer, improviser, and director from Ann Arbor, Michigan. Even before he could hold a pencil, he dictated stories to his parents.

He currently lives in Chicago after time in New York, Los Angeles, England, and a dozen fantasy worlds of his own creation.

His debut novel, *Pricked*, was written during his studies at Cornell University and Oxford University.

WWW.SCOTTMOONEYWRITER.COM

#TheEndoftheRose
#TalesfromthePoisonedApple

www.ingramcontent.com/pod-product-compliance
Lightning Source LLC
Chambersburg PA
CBHW030747190726
48285CB00003B/736